Mary Lee Settle is one of this country's finest contemporary writers. Winner of the 1978 National Book Award for *Blood Tie,* she is now gaining widespread recognition for her other works, rich with insight and powerful storytelling.

In the novels of the Beulah Quintet, people confront the conflicts, tensions, and meaning of freedom in different eras. Vivid, beautiful, daring, elegant, and refined, these novels are linked by bloodlines, kinship, and by the bold ideals that have challenged humanity for centuries.

THE BEULAH QUINTET
Prisons
O Beulah Land
Know Nothing
The Scapegoat
The Killing Ground

PRISONS

Book One of
The Beulah Quintet

Mary Lee Settle

Introduction by Roger Shattuck

BALLANTINE BOOKS • NEW YORK

Library of Congress Catalog Card Number: 73-78614

ISBN 0-345-29312-6

Manufactured in the United States of America

First Ballantine Books Edition: April 1981

Ten revolutionists in a regiment is enough to bring it over, in a red hot political atmosphere, to the side of the people. Not for nothing does the staff mortally fear tiny underground circles, or even single individuals. This reactionary general-staff fear, which imbues the Stalinist bureaucracy throughout, explains the mad character of its persecutions. . . .

The Revolution Betrayed
—Leon Trotsky

INTRODUCTION

The Beulah Quintet does not fit. But it works. It works superbly as a set of sustained and exciting narratives that probe a history about which we know far too little—our own.

These five novels in sequence do not fit our expectations of the *roman fleuve*. They do not belong to a single era as in Balzac, or to one central character as in Proust, or to one Mississippi county as in Faulkner. They relate time, place, and persons in a looser and larger structure than that of any of those masters. Furthermore, Mary Lee Settle's lengthy and fruitful research into the web of occurrences we off-handedly call "the past" has produced stories that do not lie easily under the label "historical novel." History bathes and floats the events, yet it never overwhelms the restless characters as they learn about the ways of the world, pause long enough to love, and pursue their ideals to unexpected ends.

The five novels work—singly, and even better in sequence—because Miss Settle blends tone, texture, and timing in paragraph after paragraph of strong yet unobtrusive prose. It is where all good stories start.

I saw him then, mighty Cromwell, setting his horse high above me, followed by only a few officers. He had dirty linen, and his hands and face were streaked with mud from hard riding. He was smiling down on Gideon. It was a sweet smile that belied the stern lines of his face. His eyes looked as a man's who falls into secret melancholies, apologetic, sodden eyes, with much need in them. I would have said a drunkard from them and from his swollen face, but it is not so—not for so common a lover as strong drink.

Johnny Church's fresh voice in *Prisons* evokes the violent paroxysms of the English revolution as well as its lulls. After his death at twenty by firing squad, Johnny's "democratical notions" reverberate through the four following volumes of the Beulah Quintet set in the Virginia Territory. As Virginia wins independence from the crown and later undergoes painful division into two states in the Civil War, Johnny's ideals of freedom and charity pass through the turmoil of history in succeeding generations and modified form, yet somehow unchanged. The power of Miss Settle's saga grows out of her sense of the heavy odds against which this continuity has been won—and against which, as well, every major American novel has been written.

These odds are caused by the scattered way in which American culture has evolved and by the difficulty American novelists have had in finding a world to fictionalize that is as rich in social and individual meaning as that of the great English and European masters. When he wrote about his visit to the United States in 1830, Tocqueville made frequent use of the French word *formes*. What struck him was the absence of *formes* in the new democracy—of customs, rituals, and conventions of behavior that give a culture character and coherence. In the same vein Lionel Trilling has pointed out how Cooper, Hawthorne, and James each said in his way that American society is " 'thinly composed,' lacking the thick coarse actuality which the novelist, as he existed in their day, needed for the practice of his craft." Miss Settle is descended from these writers and has their needs. In the closing pages of the last novel in the Quintet, she refers to "the price of freedom" that has dogged her principal characters. She means something closely akin to the absence of *formes* on this continent.

This is the challenge Miss Settle has met head on. For her subject in the Beulah Quintet is the direct opposite of American society as thin gruel. The pivotal events around which her story takes shape are ritual, almost primordial happenings: feasts, public ceremonials, formal balls, marriages, battles, violent deaths, funerals, and even mysterious descents far underground into the darkest entrails of the earth. The crucial scenes of the series give mythic scope to the classic American pioneer story. Through three centuries we can follow the full-bodied conflicts and tensions of characters who both value the constraint of such *formes* as they find around them and fret to get rid of them in a recurring quest for freedom and a better life.

The quest begins in seventeenth-century England. In *Prisons* Johnny Church, a sixteen-year-old boy, leaves home and his father's hard-won land in 1645 to fight on Cromwell's side for freedom and conscience. In those tumultuous times the new experiences of love and battle reach him almost simultaneously. Johnny comes to understand his revolutionary ideals only when his superiors, including Cromwell, betray them—and him. At the end, facing execution along with his friend Thankful Perkins, Johnny achieves serenity enough to reflect that the "metaphor" the two of them have lived is also a "kind of lie"—not a vain but an essential lie.

A hundred years later, in *O Beulah Land,* Johnny's ideals come back to the land and to a homestead. Johnny Lacey, his descendant, moves his family from the Virginia coast to a valley west of the Endless Mountains. His wife never loses her nostalgia for elegant Tidewater ways. With few slaves, threatened by both Indians and white frontier bandits, Johnny establishes a flourishing estate that his tenants name "Beulah" after dipping into the Bible for guidance. When he is elected to the House of Burgesses in 1774, he knows he has founded his "dynasty."

On the eve of the Civil War in *Know Nothing,* the ideals and the dynasty have been partly compromised. Peregrene Catlett, descended from both Johnnies, is

troubled about the slave-holding that allows him to
survive in a changing economy. Yet he cannot change
his way of life. All his children abandon the estate.
When the second son, another Johnny, returns to
Beulah from the West, his sense of duty binds him to
the land and permits him only a brief interlude of tenderness with the cousin he has always loved. Johnny
resigns himself to fighting the war for the Confederacy,
knowing that some of his family and some of his loyalties are on the Union side. He leaves no heir.

The Scapegoat portrays several reduced offspring of
the Beulah dynasty facing one another in 1912 during
a bitter strike in Lacey Creek, a downriver coal-mining
community. They are barely aware of their shared past
and blood. The arrival of the fiery agitator, Mother
Jones, precipitates a confrontation between miners and
strike-breakers, followed by fleeting violence into which
everyone is swept. Mother Jones' earthy speeches revive
ideas of freedom and conscience in a society corrupted
by Southern resignation and Eastern money.

Hannah MacKarkle, the central figure in the last
volume called *The Killing Ground*, has left her comfortable heritage in West Virginia for the sophisticated
pleasures of New York. The inexplicable death of her
brother Johnny in jail one Saturday night brings her
home and turns her into the chronicler of Beulah's col-
lective history—the people, the land, the ideals. Gradually she discovers that both sides of her family go back
to seventeenth-century England and to Johnny Church's
facing the firing squad. Her battle consists in the work
of assembling that confused and half-obliterated past
into a story, a story close enough to truth and significance to be told with conviction.

The themes that span and unite this extended narrative necessarily have epic dimensions. They also
assert themselves in very down-to-earth ways. For in-
stance, you cannot read these volumes comfortably
without a map, for the larger action turns on a constant
awareness of the surrounding land—the whole territory.
The colorful names (Fluvanna County, Dunkard Val-

ley, Fort Necessity) underscore the high relief of the countryside that shapes the lives of the people on it. But far more than beautiful or rugged landscape is at stake here. The Beulah Quintet takes its title from a well-known gospel hymn whose words are adopted from Isaiah:62.

> O Beulah Land, sweet Beulah Land,
> As on thy highest mount I stand,
> I look away across the sea
> Where mansions are prepared for me,
> And view the shining Glory Shore,
> My Heaven, my Home, forevermore.

For early settlers the Virginia Territory represented the Promised Land, the dream of establishing freedom and a life of plenty in the wilderness. Beulah, the Old Testament tells us, means "married." At the end of *O Beulah Land* (the second volume), the carefully chosen Beulah estate founded by Johnny Lacey does for a time permit a marriage of the real and the ideal in a reasonably harmonious community.

As the hymn implies, the myth of America has always been above all a myth of land. The land one struggles to reach and to prepare for future generations holds out the promise of a better life. Alas, the counterpart truth is too often forgotten: land corrupts as well as inspires. The burden of land one owns and has settled can soon stifle ideals and promises. Miss Settle does not flinch from telling the whole story. The Beulah estate under Peregrene Catlett in *Know Nothing* goes sour because of slavery and because of a smug and constricting sense of duty in a landed gentry that has lost touch with freedom and even love. When later applied to the bustling commerce of West Virginia with its coal mines and country clubs, the stirring words of the Beulah hymn turn ironic, even bitter. The most searing sentence in the whole series comes from Cousin Annie in the middle volume: "The satisfied are unjust." The

Promised Land, when we settle there, brings our undoing.

This cycle of restless quest, settling down, and renewed quest spreads out into a temporal sequence—the ancient and irreconcilable conflict between Antigone and Creon, between rebelliousness and security. Miss Settle's narrative alludes several times to the classic figures. She has even pointed out—a little impishly I suspect—that during the Revolution there were two American folk heroes: Brother Johnny, the legendary colonial soldier representing youth, equality, and freedom; and Uncle Sam, the father figure of authority and age. Antigone and Creon appear in surprising guises. The Beulah Quintet traces the story of Brother Johnny's gradually losing out to Uncle Sam as the frontier froze into "real estate." The series also shows how we have kept Brother Johnny quietly with us—as we must.

In effect Miss Settle recasts the bipolar Antigone–Creon conflict into a more complex situation, closer to those of us who are not rulers or noble orphans with a king for uncle and guardian. The successive generations of the Beulah Quintet set before us not two but *three* closely related antagonists: American history with its interlocking opportunities and oppressions—our version of fate; the lone individual seeking his place within these engulfing forces of history; and the intense cluster of persons we call "the family" doing its best to mediate between society and the individual and usually caught itself in a strong seesaw motion between stability and instability. The three antagonists are evenly enough matched to keep our eyes open as readers to all aspects of the action. In the stunning barroom brawl near the end of *O Beulah Land,* the tall stranger is challenged and finally silenced without bloodshed after he calls Johnny Lacey "a diehard Tuckahoe Episcopal ruffle-shirt Tory king-lover." The situation that gives the scene far more than ordinary cinematic tension fuses strong political convictions about what the colonies should do in 1774, the dominant place of the Lacey family in the valley, and the ornery individuality of two frontier mavericks willing to risk a fistfight and a shoot-out over words. The Beulah series enlarges the Antigone–Creon conflict without reducing its drama.

Miss Settle composes her story with a remarkable freedom and variety of narrative styles. *Prisons* is told in the first person by a young man, living and remembering his own story as he goes along. This first-person mode does not return until sections in the last two volumes. Elsewhere the action is told in a flexible third-person voice that moves at will into the minds of the characters and back out again, sometimes to tell us explicitly what they do *not* know. This multiplicity of points of view is appropriate to the semi-independent nature of the five volumes. It also coheres around the clear line of the action in its Virginia setting and around the depth of perception that lurks everywhere in the detail. In *The Scapegoat,* headstrong Lily, daughter of the local mine owner, has taken up a young Italian miner in order to educate him. Eduardo is fascinated by the blond girl, always dressed in white, and equally wary of her. "After the black-haired women with their dark pools of eyes made huge by shadows under them like tearstains, she seemed the color of disappearance." Such touches create a texture of writing that is finally the signature of the whole quintet.

Much of the striking detail in the writing comes from the relentless instinct for concreteness that has closeted Miss Settle at frequent intervals for solid months of reading in the British Museum and in libraries and archives throughout Virginia. A 1980 interview suggests the thoroughness and imaginativeness of her historical research.

In the state library in Charleston, I found 5,000 pages of records of a Senate investigation into the West Virginia mine wars and the Holly Grove Massacre. Instead of taking notes I recorded fourteen hours of tape by reading key testimony aloud. That way I could hear the language. Everyone said there was no record of Mother Jones' speeches because she always spoke extemporaneously. Right at the end I found stenographic transcriptions of three of her speeches to the miners. A court reporter made them for Brown, Jackson, and Knight, the coal owners' law firm. They wanted to indite her for sedition. They didn't get her on sedition, but they left me the clues to Mother Jones' rhythms, her phrasing, her vocabulary. From that I could build both her character and her speech.

When investigative research and the imagination work hand in hand, the resulting fiction allows us to perceive the events of history from inside. Mother Jones comes to life with the grainy vividness that makes Cromwell fully convincing in *Prisons*.

The pacing Miss Settle uses in her constantly renewed tale of settlers and wanderers constitutes another element of stylistic texture in the quintet and also of its form. The action of *Prisons* covers two days and two nights in 1649 during which the retrospective narrative draws out of itself the essential scenes of one man's short life. *O Beulah Land* moves in great strides from the American wilderness back to the streets of London, then over again to Tidewater Virginia, and finally out to a western settlement defending itself against the elements, Indian raids, and other hardships. In *Know Nothing*, three sequences each twelve years apart portray the pathetic-heroic tribulations of the last two generations before the Civil War. The events of *The Scapegoat* converge, sometimes at breakneck speed, sometimes at a near standstill, in seventeen hours on June 7–8, 1912. *The Killing Ground*, reaching the "present" of its own composition in 1980, shuttles back and forth across a twenty-year interval whose gradually revealed content transforms a woman's character and establishes the narrative context for the preceding volumes.

The restless movement of this three-hundred-year chronology carries a significance very different from that of Faulkner's convoluted narratives. He rarely allows a major event to happen straight out, on stage and on schedule, before our eyes. It is usually retrieved from an elaborately reconstructed past, sometimes by a character thrust suddenly forward to a future-perfect consciousness in order to supply this backward perspective. Whenever the story line ventures close to a crucial occurrence, the narrative pressure collapses or is interrupted in such a way as to prevent the stream of time from flowing into a simple present. The sometimes frustrating fascination of *Absalom, Absalom!* lies in the frequency with which Faulkner engages in a narrative equivalent of *coitus interruptus*. Sutpen, a self-made man of mysterious ambitions and innate courage and shrewdness, never achieves a moment of satisfaction. The shape of the story as much as its content tells us that this larger-than-life adventurer cannot touch life long enough to grasp it.

In Miss Settle's novels, on the other hand, the swerves and jumps in the story do not deprive time of its ability to catch up finally with the present at a point where, for a rare bright interlude, it coincides with the character's consciousness and experience. Like parts of a liturgy, her deliberate narrative gestures certify the occurrence of a few major events following an interval of high suspense. "My mind twitters," Johnny says to himself near the end of *Prisons,* waiting to be shot. In spite of his intense anguish, both he and we are there, in full awareness, when his death comes in the form of three brief and fully eloquent sentences on the last page. In *Know Nothing* Johnny Catlett and Melinda desire one another through thirty years and four hundred pages of obstacles raised by themselves and the society they live in. When finally they can come to one another, just once, in full physical embrace, there is not one shred of uncertainty or narrative evasiveness in the sentence that records the moment. "After the longing they hardly needed to move."

Both Faulkner and Miss Settle would reject Parmenides' perennial notion that "True being is timeless." Faulkner's entire universe suggests that even the most imaginative, or energetic, or reflective of human minds has no access to "true being"—if indeed it exists. His characters spend their lives circling around it in exhausting, sometimes spectacular loops that constantly breed further loops of memory and speculation. In the Beulah Quintet, Miss Settle's narrative loops—rarely so compulsive or so extravagant as Faulkner's—establish a distance and a perspective from which the action can at intervals return to the straightaway of experience. True being is not timeless. Rather we come upon it when the stream of individual consciousness coincides briefly with the stream of time shared with others. These interludes are not hushed epiphanies as Proust and Joyce celebrated them, moments projected out of the domain of contingent consciousness. They remain *in time*. After long preparation and many missed turns, a perceptive individual may participate fully in a recognizable event of genuine significance to him and to others. It is a rare accomplishment in modern fiction.

Thus Miss Settle's free treatment of narrative form and individual time leads the story intermittently to the same ceremonial, almost archetypal happenings of celebration or loss that testify to her sense of *formes*. The convergence has a tightening effect on the economy and power of her novels. Part of the writing creates a kind of ontological suspense around the events it depicts, because the characters themselves cannot endow them with full reality, full existence. In other, rarer passages the action approaches certain heightened, ritualized moments and enters them long enough to give us a glimpse of "true being" as well as a sense of social custom. Both the private and the public sides of the Beulah Quintet contribute to one insight: life, or perception, comes in strong flashes. The corollary: don't fall asleep in the intervals.

At no point in her writing does Mary Lee Settle become an anti-novelist or a player of literary games. Be of good faith, she says quietly, for I can help you see that everything is significant—the shape of a girl's fingernails; the way a man sits his horse or his car; the excited gestures of frontier children as they smoke snakes out of a rock pile. We may not be able to notice everything, as Henry James counseled us; but Miss Settle, patiently and convincingly weaving history into her *roman fleuve,* reveals that nothing has to be lost for good. The Beulah Quintet represents an act of faith in the novel, less as vicarious experience than as a source of energies we can carry back to life itself, to our lives. Literature in its highest form does not distract us. It puts us on our mettle.

ROGER SHATTUCK
LINCOLN, VERMONT
NOVEMBER 1980

I AM twenty today. There is only Thankful Perkins to tell it to, but Thankful is asleep. He has that soldier's way of catching sleep when he can. His head is bowed on his tarnished beaten iron breast and jogs in rhythm with his horse. His pot has fell over his eyes. His hands rest on the pummel and move on their own like little animals or when a child sleeps and its hands go on playing in a dream. How small he is. He looks fourteen, and lost in this great flat valley of the Thames. Who would know, watching him ride along there with his mouth fell ajar, that he is as fine a soldier as I have ever known and so compassionate and loving a friend? Why, he can speak with the tongues of angels, and he has, shining sometimes in his dirty face, the wonder of one newborn every day.

Twenty—being twenty takes me home to all my birthdays, for in truth, when I chose to go to this war, I carried all within me. I think it is no choice, to go abroad or stay afusting in a birth house, as I once thought, for the answer is that a man does both. We who ride here carry our staying within us to comfort or damn us. Oh, we choose that indeed, the comfort or the damning. There is little other that has not been stripped away from such men as we are but this slow and endless march, one foot before the other.

I think I have been at war all my life, riding, riding, for in truth more of a soldier's life is riding and waiting than ever skirl of pipes or beat of drums. The dull plodding of the horses ahead, flung out like a narrow black

1

ribbon across this misty plain, this time like space passing, charms such things back to me; such pictures sting
my eyes more real than any Thames valley.

I would tell it all to someone to unburden me. I
would pray words and wit to tell. I would sit down by
the fire with a friend or a wife in a long evening and
have the ease to do this sometime, in some fine latter
day of peace. I would do so when old, but that's a
far-off lonesome cry from here. Now I must ride rear
guard with Thankful and only dream to pass the time.

Not all of the time of war can staunch this anger
within me that rises pure from some fire so deep that
I cannot know its source. Of all the wars men fight,
civil wars rise from no great single matters, actions of
the king or Parliament, or this or that, not down here
in the sullen mud. They start in houses, houses like my
father's, and in men's breasts where outrage grows and
grows, and blooms in the heart, and bursts over a
countryside. What we have in common here is not the
root, but the flower of it, the anger.

Seek your own taproot. I seek mine in my father's
house, in his eyes that told me little, in his hard hands
that told me much, or in glimpses, the glimpses that we
have in childhood, when we are small and those who
rule over us are too tall for us to see their eyes, but
catch from hints, from gestures, from some night of
passing habit they have long forgotten, a few words
to treasure and wonder at.

Aie, I think I would begin by telling how civil wars
are fought with little boys, and maids and old dis-
tempers haunting us from behind doors, in other rooms
where we are not allowed to go. Did this long riding
begin even then when I, a five-year-old Tom Fool, rode
there all bundled up and close to Charity's warm breast?

It was the Christmas of 1634. The old men said it
was the coldest winter ever in their lives. The snow lay
deep and still all that winter. In Henlow Wood the
dead branches in the distance fell tinkling like glass
bells, and they said that a man hanged in chains in
November was still there that night, frozen like an

icicle. He did clang and clang against the gallows, and you could hear him in the night, tolling and crying.

We set out from a dark house, for my mother had put her foot down on such Babylonish festivals. I remember how she would spit the words "Christ mass" out of her mouth. All I saw behind us as we started out was the shape of Henlow, my father's house, under winter and snow like a deserted hill behind us. I think my father must have said I should go, though Charity liked it not either and grumbled at Lazarus, who led our mule, urging it on through the snow under the black night and the wild stars. My father would have done this to spite my mother, for I often heard him say that between the saints she gathered around her at Henlow and the sinners who robbed him blind he would end up as beggarly as they were. There was something beyond that, though, something behind his disapproval and the bitterness in his voice when he spoke of it, that made him proud of our connections with Lacy House.

Charity's lap smelled of old winter piss and warm wool, the smell of safety. She told me often that my mother and my aunt had nestled so in her, for she had nursed them with her milk and had come with them to Henlow when my father plucked my mother from the county family of Cockburn, poor and half dead like an old tree, and married her. It was hard to think of them lying so upon her, my mother now so old and yellow, my Aunt Nell, Sir Valentine Lacy's wife, so beautiful and like a fairy princess. She told me that my father had married wisely, as he did all, when he bought Henlow of Sir Valentine. He needed not dowry of my mother, but he did need blood, and so I was born into the gentry by the skin of my teeth. Even now I cannot imagine my father mounting my mother to get me upon her.

With Sir Valentine it was different, Charity told me. He would never have seen my aunt that day when she was fourteen, wading in the creek to tickle fish, had the king not ordered the gentry to leave London and live on their estates. Sir Valentine counted it a blessing, for he liked not the mincing precious court. He said he had married one dried-up woman for her dowry, and when she died, it gave him leave to please himself.

She told me that Nell had run away that day like a wild thing from the straight lacing of her older sister's watch upon her, and he did pluck her straight out of the water and take her to Lacy House like a captive water sprite, and that's how we were kin.

I never heard my father say a good word of Sir Valentine, nor Sir Valentine of him, yet he would command my mother to take me there. I had climbed the boulder steps of Lacy House, with my cousin Peregrine floundering beside me, up toward the black door with its ancient nails, since I could remember. I would put both my hands on the next step and hoist myself aloft toward my Aunt Nell, astooping there with her soft arms out to me, and she would croon, "Come up, come up, my darling, my knight, climb the castle wall."

We played so until I rushed into the sweet safety of her belly and her arms and nested my head in her breast, with her hair shining above me in the sun. 'Twas not my mother's way to play such foolishness, for she was already old when I was born. She must have been born so, I think. My aunt, who mothered my cousin Peregrine and me too, was only seventeen then and mothered all. I already had a secret self within me, and secret prayers, for even as I rode along in Charity's lap, I thought my prayer was answered that I was going to Lacy House to climb into my aunt's arms again.

That night ariding we saw a great star like a cross in the sky. Lazarus called back through the cold that it was the Christ Child come down on mother night to be born again. I could see his breath in a cloud, bringing his words back to us like a ghost. As we rode, Charity forgot her sullenness, and we laughed to see the ghosts of our own breath dance together in the frozen air. I heard her call to Lazarus with a rumble of her chest against my ear and a moving of her huge soft dugs, "For the love of the Lamb of God, hurry. 'Tis as cold as charity."

"Aie, as a witch's tit," his voice came back. "Hark," he called. "Hark, the hanged man's ringing in Christmas." I could hear the corpse like a clapper against the gallows.

"For shame of yourself," Charity fussed with him. "You will frighten the life out of the child."

He paid no attention to her, for they had been married all my life.

"I pulled a mandrake from underneath the gallows, and it shrieked like a man." He went on talking and trudging, up to his waist sometimes in drifts, a dark figure with a lantern that spilled a swaying light onto the white snow. I was so contented then, all swaddled there, feeling the animal under me as I do now, the life of it. The mule's twin breaths played in the lantern light.

Lazarus had already told me much about the mandrake root and shown it to me, shaped like a man. He said he had found it that way, and I thought he had forgot that I had watched him help the man out of it, as he called it, while he carved and chanted, "Arataly, rataly, ataly, taly, ali, ly," over and over again. When my mother heard me singing the chant later, she hit me on the head with the stick she used for the maids and made me kneel upon the cold wood floor and ask God's forgiveness.

But that night when he reminded me of the mandrake root, I thought of the roots of men and how he said they too were deep in the land, like the trees that reached as far beneath the earth as we could see when they rose into the sky. I could see my father, sitting in the dark house behind us, trying to grow his roots downward, and covering the house slowly, like ivy. After a while the night, so cold and clear and full of peace, enchanted us, and we moved, slow and silent. I went to sleep.

I was turning in a burst of warm yellow light from many flambeaus as my aunt took me from Charity and walked into the hall; the warmth and wet of her kisses were on my face. All around us there were shifting strangers, all moving and changing, in red and blue and gold, and all crowding near us and calling out "Merry Christmas!" Christ mass. I clutched at my aunt and tried not to hear the evil words. They shamed me, and I thought the voices loud and silly and false. She felt me cringing to her and called out, "Make room. The child is cold."

I hid my face in her breast as she carried me through the hall and the noise. I could feel the light of it but dared not look again, until she laughed and picked me off like a limpet and held me up before the fire.

I thought that summer had burst by magic within the great hall of Lacy House. I remember that all that green and light swam before my eyes and I was afraid that I would cry. Why, I cannot forget the wonder of it even now. There was ivy growing up the walls, and bays sprouted from the lintels of the doors, and everywhere were great sprigs of holly grown and moving in the swirl of folks and yellow candles and pitch-pine torches. It smelled of summer, but of some strange summer of spices, a cave of captured summer. There was music of pipes and lutes and tabors, and the middle of the room was atilt with dancers, all wanton, charming the winter away with the bang slap of their feet. They were tricked out in big crowns of myrtle and bay, and their knees were alive with tinkling bells. I was in it, in bells and lights and spices. My aunt put me down. I turned and clung to Charity's skirts and had a most unseemly urge to stick my thumb into my mouth for comfort and shut the whole wildness out by burying my ears against her familiar fat leg.

"Holy Jesus, what a sight is this!" I heard her say above me. One in bells and a thousand ribbons grabbed her for the dancing, and she struggled with him, laughing fit to kill, and stomped away and forgot me. Then there were only legs moving like tall trees gone mad under the green roof and the branches high as Henlow Wood. Peregrine had been forgot, too. He came and stood beside me, and we held hands.

"You wear black clothes like the devil," he said, and I wished my mother had not dressed me so, for she never had done that before. She said it was to show them who I was.

I wished I were like Peregrine, all in gold silk and pretty lace.

There was a loud battering at the door, and all was still. The door flew open. Snow and night and men howled through it, carrying a huge log of oak. I knew what it was, for Lazarus had told me. He said it was to make a great fire to bring the sun back that had gone away and forgot us, and it must burn all Christmas, all the twelve days, to bring the spring, or else the spring would never come again. It took four men, heaving their muscles under their coats, to lift the log into the stone fireplace, as big as a room. We all stood around and waited for it to catch. Peregrine and I wiggled our way through the thicket of skirts and boots and prayed together for it to catch so that the spring would come. I saw the flames lick, and fail, and then, slowly, slowly, begin to eat the log. At first it flickered, and then the flames went up around the log. All above us they sang the log alive with tunes that caught as the fire and ran among them, some singing a snatch of song, then others answering them, a round of singing.

It was time to feast. Charity found me and took me to the table, big enough for all the guests and all the servants of the house. She smelled of strong beer, and her face was red and wet. We sat close, cheek by jowl. The boar's head was carried in on a platter like a table, looking alive and fierce with a lemon in its mouth and its tusks atwined with holly. I wondered then if these were like the horns my father said Sir Valentine should pull in or be ruined.

I had heard Sir Valentine say many a time, "I'll not pull in my horns while there are friends and neighbors." I used to tiptoe close and look for horns above his temples, but I never saw any, so I was sure that night that it was the tusks of the boar my father must have meant, for there they were served up for friends and neighbors, as he said.

When Sir Valentine said my father came from God

knows where, I thought it to be a place and used to look for it in secret on our globe. I found the Bermudas and Virginia of the savages with faces red as holly and India all filled with names like the spices of Christmas, but I never found that place, that God knows where. In truth, now as a man I have not found it, for him or for myself.

Charity would not let me eat the Christmas pudding or the seed cakes, for she whispered it was sinful to eat the seeds and shit them on the ground to make the crops come back; but when the cakes shaped like the Christ Child came, she had her back to me, and I did stuff the Yule baby into my mouth and waited to be struck down for blasphemy. I cringed myself down as I did always when I was beat, and when nothing happened, I thought God had not seen me do it.

All along the table Sir Valentine and my aunt served the servants, as King Wenceslas the beggars, from a huge silver bowl of wassail. The hot ale and the spices made my head hollow and the table not like wood, but like some stream that flowed with food and branches. I could hear the sighing silk of my aunt's dress as she passed.

Then Sir Valentine stood at the table's head, oh, a fine ruddy man there all in red satin with gold lace around a wide collar; I thought his head looked served upon that collar as the boar's upon the platter. His hair was not yet gray then, but autumn color, and it fell in lovelocks around his shoulders. I knew that color, for my aunt said that I, too, had autumn-colored hair. He stood there, a big man with a face that could be cruel, but was not so that night, and toasted all his people, as big and fine as a king in his house. Though I knew it all to be sinful, it was the happiest time that ever I had had. I fell asleep in Charity's lap, and when I woke, something fearful in that room had waked me.

Sir Valentine and the men had set the dogs at one another in the middle of a ring they made with their bodies. They had took off their fine coats, and they sweated and yelled as the dogs growled and tore each other's flesh and sprayed blood on their linen shirts.

"Set him on!" one yelled. "I have a hundred pounds on the pocky cur!"

"Odds fuck. He shits with fear as if the devil were in him."

"Go on there. Put a sprig of holly under his tail to mad him."

I heard a dog yelp, once.

"A pox on him." One man turned back to the table, disgusted. "He cringes."

My aunt called out, "Enough!" Peregrine was crying in her lap. She looked along the table and read the fear in my eyes, too, and set Peregrine to his nurse. She came and held me up and danced around the table away from that awful center of the floor where the dogs tore the peace of the night with their jaws. She held me under the mistletoe that hung from the door. She smelled of ale and spices as if she had breathed it in and become a part of the air.

"Come kiss me, my connie, and earn the mistletoe."

I kissed and clung to her, and she reached up for a berry that I had earned, but Charity slapped it out of my fist and shrieked as if she'd caught the dog's fury.

"Nay, touch it not, that pagan thing! 'Tis the very forbidden tree from the Garden of Eden. Nell, you have lost all shame among these people!"

Her voice made all the room still.

I heard Sir Valentine yell, "Call off your dog." He dragged his own off by its ruff and kicked the other away. The dog slunk, growling still, under the table. I was held there under the mistletoe and would cry, but Sir Valentine took me from my aunt's arms and carried me against his bloody shirt to his seat at the head of the table and crooned as soft as a woman would, "Aie, come then little preacher among the men. Damn me, blood's thicker than fool religion."

I sat upon his lap and saw, for the first time, my new black clothes against the soft white satin sash he wore. He gave me wassail upon his knee until I was asleep

again. Once I felt him lift his body from the chair and
fart a great fart and say, "Damn me, 'tis me own house."

There were several fine gentlemen still sitting up
around him. One staggered away from his chair, and I
could hear him piss into the fire and make it sizzle.
Some lay already with their heads pillowed in their long
curls upon the table.

I floated in someone's arms through the green gar-
lands and then along a dark gallery where a candle flickered past faces of paint that stared at me. Then I was
in my bed, and my aunt did tuck me in, and held me,
and smelled so sweet.

I said for her the prayer she had taught me to keep
me safe in the night. She let me say it beneath the
covers, not kneeling on the cold floor.

Christabus mumblebus, cold as a haddock,
I lie here sweet Jesus all safe in my paddock.
Send angels to hold me all night in their keeping
And take me to heaven if I should die sleeping.

She said, "Good night, little colt," and kissed me
many times again and rocked me, and I sucked my
thumb all half-asleep and fondled at her breast.

In truth, I know now that civil war can split a small
boy's heart. Who was there to tell me that I was in love,
for if that passion is the taking up of lodging in a soul
and mind, she already lived in mine? I could call her
to me, the sound, the color, the smell of her, the way
her clothes lay across her breasts, the soft touch of her
hands, the halo of her hair around her head as she
leaned over me. Only then I thought her large and almost stately, though she could change from that with
the sweet laughter that came so easy to her mouth. She
never did stink or spit as all the others did who lived
so high above me. She smelled of lemons and sometimes
balm of flowers. I only knew then that she took the
light away as I heard her going back through the gallery.
The rustle of her dress faded away and left an empty
silence in the strange room.

I knew then that what I did was wrong, for my mother had told me there was only one prayer to keep me safe from the wild, harrowing noise of riot that rose far away in the dark house, the frightening sound of men let loose in their passions. I could hear the dogs again, barking and growling. I got out of the warm bed and knelt upon the floor and said over and over again the Lord's Prayer, for my mother said it was the only one that God would listen to because it was wrote in the Bible, that and my own prayer words that God put into my heart. But there were not any words. I thought I had sinned too much to hear my heart. I huggled and cried there beside the bed and punished myself with cold.

I tried to pray that God would forgive me my sinful happiness among such tinsel baubles. I could taste the Yule baby in my mouth still, and I prayed that the taste be took away by the blood of the Lamb. I thought how my eyes had sinned, and so my ears and nose and mouth that first kept silent and then did peep and then did sing out loud around the Yule log. I hit them all with my fist. I hit my eyes and nose until I could taste salty blood and snot and hit my ears until they rang, and as I drifted off to sleep, I wet the bed for the last time I ever did, and my own piss warmed me.

It was the Christmas bells of the first dawn, a pale pink streak in the darkness on the horizon, that woke me. Away over the snow I heard the call of Yule, Yule, Yule, across the vast white fields. It was a call of snow and birds, that Yule, Yule, Yule of the people coming from the church. The whole house was dead still, and I never felt so lonesome in my life.

HOW is it, Johnny?" Thankful has woke up.

The fog is so dense here that the valley is hid behind it, and we could be but a few men riding in limbo, and not a mile-long army. I can tell it is level only because of the ease of my mare's muscles. We must be riding now alongside a stream, for I can hear water and must bend away from the brushing of wet, leafy branches that loom black out of the mist. The rain hangs here among the leaves, slowly plashing. It is all mute, but for the dripping of the leaves. We move through heavy, slippery mud.

"Sodden," I tell him.

"England will ever celebrate a victory with rain." He turns his head away. I can see only his black form and, ahead, a few black forms disappearing, fading into the fog like ghosts.

Here am I, a grown man and a soldier for four years, riding the child within me as I once rode pillion with Charity and led along by Lazarus, on the way home from the feast, the lilting of the prayer my aunt had said with me, and all the rounds and carols asighing in my head. Ah, well, I have seen many a soldier die calling for his mother in the dark.

There seems to be no time between the sucking of my thumb and the fondling of breasts that late I had suckled, and I was standing all alone in the middle of my mother's room, learning of my Latin and my Scripture. I said my *amo, amas, amat* and my *hic, haec, hoc* and saw her nod her thin, pale, fragile head to the sound of it, spinning ever at her wheel. She had the pitting of smallpox upon her face, for we had been struck down in the summer, and she had caught it nursing in one of my father's villages. The village was wiped out by it, and she was the only one who would go near to pray with the dying. She said that God would protect her; but he did not, and she had nearly died and never was the same after. Charity told me that she had once been as pretty as her sister, but I did not believe that. I wish I could have loved her more. It is a loss to us, but I feared her thin yellow hands, the bones bit in my flesh. I hated her sad voice and the easy tears that seemed forever swimming in her eyes. Later the tears would harden and glitter and all her body dry into a whip. She was to become the sternest soldier of us all. Untouched by any of us, she turned to embrace the phantom of a cause. It became more real to her than any blood and growth around her. It drew my father to her at long last, and I would come upon them when I was older, speaking together like men; but they were quiet when they saw me, as if the matters that have finally launched me here into this valley had naught to do with me.

That was all later. I remember her then, in her room listening and spinning, big with another child that would, as all but me, be stillborn. There were already three tiny graves, and there would be four more. I became a thing of ever greater value to them. She called this stillborn family my brothers and sisters and told me that because they had died before they were baptized, they went to limbo. Limbo was foggy, a gray plain, as this we ride in now, all full of the stillborn waiting for the Last Judgment.

Lazarus said it was the curse of the land that she and my aunt should bear no more sons, for we owned church land, and such usurping families of the Lord's land could never prosper. I could not believe him, except at night when the wind blew and made the field bell ring. I knew it was the ghosts of monks ringing for prayer. Lazarus said he had seen them many a night, filing across the courtyard into our stable that had been their refectory. Once Peregrine and I sneaked into the hayloft to wait for them. We heard them coming, moving across the hay, but what we saw was only rats, looking for food.

I was shedding belief in Lazarus by then. He had said that the mandrake root he carried would make him rich, and he was the poorest scarecrow I ever saw. When I teased him about it, he said no, not rich as I knew, but another way, but what the other way was he would not say. Oh, there were many things he told me. He told me that my soul was a bone within my body and that when I died, it would seep out of my big toe like a mist. He said that the Father lived in London, and the Son in the sun, but as for the other fellow, the Holy Ghost, he knew nothing of him or where he bided.

How a child can love and hate and fear and none around him know it!

My mother's preacher who stood above me and taught me with a nodding of his head and a stick in his hand was ugly. He smelled of rancid balsam oil that he kept on a dirty soaked rag about his neck to protect him from the winter ague. Indeed he knew the Bible, but his Latin was confined to *amo, amas, amat,* and *hic, haec, hoc.* I said it until it rang in me. When I could declaim all of the Fifty-first Psalm, my mother gave me an apple, for she said it was her favorite.

I thought his face was what the devil would look like, for Charity said the devil could be recognized by one face before and another behind. He had such a double face, one red and ever dripping snot and sanctity and the other, behind it, peeping through and ever watchful. He would look so at my mother at her spinning wheel as she bent her head to take the loaded distaff from her maid, but when she looked up again, he would hide behind the redness and prod me into chanting. How can we forget so soon as we grow away from childhood that once we were not fooled as I saw my mother fooled and blinded?

All the grown seemed so big to me then. Later they

seemed not to change, but to begin to shrink, rather, and grow younger as I rose to meet them, as a high tree branch; so a part of an unreachable life seems to come down toward us, until by the day we can grasp it, it is hardly fit to hold our weight. The mysterious chest that we can hardly see over becomes a seat to sit and gossip on.

I spent what seems a lifetime in the middle of that bare floor until my father noticed what was happening. He said, "Take from the devil what you can use for God," and he did set me on my first pony and send me off to Lacy House to learn with Cousin Peregrine of his tutor. At first Lazarus took me, and then I rode myself six miles each morning along the edge of Henlow Wood until the road was as familiar as the veins of my wrist.

There Peregrine and I stood together as two soldiers against much beating and much Latin and less Scripture. Peregrine was beat most, for I had already in me a shameful love of learning. I can see Peregrine now, his hair all tow-colored, his face set with fury and pain while the tutor went on beating until he finally cried and clutched his legs and tried to claw his way up to his heart.

Our ears seemed ever ringing and red. Within earshot means not whistle of bullets to a boy, but the shooting out of hands to twist our ears and force us to the floor so we confess to the bare boards all our mistakes and wandering minds and mischiefs. It is strange to me now how the sight of that man is blotted from my mind. He was handsome, and he drank much wine. He taught me more than any in my life, and I cannot remember him except as a voice reaching me and offering secrecy and knights and kings, and worlds at the world's end and ships that sailed beyond the windows, and singing powerful words.

My aunt seems not to be there ever. What would I tell of her then? She is a part of the world of summer, not the schoolroom and cold fingers and the dull scratch of hornbooks.

Oh, once in a great while she would reach her hand into that prison and pet me as I passed and say, "My poppet." All her attention had been cut away from us. Once she knelt and fondled us, one in each arm, but we were already trained away from her and grew stiff in her arms and watched each other, wary. Over us, we heard Sir Valentine call, "Nell!"

She ran one way and we ran the other, and I heard him laugh. But he must have been roiled with her, for he usually called her Nellie, and seldom Nell, and when he did, 'twas like a crack of a whip and she jumped to it.

Oh, hell, cry up the setting dogs, hares, connies, heat and all. At least I need not fool my own self, here, so late. It is summer that returns most to me, with all its beauty and cruelty. Boys live their most secret lives in summer. It is when the powerful cannot find us. When we saw them at all, except sweating and tired at evening prayer or half-asleep at morning prayer, Peregrine and I followed our fathers on our ponies when they hunted and listened to the bugling of the dogs. Their perpetual quarrel seemed left behind with the winter. In summer it was grown over by the tall grass and beaten by the sun, thrust down until harvesttime was over and the doors closed their feuds into the prisons of their houses.

For the rest, Peregrine and I ran wild, won tosses, races, and had such fights and plots and slipping out of windows as boys do. We ran the swans up to hear the fierce creak of their wings, thrust into the helfer, smoked country weeds that Lazarus told us of, argued the shape of the world, lay and let the warm sun caress our cods to sweet release, and left our sinning in the stream among the trout and proudly watched them rise to our seed. We seemed the same, but already there was in me a loss I never saw in him. I carried some sorrow already that he knew not of, and it would make him fight me when he saw it in me. He could do things I could not. He could steal, but afterward share his loot with me. Gesture touched him not within. He could already do all required of him, as formal as a dance, and watch himself and laugh. That was what I could never do, for I was reared more solemn.

It was rude, a life of mud and dung and green fields, the fine shriek of the animals we trapped. What we learned then, we learned in long private days that seemed never to end. Only Lazarus came into those fields of summer with us. We ranged afar with him, and he picked herbs and taught us charms to catch fish and women. Lazarus called himself a cunning man, but he was the least cunning that ever I saw. He told us that he could rub himself with secret oils and fly at night like an owl. Indeed, he told us that he had looked in upon us at our windows at night and hooted for us to come out. Once I was sure I did, and flew with him all over Henlow Wood and lit in the top of a tree. I can still see it, down below me, spread out as far as I could see and dark. He never let us go into the wood, for he said the woodfolk there would eat us and make drums of our skin. He said, "Hark in the night and you can hear the drums."

He never told aught of this in front of Charity, for she laughed him to scorn, but long after she had done nursing me and been sent back to live in their village on the edge of Henlow Wood, she would make me swallow such evil potions Lazarus made that I gagged at the foul taste of them. She said they would cleanse the heavy winter humors from my blood.

Peregrine and I would squat upwind of Lazarus' stink and watch baskets grow in his hands, as his father and his before him had taught him to weave. He made them from the river reeds. They would snap like fans as his hands flew, and bend, but never break. He would talk the whole time he worked. No one else would listen to him as we did. He said that in the winter a black dog ran into our milk house and when the maids cornered it, it was eating a round cheese. They were afraid of its big yellow eyes and called the men from the barn, who came in with their pitchforks, and killed it. The dog's body turned into a ragged man, right there in front of them on the milk house floor. He said it was kept from me for fear of frightening me, but that he thought I ought to know.

I know now that Lazarus was simple in his head. Sometimes the men would take him to the alehouse and get him drunk and make sport of him and Charity would go and get him and bring him home. He was not always so, she said, when my father told her to marry him. She said that he was handsome as any man she ever saw. But when we sat upwind of him and listened to his stories, his head had grown bald as a coot's and his body rake-thin. His mouth stretched across his face as people said the jack-o'-lantern looked when they saw it flickering all alight before them to drag them into bogs when they went abroad too late at night.

I know now it was some distemper that had made him so, but then I took him at his word and thought he was bewitched.

But I remember most his hands that seemed to have sane minds of their own as he wove. There was not an animal wild or tame, not a hell-driven horse or cringing dog, that would not trust his hands or come and eat from them. My father used him to tame the new horses to hand and to lead my mother when she rode.

Charity said he had gone out one night and slept in the fields and the fairy queen had given him mad honey. He came back touched. He did have an uncommon passion for mad honey, though, and could make it himself, but he never gave us any or told us where the fairy village was he had slept in.

Peregrine and I dared each other to go and find it.

How still it was that day. It had rained much, and the cow paths ran with water. We sloshed along them to make noise against the stillness. Not even a bird sang. We lost ourselves in a copse, and I wanted to turn back, but said not so because it was a dare. Beyond the copse the downs opened out where we had never been before. The whole meadow before us was a blanket of primroses. Once it had been plowed, for we could feel the hummocks under our feet.

We walked up a rise into the wind, and there, far

away below us, the slanting sun etched a circle so that it stood out in shadow from the waving grass. We stood there, both afraid to walk down toward it.

Peregrine said, "You are afeard."

I said I was not, and we went down together slowly, lagging our steps. We felt the stone walls of what had been a house before we saw them. Peregrine stumbled and hurt his knee so it bled, and tore his breeks. We had to fight our way through low brambles. On top of what had been a room, all filled in with fallen stones and dirt, a small gnarled tree had found roots and grew there alone. There was no magic anywhere. We stood on top of the fallen rubble of old stones. I think I have never felt such peace in my life and have ever tried since to learn within me what that peace was. I can only remember that it was a welcoming, a charm of loneliness assuaged and overjoyed for company. We never said a word to each other, only stood, then sat and clutched our knees under the scant shade of the little tree. How was I to know I was being more blooded there by silence with something I could not name than all the splashing of fox blood on my cheeks to make a man of me?

Five minutes, an hour, we sat there, what does it matter? It was a place that had been cherished and had bred many and was now deserted. The sun was low, and it was time to leave. Nothing had happened. Nothing happens at such times as that, but a knowledge in my loins and heart of what a lost place is when the people who have made it have been thrust out and it is left to a gnarled tree, and the hummocks grow over with grass and primroses, and the wall stones fall so slowly into the empty rooms and make little haunted hills for boys to find and sit on, waiting to be frightened.

It was haunted indeed. When we got up to go, we could not move. We did not tell each other at first. We walked around the circle of the room, but as we tried to pull away, we seemed to move against a current. The brambles caught us and flung us back. Peregrine began to cry and said his knee hurt, and I held onto him as much to give myself the strength to pull away as to hold him up. We freed ourselves together from the holding of the air, the silent mourning "Come back, come back," a sense of crying. That mourning and the charm of it clung to our backs, and I began to cry as if I had heard the single tone of all the world's desertions. That offended Peregrine. He broke away from me, and we stumbled separately across the hidden hummocks and the treacherous downs until we fell panting at the top of the rise again.

The sun had changed and no longer etched the circle with shadow. As far as we could see, there were only the rolling downs, no village, nothing, and in the distance many little isolated thorn trees, so I could not tell which we had sat under.

Peregrine teased me and said I made it up, and then he suddenly bounded up and ran away and I went home alone to evening prayers.

When I told Lazarus and Charity where we had been, he said, "Aie, that was the very place where I was."

Charity said, "No such thing. I found you out by the old monks' farm, you fool. 'Tis only one of the old villages they found, and not so old neither. My father said his father went there oft when he was a lad and got my mother on my granny there. It was deserted when the enclosures came." She laughed at us. " 'Tis only part of Sir Valentine's deer park."

I believed Lazarus, and Peregrine Charity, and that was the difference between us. After that he began to say we had not gone there at all, that I had made it up. I was made shy by what had happened to me there, I think. Why else would I have picked a fight with him? He bloodied my nose, and we fought, rolling over and over in the dung and fallen hay of the stableyard. Sir Valentine came running to cheer us on.

We could hear the stablemen calling wagers over us as we tumbled in the dirt and tried to bite each other. When we were exhausted, Sir Valentine pulled us apart and asked why we did quarrel. There were no words for it, so Peregrine said religion, and it seemed to satisfy him.

He pulled my sore ear and said, "Ever the little Puritan." My mother had told me it was an insult to call one that word, and I tried to pull away; but he would not let me go. "We'll wean you yet away from your mother's apron strings," he said and took us to see the killing of the hogs.

The bonfire had been lit. The first huge hog was trussed up by its hind feet, screaming; its heavy head trying still to tusk the men who came near, its prick long and hard with fury. One of the men leaned forward and hit the member until it seemed to fence with him. They stood in a circle around the animal and moved away to make room as the squire and the two bloodied and dung-covered boys walked among them, still panting from the fight.

That day such matters as tugs-of-war between kings and parliaments seemed no concern of theirs who kept to the harder masters of poverty and ignorance and work. All that quarrel among the great was as far from them, as capricious as the sun and rain that came or did not come, fed or ruined them as God willed.

But I knew then—oh, I did, most clear it comes to me—the deadened patient fury in their eyes as we came near. When their masters reached down to pluck them into war, men like Sir Valentine standing there all stupid with good fellowship in the circle knew not they plucked them from such soil of patient, biding country anger.

They learned so young the honing of the killing knives as they worked the treadle of the whetstone near the hog and heard the singing blades. Their hands were tuned long since to the quick slash across the throat that cut the screaming of the animal. It was a legend of Sir Valentine's, watching them slaughter, flay and singe the hide, catch the blood for pudding and the gall for medicine, wasting nothing, that they would not make good soldiers, for they were kept by ancient law from the carrying of swords and could not learn what he called the arts of arms as we did, parrying and thrusting at our fencing lessons. He, and those like him, could never see that those country men had more efficient arts by their necessities than all the gentlemen who chased the fox the dogs killed or shot the deer and left the cutting of its throat to their huntsmen. I think they have hid long centuries of their contempt as we reached down from our heights and drew our white fingers through the blood and, playing at death, streaked our cheeks.

I saw the fury in the hog's eyes turn to stone.

My father knew better. He had learned no *amo, amas, amat* but "dog eat dog" in hungry London streets.

T HESE drifting dreams of me, a child, these growing pains, seem all luxuries now as I ride here, my coat brackish and heavy with damp, my back chilled, my fingers numb against the leather reins. Midafternoon in May and it is a cold twilight, this day flung back to winter. Oh, England, what a capricious bitch you are! The fog has muted and faded us, leached out our color and sound. How far ahead this long snake moves I know not. I measure distance by the rump of the horse ahead, and direction as a nerve that runs through us, horse to horse, faint, very faint.

All that I could glean of what my father was, Thankful there knows in his bones, for he was an apprentice, too, before he came into the army.

I thought my father very old when I was growing up. He had lived under three reigns, Queen Elizabeth, King James, and then King Charles, and he had bandy legs like an old man, though his shoulders were broad and strong, as one who has lifted many a weight in his time. He was apprenticed to a tallow chandler in Cheapside when he was ten years old. He slept beneath the counter on straw and listened to the London rats come up from the river at night to eat. The old man who prenticed him used him as a crutch, for he could not move without his shoulder. Once they saw the old queen pass in procession, Queen Elizabeth, painted, he said, like Jezebel and wrinkled as a witch.

He told me once of darting among the crowds with the other apprentices to see the new King James pass by, all swaddled up like a great baby, his full armor underneath his state robes, because he had a deadly fear of assassination. In truth, he said he went to see the wild Scots who rode with him, for he had seen the Virgin Queen, and after that a poor Scot of a king was nothing. He said the king had been a surly man and, when he saw the gaping crowd, growled in his foreign Scots' tongue, "By God's wounds, what would they have of me? Must I pull down my breeks that they may see my arse?"

But he too had wounds made in him by his father's murder and his mother, Mary, Queen of the Scots. Why, if one who is a king at one-year-old has such deep wounds he scars a country with them, how can I but beg Christ's mercy upon mine?

My father used his to make himself rich. I saw him climb and claw his way up some Jacob's ladder of advancement until he was a country man and owned land, all enclosed, heart and all. He was goaded by his own hunger, by cold, and by a strange and ever-present conviction that he was born too late. I cannot still conceive that feeling of his, to be born disappointed and too late, for I was born into such a ripe time, a time to take into my hands and mold more to my liking.

My father was already thirty-five when he bought Henlow. It was neglected, forgot, nearly fallen down, but he bought cheap of Sir Valentine, who ever needed money and had more land than he knew what to do with or cared about. He had got it of his family who had got it of the church in the old days when the Catholics fell. In truth, our map of England and our gentry are made of old politics. How strange it is to think of those two men, one old county, one new, six miles apart in wild Northamptonshire, kin and nearest neighbors, though Henlow Wood stood between their kingdoms and they fought for the hanging tree that marks its center as kings for countries.

My father said that when he saw the ruins of Henlow the first day, he knew it was to be the beginning of his house. No man had lived in it since it was a priory when the monks had fled. Since time remembered it had been used as a cattle barn, for the great hall was still roofed and dry. All the rest of the buildings had fallen, and only the walls were left, some used as sties, some to store manure and lime for the fields. The ancient almshouse was a bier for cows. He had moved into it at once, squatting there like a beggar who has found shelter and, seeing the walls grow around him, building like a man besieged. Sir Valentine said it was the most troublesome damned barn that ever he sold, and when my father found coal beneath the land, Sir Valentine stayed drunk for three days.

I grew up to eight years old to the sound of hammers and saws and the tap-tap-tap of masons' mallets. Sometimes when I would wake on winter mornings, I would think it rained, but it was only that tap-tap-tapping as my father constructed a world for himself safer than any he had known before.

On the night the final scaffolding came down we feasted for the first time at Henlow. There were many gentry that I did not know at table, and much spilling of wine. My father drank seldom, but when he did, he drank much, as a good horse takes its fill and then needs little again for a long ride. The waiscoting shone in the firelight. The long refectory table he had found there was covered in white linen. The new glasses my father had brought with him from London shone and glittered; the new leathern Spanish chairs smelled sweet and rich. The damask had been hung that day, and it flowed down over the windows like red wine.

My father made me stand before the company in my new clothes, and this time he had defeated my mother, and I was dressed in velvet, all nut-brown. I had to declaim a Latin poem to show off my learning. He served me up that night as he did the silver bowls and the pewter and the knives and the newfangled forks they had begun to use at court, though my mother said he went too far and most of the company would not know how to use forks and God knows I did not. Sir Valentine said fingers were made before forks and would not have one at his table. They were there only for show, to shine upon the linen. No one used them. I watched, wanting to see how it was done.

My father's new scutcheon was carved upon the chimney, for he must have arms as all the others in such houses. He had took to himself the ancient crest of Henlow, the three pine trees and the portcullis, its meaning long lost in time. He did have the wit to have a lighted candle carved within the center to remind himself that his fortune had a mortal base, though my mother told all that it was put there in thanks for God's bounty to us.

As we sat at table, something, some flick at my father's pride, was said. What it could have been I know not. He rose up so high above me that I thought I had done wrong and he was going to strike me. But instead he spit upon his fingers and doused all the fine waxen candles. We sat silent and cold, all the company, with the fire from the big hearth flickering on the walls and all the rest darkness.

When he spoke, his voice was softer than I had ever heard it.

"I have seen," he said, "a thousand of those lit before the mincing king, and I who made them early in the morning and held my fingers over the hot wax to keep them free enough of cold to work must stand without and never warm and see the people dance."

Later that night I stole from my bed and crouched

in the gallery over the great hall and watched the men below as they smoked around the fire. My mother had told me that tobacco drove men mad; I think I was waiting to see them go mad and caper about the room in their dark clothes and piss into the fire as the men did at Lacy House when they were mad with drink. I prayed a little that they would go mad before I fell asleep there. I remember itching under my shift but dared not pick the little flea for fear they would hear me.

Now there is a blot on memory, and now I see them there. What they were saying waked me, and I could never forget again what it was.

One stood close to the fire and kicked it and made the sparks fly up and light their faces.

"June, by Christ, and must needs a fire," he said.

One settled in his chair. The new leather creaked. My father said, low, "I hear a horse."

Yet I heard nothing but the rain, pounding on the roof—no howling of the dogs, so I knew he was wrong, and no one came.

"The Scots will not have it so, I tell you." That was a red-haired man with a full tawny beard.

One roused himself who seemed to have been sleeping. "Trust a Scot and trust the devil," he said, and fell adozing again.

"So we have sunk to this, that we look to the Scots for help. We will stop this king ourselves," the red-haired man said, and I thought my father would call him down for speaking so of the king in his house, but he did not.

"How so?" My father laughed, and I could see by the hunch of his heavy shoulders that he held fury in him.

"They say he plans to stop men settling in Virginia and New England."

"In God's name, why?"

"He cannot force the Prayer Book into their hands so far away. He fears a freedom of religion grows there he cannot control."

"Control! Control!" the red-haired man burst out again. "Does he think of nothing else? He'd tie the lid to the pot to keep the steam within."

"Oh, 'tis that damnable archbishop holding one ear and the queen tother. They ride him by his ears like an ass."

All this had waked the sleeping man. "What of our investment if we can send no settlers? Every man here has invested in the New World. We must protect that or be ruined."

My father lifted up the ale from the fire and poured it smoking in the tankards they held. I could smell the spices.

"Damn me. What choice have we?" Most of the time I knew not who spoke what. They were only voices rising up to the gallery. "On one side a foolish king who peels the land to its bones—would you have us choose other and let every wild-worded rabble-rouser loose? How would we control them? Why, your own woods are full of men who would cut your throat for a penny."

My body shivered from something more than cold to hear them speak so, as when a person walks over your grave.

No one answered, and the red-haired man went on grinding his ax about the king. "I tell you, while he is being rid by the Catholic queen, we will be pushed into choosing other mounts."

"And loose anarchy in the land, and every damned tinker and cobbler and tallow chandler rule over us?" There they sat and spoke so in my father's house who had been a tallow chandler himself, and he said nothing. I was ashamed for him.

Another rose and stretched his arms. He made a growing shadow from the fire that flowed over me. "We will control them." He laughed, but angry as my father had been. "We will use their hate of the arch-bishop and the queen."

"And then?"

"Hell's fire." He laughed again. "There is always that."

"Do not joke at such things." I was surprised at my father's voice. "You speak as a cynic of religion."

"I do not," the man answered him, "but from the bottom of my conscience. While we are slowly imprisoned in such stupidities as who should bob to the east and who should bow to the west and such like matters that the royal fool does call religion, it covers over ruin and our liberties. Who can live so? Why, even here we shiver in our boots for lack of trust that one may overhear us. What kind of life is that for a man? 'Tis spiritual whoredom. The queen's a Catholic whore, and that little mean scholar Laud but uses his old quarrels of religion so that London courtiers can bleed us white. 'Tis no wonder we county men do hate their masks and dancing and gaudy shows at court. We pay for them."

The red-haired man laughed and leaned over to pour himself ale. "Aie, there's many an honest Christian carries his beliefs in his pocket."

"He says he is the happiest king in Christendom."

"He is like a sow that lies under a tree and eats the chestnuts but knows not nor cares where they came from."

To call the king of England a sow! I clutched the railings and prayed that they would not be struck by lightning, as Charity told me had happened to a man in Northampton who blasphemed the king and was struck as he stood and was shriveled up and black as burned meat, she said.

"They say the queen and her Catholic friends do act in the masques and prance half-naked as pagan gods and goddesses," said one who had not spoke.

"And no one at the court can tell which is which," the red-haired man said. "Enough of this. Would you lie down with her, the very whore of Babylon, and see us driven into such impotent meetings as this, whining around fires in country houses?"

So it was a meeting and not a feast as I had thought.

"He speaks well," one said.

It seemed to release them all. Their dark forms moved and stretched. One reached into the fire and lit his pipe. I saw his face aglow and thought, aie, now they will stop this drivel and go mad.

"I have slept with many a whore, but I will not with the whore of Babylon," my father said. There was a little laughter, and it died, and they still waited. I had not heard my father ever speak of whores and with such ease among men. I liked him then, as a stranger we feel warm toward by the ease of his laughter. I think I slept then and was waked, almost too cold to move, by the opening of the great doors and the sound of the wind.

I saw a cloak, and heard the stamp of feet below, and thought in my half dream that it looked like the devil, for they had built up the fire and it flung the stranger's shadow as if it haunted all the room. I watched it grow smaller as he walked to the fireplace, and then it was only a man, younger than the others, stamping before the fire and cursing the foul night without and steaming by the flames to warm himself while my father poured him ale.

The clock struck midnight, and I was afraid of the witching hour.

"I have rid harder than ever in my life," he spoke to the fire, and then he turned to the others. " 'Twas done, I cannot believe it."

"It is unthinkable, that it should come to this," the red-haired man spoke.

"They were condemned—as harsh a condemnation as I ever heard for writing what was no more than a sermon, to stand in the stocks at Palace Yard and have their ears cut off, and then to solitary confinement for the rest of their lives."

"All three?"

"Aie. Prynne, Bastwick, Burton, all three."

"These were no common felons, but respectable men, a doctor, a lawyer, a merchant. . . ."

"Has it at last gone far enough to dark our blood?"

The red-haired man put his hand on my father's back, whom I had never seen touched, and my father let it stay there, as a boy with a comrade.

"Aie, far enough," he mumbled.

"They will not dare to carry out such a sentence."

"I saw them do it." The traveler was near to crying. "That good old man. I could not believe what I saw. It was a bright, hot day today in London." His voice was quiet, as one telling a story, and he brought up to me the London I had never seen, a mixture of Cheapside and rats, and golden towers and palaces, princes and princesses riding white horses, and knights in silver armor, and silks and satins and the blowing of trumpets, and all, always in the sun, with the white banners whipping in the wind, not this, this new thing, of old men standing in the stocks, and preachers, too.

"I never saw such crowds. They did broadcast rosemary and sweet herbs 'til all the Palace Yard was covered. I could not get near enough to hear them, but the word passed through the crowd that Prynne was preaching of Christ through all two hours as they stood clamped there in the brutal stocks. Burton was dressed as for a wedding, with fine white gloves and a nosegay in his hand. I could see hands passing up cups of wine as they say the Disciples did to Christ on the cross."

" 'Twas vinegar on a sponge."

"A mistranslation."

I feared they would get into that Scripture picking my parents seemed to like so well and ruin the story.

"A woman climbed up and kissed Burton and held him while the crowd cheered. A man beside me said it was Mrs. Burton. After two hours the executioner walked out, and I saw the crowd around the stocks part and turn their backs on him. He cut off Prynne's ears first and branded his face with the letters *S L* for Seditious Libeler. All was so quiet I could hear from that far the sizzling of his face and see the smoke of his flesh rise up. He moaned, and the crowd took up the moan and carried it as if some great beast had been hurt and groaned for pain."

"Think you the king heard that?"

"The king was hunting in the country."

They waited for the young man at the fire to tell more.

"Bastwick, the doctor, had brought a surgeon's knife and tried to instruct the executioner, but he would not be instructed and cut so the blood coursed out and ran down their clothes and into pools on the stone pavement. Burton was begging the women not to dip their handkerchiefs in it as that was blasphemy and pagan practice."

"God damn me. What a stupidity is this, to make martyrs of fanatic ranters." I was beginning to recognize that man when he spoke, the one who had slept before. He had a piping voice, small for his heavy body, and moved slower than the rest.

"These were no ranters, but honest, upright men. I am ashamed of my country." The traveler turned again to the fire and fell acrying against the stones, as if he had finally come as far and seen as much as he could stand and was at end of his strength. It was my father who held and comforted him. I think that shame and outrage have more to do with civil war than all the great events we can look back upon. I had never seen a man cry before, and that so brave a man who had rode all the way from London through the night.

"One more thing and one more thing, and one thing always. Never enough." The red-haired man spoke even more angrily than he had before. "We get used to these oppressions when they come separately, as bitter pills, and one digested and forgot before the next. That damned blind, deaf Sodomite! What will finally break us?"

"I care not for such speaking of the king before me," the piping voice spoke up. "Damn me. I am an upright-enough plain-speaking Parliament fellow who wants to protect his investments, but this goes too far. Is there wrong in that?"

"Aie, there's wrong enough." The young man had turned from my father's arms. "Care you not that our liberty of conscience is trampled and we are whored. . . ."

The other jumped from his seat and yelled, "Liberty of conscience I hate as bringing anarchy and atheism upon us! I like not serving under narrow archbishops, nor will I under blind authority of bigoted Presbyters; they are but two sides of the same coin."

"That is not the choice. The choice is between liberty and authority."

"You would have freethinking Antinomians light fires all over England and make it a land of libertines?"

How they threw those strange unpassionate words at one another so passionately I could not fathom.

"I am proud to be called libertine, sir." The young man's words rang as in a sermon, and they stood with their necks forward and their faces red, ready as cocks to fly at each other.

Anger seemed easy, with easy words in that man's mouth, but it was in my father's blood and muscles and his bandy legs as he said, quieter than the rest, "I think the king is mad—that for the accepting of a little puny Book of Common Prayer that all might think alike and pray alike, and for a little bobbing at the altar and holy rags, he'd drag us down to this. A way must be found. . . ."

They stopped arguing among themselves and listened then, listened to my own father.

"He must be maneuvered into calling back the Parliament."

"After eight years?"

The man at the fire, now warmed, fell into a chair beside it and began wrenching at his boots. My father stood before him and clasped a boot between his legs. The man pushed at his ass to get the boot off as he spoke. "There is some talk of that already in London, that if the Scots accept not the Book of Common Prayer, he will call the Parliament for money to go to war against them."

"Against the Scots? Why, not even he will hear. . . ."

"So that is the way," my father said. "Aie, we break

too soon into factions of our own, mewling here like maids in love."

"Who is near enough the king to put such a flea in his ear?" and all impotent again, they fell to staring at the fire, and smoke from their pipes curled up in its light.

"The Fairfaxes, the Verneys, and the Earl of Essex, that stolid son of a wild father. He could be king today if his father had succeeded in his rebellion."

"Would that he were," someone said.

As they quarreled and drank among themselves, I saw a different thing. I had seen a man standing in the stocks at Northampton when we went to the fair. The blood was clotted black in the sun where his ears had been. He screamed of Christ the while but seemed to curse the ground with his name, and all the faces, hard with hate, around him did the same. In truth, I never saw religion as more than manners and politics and used as a stone wall of willful strength by my mother when I was a child. If you knelt one way for prayer, you were a king's man; if the other, you were for the Parliament. If I dive down within me for something like the light that Thankful Perkins there carries, I see it not in churches or in the moan of angry crowds, but in other, secret places, where the child's eyes see. Thankful keeps that clearness; ah, I wish he would wake again and talk to me here as we ride along.

I have only glimpses of that light, as most men do. Some do treasure such glimpses, and some do fear them. Mostly my vision is through a glass darkly; but there are rifts, and deep within my childhood I carry in me those glimpses of what I know to be face to face with God. Once I passed by my father's chamber and saw him sitting by the window there. He was praying silently into his hands, as if the words dropped there, and when he raised his face to the sky, he had in it a tough and leathern joy of his own, but I never knew what caused it and never saw him so in company.

I must have slept again, huddled there in the gallery, for I remember nothing more until my mother clapped her hand across my mouth and hauled me to my feet. She whispered that it was evil to eavesdrop, that little pitchers had big ears, and that I would go to hell. She dragged me, already, at eight, too big to be carried, along the gallery and thrust me into my chamber. I found my way in the dark to my bed to lie there and wish my aunt would come and kiss me good-night. In truth, I think I have wished that every night of my life, but even though I told the rest, how could I tell that to any man?

God knows there was none of such meetings at Lacy House. When I crossed each day by Henlow Wood, I crossed a Rubicon of expectations. There, in the long days, I prated passages of Virgil to the tutor, for I kept words in memory then as a sponge sops vinegar. As easily, for the other end of the seesaw of my learning, I prated the Epistles and Psalms after evening prayer for my parents, my father sitting staring at the fire, my mother nodding. I remember little of her voice in repose like that; I hear it always with the thin edge of urgency with which she ruled a roost of women my father came not near. But one night she sighed and asked me to declaim for her the thirteenth chapter of the Letter to the Corinthians. My hand lay upon the arm of her chair, and when I spoke the words, she lay her own yellow hand over it and lay her head back, and tears fell from her closed eyes.

I had long since fell out of love with Lacy House. Too many fine mysterious things had grown domestic in the light of too many days. I saw Sir Valentine grow fat and bald as Lazarus, though he wore a fine periwig. Usually by afternoon the wig had become drunk and slipped and staggered around his head and sometimes fell to the floor. He seemed to me to have changed in a day from that comely ruddy man who had held me on his lap at Christmas to this bald mountain who could hardly sit his house, for I reckon the vision of youngsters to care not for the saving compassionate slowness of change, but to see all one way one day and one way the other.

My aunt seemed not to change, though, except that she grew ever younger and smaller. How was I to know then 'twas me agrowing up to her and reaching to her shoulder nearly at ten or so, tall for my years? I had a fine contempt that she would fawn so upon that old man. How could I fathom then that she was only twenty-five in years, for she had been married to Sir Valentine at fourteen and loved him as I love her, for the first kindness she had known and for his smile like a blessing upon her after her lost and lonely childhood unmothered at Henlow? Sir Valentine had doted upon his child bride, and child bride she remained to him and seemed untouched by much at Lacy House.

I went not ever to their chapel when they prayed. There was an unspoken truce between the houses that I should not. I came there after morning prayer, and before the evening prayer I had long gone to my house. But often I peeped into the chapel because it was so beautiful—the carved face, the golden candlesticks on the altar, the chapel to the pagan goddess, Mary, that they had made in their ignorance of Jesus' mother. She stood, in a blue robe that fell like water, all painted with gold stars, and her face was the face of my aunt. Sir Valentine had had it carved so in the first flush of their marrying. There she stood, at fifteen, her eyes cast down at the babe in her arms, a candle lit before her that brushed her face alive with its light.

I began to see that the stillness of Henlow was busy, industrious, something more solid and more pleasing than all the noise and riot of Lacy House. That June night when the man rode out from London to Henlow had been the first of many such meetings. My father grew stronger, surer, as if his taproot had indeed grown down and he drew strength from his earth. He was finding a way for his new strength and his ambition to reach far beyond the confines of his house. There grew in me a compassion for him I had not known before, for his strong voice in the night, for his silences as he stared into the fire, one leg upon a stool, for though he seemed to have forgot, in his new direction, the hunger of his childhood, it stayed in the bandy leg that often hurt him in the winter. Then he limped and dragged his powerful upper body like a sick hound that hauls itself along by its great shoulders. I thought his silences to be like mine, an untouched world. I was already then carrying a secret pocket book and writ down there many fine lines and thought myself a poet. But I ever kept the pocket book hid, for I knew that if they found and read it, my father would beat me for such courtly fripperies as poetry, my mother for religion, Sir Valentine for unmanliness, and Peregrine, God knows, would try to whip the scholar out of me as he always had.

There were things I tried to whip out of him. We saw the same things, but he learned to use them, to charm and shrug, and when I spoke against such practices, he laughed me to scorn. What was it offended me so? I cannot say, even now, though I know it is a quality I have fought for four years now. So much for sale? Or was it a jockeying for position that spread from the great hall to the winery to the bakery, among the grooms? It was only a whiff of something that usually I tried to brush away, as I do now these wet leaves that flick against my face.

Something, a weariness at being confined to the country, was at Lacy House and crept along the corridors in those times when Sir Valentine did not keep company there. But that was seldom. When he did keep company, the men fought easily. They seemed caught in tedium. They were ever genial but seldom tender. Their astounding pose of ignorance was worrisome as a sickness rather than a fashion, for most of them had been at Oxford, and some at the Inns of Court.

'Tis strange how little I see my aunt among them all this time. It was as if she lay then in my heart waiting, forgot for a while, as a stream that disappears and flows underneath a meadow and then finds a fall to release it so that it seems to come from no place like a new spring, a holy well, and courses stronger in new lands.

Ah, God knows what is hidden in the heart until there comes a long day's journey, a night without sleep. It is like the first waking, surprised to a dream of things so long forgot.

I tried hard to take on a thick hide there of the learning my father yearned for me to have, though he cared not for it. How much of hidden shame there was in the learning of swordplay, aie, and I know now what play it was. I took upon me to grow my hair and thrust out my silly hairless chin as arrogant as I could to ape the others, to bow, to scrape the hat to the floor, to turn out my feet like a fashionable duck. Oh, I turned, at least for all to see, a fair young coxcomb. Aie, I even tried to grab my father's hand once and shake it in the new way of fashion, but he fetched me a clout across my fine ear, and said, "Leave off your pulling and hauling at my paw!"

Now it all splits into pictures, fragments, and one day, what was it? I was running along the gallery to the schoolroom at Lacy House where I had left my shuttlecock. The tutor, damn me, his name escapes me but he will not let me go, was standing, staring out of the mullioned window as he did much there, a lonely man, neither master nor servant, and ignored by both. I saw the shadow of the dark bars across his face like prison bars.

He caught me by my flying hair.

"You. . . ." What was it he said to me? It is gone. I know it struck my heart. It is that striking that I remember and hold still, not his words. I swaggered away from him, hidden behind the shallow ways my soul cared not for. I felt hatred for that tall, wasted man who reeked of wine. I know now that I was repulsed by his despair. One morning afterward, long after, he was found hanging from the rafters of the schoolroom. Like the coward grouse that flushes too soon, he did not wait for war.

Now I see myself riding my first horse, Pegasus, at a

snail's pace along the road between the houses that expected so much. It was on that daily ride, through rain and sun and winter and summer, that I called my soul my own.

Once, at evening, when the sun had made a mirror of a water pool in the road, I dismounted, out there where no one could see me, and knelt down beside the pool to see what I looked like, see, not glance, as I had ever done before mirrors in front of others. I saw my face, a ruddy square face, and my eyes like hazelnuts. My shoulders had begun to widen and grow strong. My hair was burnished by the late sun and fell in thick wings toward the pool. The careful lovelocks I had fondled while I read to make them curl hung down almost to the water. I looked a long time, well pleased at what I saw there, but studying as well. I saw all their masks upon me, the hair, the lace, the jacket of rich russet wool, but I saw my eyes, too, that recognized me and could not be fooled, and I thought, who knows what lies behind this face they find so comely? I know, but cannot tell, and no one else in the world is like this. This is the first time since the expulsion from the Garden of Eden itself that this boy has knelt so by this pool and seen his face. Pegasus nudged me and threw me forward into the puddle. The face I had admired so came up covered with mud, the lovelocks were lank, the russet coat a sodden mess. I thought it a judgment of God's for my vanity, not just an impatient horse.

When I came in late for evening prayers, I lied and said I was chasing a deer and Pegasus had stumbled and throwed me headlong into a stream. I would not have told a soul what really happened, not only out of shame, but because it had happened in my world, the world between the houses where I drew my own shadow.

These are all snatches, as we remember snatches of old songs that bring back glimpses of the singing of them. So much eludes me, the long, gentle, senseless days, the grace—I had forgot the grace.

I THINK we are rising out of the fog. I can see two horses and their shadow riders, now four, now six horses ahead. The fog grows white and thinner. We scramble slowly up from it out of the creek bed onto the flat plain. Behind us it still lies along the streams, the rills, the branches like long veins that stretch so quietly along this land and hardly seem to flow until they meet together in one strong quiet River Thames. I know this land so well, this open bowl that we have made so long into the battleground of England. The sky lifts here from off our backs, and now the long, thin, fragile distant column stretches all the way to the horizon. The men, the few trees, even the little villages that I can scarcely yet see are drawn black, thinned by the muted day, all those small things that make a living place, dwarfed by the empty sky. No one follows us. Here at the rear guard, I see only the sinking fog behind us and empty land where nothing moves.

All I have thought of is the stuff of boys, and not fine matters. What would they tell me of how, through those bated years, this land changed its rhythm and finally burst, or fell's more like it, into war; how these fallow, empty, changeless fields came to be battlefields? Yet if I were to tell, later, when I can, of greater matters, it would not be true. It would not be what set us here in this black line, vulnerable to the cold and damp, wandering across this plain of all plains, in this time of all times. On such days we are not the Lord's Saints, as we tell ourselves, nor they, our enemies, the hosts of Midian. Though all that is, God knows, a fine language and much uplifting, it sounds far off to simple Englishmen, caked with the mud we came from. Many will say it was a fine religious war as in the old Crusades.

No, I would tell instead what soil it grew from, watered by stupidity and weary charms on one hand, and on the other by frustration and ambition. The men who fought the king in Parliament when he was finally forced to call it came from such meetings as those around my father's hearth. So many men who flocked around the king were like the men at Lacy House, men of arrogant despair at being long unused, uncalled, unformed by manly duties, until they counted it a gesture to ruin themselves. I would tell of the buying and selling of land, how the men who rioted sold and sold again to those who, like my father, waited with contempt to put them in pawn—sober, upright, cold, ambitious men.

I think there was no one to tell the king of this. Else he would not have come on so ridiculous an errand, to ask his long-neglected, festering Parliament for money to fight the Scots to make them pray as he thought fit, a war to make men kneel one way or the other as a dancing master will flick at the legs of children with his wand to train them to be graceful. My Christ, I cannot think that all this blew to flames over the flickings of a dancing master.

When, after eleven years, he saw his Parliament again, he must have seen a strange new alien seed grown there, more like the Presbyterian Scots he sought to fight than any men he had kept close to his ear all those years. There were, in his diminished forests, his sold crown lands, the church lands long usurped, so many of my father's breed. He could not know them, and Christ knows he had not wit to harness their new strength. Their persistence, their manners, the way they looked and disapproved of him offended him. He was a man of delicacy and most easily offended.

But now, what of such matters? There is a birdcall, and another. The birds know before us that the day is clearing. On such a day as this is now, a white day without sun, came the agents of the Parliament to my father's courtyard. I stood over beside the red-haired man with tawny beard who had been so long ago feasting in our house. He sat his horse as one born in the saddle and read the proclamation of the Parliament, his voice excited, ringing so loud it brought the maids and dairy men to the outbuilding doors and echoed against the stone walls.

Resolved upon the question, that an army shall be henceforth raised for the safety of the king's person, defense of both houses of Parliament, and those who have obeyed their orders and commands, and preserving the true religion, the laws, liberty, and peace of the kingdom. . . .

Some such words he read, and more, 'tis gone, but at the end, something came again. ". . . To move His Majesty to a good accord with his Parliament to prevent a civil war." The last words rang around us. I heard a horse, pawing at the stones, and then my father's voice.

"What will you have of me?"

"Can you raise and arm a troop to gather at Northampton?"

"Aie, I have been some time preparing. A hundred men, pikes, pots, backs, and breasts. . . ."

I was thirteen and fit to be hog-tied with excitement at it all. Still, I could not fathom why they should muster men and arm them to stop a war. I had heard my father say the king sat at York and had issued a call to the militia for the same purpose a month since —to stop a war. We had much word of an army gathering there all through the month of June, of much license and rioting of the mercenary soldiery that battened on the town.

I had never seen so many folks in my life as were gathered at Northampton when I rode there with my father to deliver the men. We had rode so many times before to deliver cattle to sell at the fair, but even with all its crowds and holler, the fair was nothing to this wild surge of men.

We had started out so fine from Henlow in the early morning under colors that my mother made with the three trees and the portcullis and the candle and "God Our Witness" embroidered below. We were soon almost pulled apart from one another and jostled and diminished in the crowded green by a storm of men and horses, and wagons, and every three feet a preacher. The colors were so fine. There was many a "God Our Strength" and "God Our Witness" and some "Prepare Ye the Way of the Lord," and one in Hebrew.

Finally, in the late afternoon, somehow, the wagtag had been organized into some kind of marching order. We watched them trying to step to the drums as they came along the green, dragging new pikes sixteen feet long as if they were pitchforks, tripping the men behind them.

At last my father's troop did jingle into view, and there was Lazarus. His head was like a lantern on a stick, bobbing and smiling. He was costumed like a man in a country play in a pot too big for his head, a breast and back of iron, a fine sash Charity had found for him, as silly a soldier as ever trailed a pike. I doubled up with laughter.

All day his shoulder had been clapped by my father and the county officers, telling their country boys all words of flattery, preparing to send them, those killers of connies and pigs and sheep, against the king's mercenaries, who had fought in the Low Countries those many years and would do anything for pay and loot. We did not know this, Lazarus and I. We knew that day only dumb show pride and war like county fairs.

I could not stop laughing at Lazarus that they had took for a soldier—scarecrow-skinny, rake-legged, high-bottomed, paid attention to for the first time. 'Twas not like any army had been before since time remembered, when men had been ripped from the land and pressed into service, no, not like that. He was told he was wanted, told he was needed, not dragged, as he had understood the world to be, to be broke and hoppled and rid.

This was indeed a new way, where the sun of the squire shone on the faces of the least of these, his brethren. Lazarus was as high with pride as his own stink, and I, the lord god universe's son of glory in one corner of the icy world, could not stop laughing at him. He looked up and saw me. It was as if I had pricked his joy with a pin. I can still hear my stupid, arrogant laughter.

They marched away, and that was all. At Henlow we drifted again in summer. I went no longer to Lacy House, for king's men were quartered there. I wandered that summer, flicking at weeds with a stick and waiting for I knew not what. War whispered near us, as distant summer thunder, but we saw it not. Oh, from time to time there was an officer to sup with my father, two or three soldiers in the yard to beg for food. Most of the horses were took away that summer for the army. We would hear rumors that the king's or Parliament's men had passed within five miles of Henlow and yet not know it, for the country people kept silence and cared little for one side or the other then. They hid their crops from the thieving of the roving bands.

Then, one day in November, Charity came weeping into the great hall and brought the war with her. Lazarus had come home. She had seen him in the distance, she said, wandering down the road like a man blinded, but he was not blinded, though the wounded man who leaned upon him was. Lazarus had walked as dumb as a pig toward his Golgotha. The man told her he had found him wandering in a lane after a battle, not knowing whither to go, for he had not been five miles from my father's land ever in his life. The mercenaries had been given the town for pay, and they were killing for practice, taking food and drink and plate and women. I have seen towns after them. Nothing moves, or only a few humans wander like chickens, picking among the rubble of their passing, ones they have not bothered to kill and strip. Lazarus was wandering like one of those. He'd had his ears cropped and his tongue uprooted from his mouth. He had wandered in the way of their passing, like a stone in the way of a horse's hoof. It was a village near a place called Edgehill that I had not heard of.

Charity looked after him in the cottage on the edge of the wood, and he sat there and charmed the animals to him, the piglets, calves, even the scawed deerlings, who skitter at a leaf's fall in the woods. He seemed quite happy, weaving his baskets among them, almost relieved. With some silly pride he made a basket hat to hide the holes where his ears had been. We got used to him soon again, Lazarus the simpleton, making noises in his throat like a pig's grunt.

In the spring my father sent me to Oxford. The day I went, on Pegasus, with my box and servant behind me on an old nag, he embraced me. I can still feel his arm across my shoulders, man to man, as I had seen him do with the young man by the fire that night so long ago when Prynne and Burton and Bastwick were punished in London for what all men were doing now. It was the first time he had touched me with his hands except to whip me since I was a child. My mother would not say good-bye to me, for I was being sent, she said, into the king's maw. His court had been long at Oxford, and she feared that I would be infected with his doctrine. Little she knew the king had none, only a way, not a doctrine. I saw her watching from her chamber as I rode away, still as a stone figure.

What comes back first to me from Oxford, why, it makes me laugh to think it—that I longed for an ostrich plume to put into my hat! They cost a year's living for honest men and were smuggled over for the court all the way from France. The lordly boys from Lauds and Magdalen flaunted them, though some of them were so poor they had to go to their beds until their shirts were washed. All curled and slickened, they pranced along behind the arrogant lady, the Catholic queen, and lived on glances from the Jezebel as she kept her penny court sweeping through Jericho, walking Oxford's meadows with her ladies. 'Twould have been piteous with poverty clinging to them and death so near had they not been so cruel. They'd lost all but that. They styled it fleering to take the High Street or the Broad, and clear it of the people with their swords, and tumble the old or the poor into the gutters. Even though I yearned for the plume, I hated the acts that went with it, the despising of all that was not like themselves, the loudness of their voices, how they took to a way of hesitant speaking to imitate the king, how they aped the lofty, desperate, and discontented-minded spirits of all those dispossessed king's men who were garrisoned there, rotting with weariness.

Ten of them caught three of us one night, for we had been boating and were caught by the eventide. My God, they were cavalierish enough; they stripped us of our breeks, jeered at our privies and our simple hats and small lace and our country voices and throwed us in the water. While I shivered there naked and they played king on the shore, they shamed me into an anger I had not known before and cannot lose ever. It pushed me into all the schoolboy rebellions. How brave we thought we were to write upon the walls at night until the watch caught me and Laodocious Martin who died at the siege of Taunton writing *Astrologia non est scientia* upon the door of Lauds and took and flung us into jail, for they loved to catch the gowns and knowed no difference between us and Cavaliers, nor cared much. All we got was a whipping from our tutors, who wielded mighty whips and said it was the writing up of newfangled democratical notions that the king might see as he passed and so be offended. Democratical was the most evil word at Oxford when the king was there, and little better after.

'Twas not only newfangled notions, but words too, words that rolled and tumbled through us in a new way, as we took to the heady speech of the new dangerous men. How was it, Johnny, for the lack of a feather and some tricks of country speech and simpler ways than they that you entered so into those new and urgent ways? A boy needs friends, and I was fourteen and something wakening within after all the words I could not say at Henlow or at Lacy House.

If the king's fanfarons aped him, my dear friends and I aped Freeborn Jack Lilburne as shamelessly. Why, it was like a dawn breaking for me to hear all that martyr's words, unspoken even in my wildest thoughts before, and now printed and hid beneath my pillow, to be learned with more zeal than all the dusty mumblings from tutors' mouths. We kept, my friends and I, many a late vigil over these new things and thought to change the world.

Why, I would even stand alone, in my room, fourteen years old, and not pretend, no, more than that, be at that moment Lilburne himself when he stood before the court of the Star Chamber, whose very presence had silenced the bravest of men. I would say his words, whispering so my tutor would not hear me, that had rung out there when he was only twenty-two and stood so with his hat foursquare upon his head to shout defiance to the greatest power in England. It became my creed, more sweet to me than any I heard chanted in the Oxford churches.

For what is done to anyone may be done to everyone: besides, being all members of one body, that is, of the English Commonwealth, one man should not suffer wrongfully, but all should be sensible, and endeavor his preservation; otherwise they may give way to an inlet of the sea of will and power, upon their laws and liberties, which are the boundaries to keep out tyranny and oppression; and one who assists not in such cases betrays his own rights, and is overrun, and of a free man made a slave when he thinks not of it, or regards it not, and so shunning the censure of turbulency, incurs the guilt of treachery to the present and future generations.

For that, in his youth, he had been flogged from Saint Paul's to Westminster, stripped to the waist, and tied to the back of a cart, while he preached Christ and liberty to all the crowds who lined the streets as long as he had strength and lit such fires that day that still do run through this army.

To think those words were said so, in English words, and by so young an Englishman. Why, it is such a thing of pride that long after all words of kings are forgot, these will stay in English hearts.

Outside that child's play of our democratical whisperings, 'twas all bowing and scraping and never a hat upon the head as a freeborn man and equal to all in the sight of Christ, but always aflourishing in the hand, swords clanking and many deaths from a thing as fruitless as exercise of honor in that terrible child's play court, and tutors running, gowns flying like blackbirds' wings, after boys who could have been their children, and all for pride of birth. Much time was spent in the setting of figures for the court ladies of what the stars foretold.

But John Wycliffe who had translated the Bible into the English tongue so that all men could hold it in their hands had walked there. When it all offended me, I remembered that. I passed Harvey often in the High Street who had discovered the circulation of the blood. He had opened the gate of his body and found his blood awhirl, in a space, as rushing and circular as Copernicus had seen when he studied the stars.

I saw the king once, standing on the porch of Saint Mary's, only a glance. I was afeard to look more. What is it in us makes the heart quake at the sight of kings? He had a leady look from some illness, and long petulance from childhood was left over and forgot in his face. He was lingering there, speaking very deep to some man whose back was to me. He wore that day a long brown periwig and a simple brown or purple coat, I can't remember, but a dun-colored velvet hat, all plumed.

After two years, in the early spring of 1645, my

father called me back to Henlow. He did not tell me why. I think he wanted to hide me from the war, though he could say nothing of this to me. He had changed much, grown bitter as I had not seen him before. Nothing of how it went was to his liking. As many such men as himself, he had taken a step toward liberty, found it contemptible, and drawn back again.

"Damn me," he said, "the army has been took over by the hottest heads in England. They have sewn the cockle of heresies, and every rabble thinks himself a fair Lilburne to petition Parliament and importune his betters for every manner of damned foolishness. Why, they'll turn everyone against all the nobility and clergy and gentry in the land and destroy the monarchy itself. That is not what we meant when we started, but to chastise the king—to trim the tree, not strike so near the root. How can any prince be a king only of beggars, tinkers, and cobblers, for that is what they are reducing this land to?"

He did not say tallow chandlers. At least he did not say that. In short, the war had cost him too much of what he had built at Henlow, and he was afraid. The stone walls that were to stand for centuries of his house had grown frail as a wattle hut in his eyes.

CHRIST in me, now I come to it and relive it, that which had grown in me and then became what Thankful calls conversion, though in truth, God knows it was made of no great visions. But I would tell the world, it is more powerful in my head than all this day's or any other day's riding that came after.

On the morning of my sixteenth birthday, I knelt before my father for my daily blessing as custom had forced me to my knees all my life on the cold stones, and I had never before thought anything of it. When the servants filed into the great hall and morning prayers began, it seeped into my ears for the first time that my father spoke plain before God as if he had a closed contract or covenant with him. The servants creaked that day as always, let wind, sighed, and scraunched their eyes, kneeling so not from conversion but toward the direction of the pence and the food and the bit of ground, and feared among them my father's power, though they were taught to call it God's. God brought the rain, the drought, but my father held the purse strings, owned the food and the roofs over their heads.

Charity knelt behind me, sniveling and grunting. I thought first, she is old, and then, no, she is crying. How can she cry so, like the drip of last raindrops, when it is my birthday? Aie, look to what annoys you most and find your innocence that can stink more, hurt more than guilt. She reminded me of Lazarus again and of my hurting laughter. That was why, when prayers were over, I followed the insistence of her crying down through the stone passage to the kitchens where the sun never came. I found her in the smokehouse bellowing like an unmilked cow.

God knows my path here has no great things along it. Instead of the voice of God as some have heard or the seduction of drums and banners, I have only a giggle, a sniffle, a few rags, cold knees at morning prayer; what noble tilting that is, more foolish I could not find.

I finally made her tell me through her tears what the matter was. My father had decided to flood their village to make a lake and enclose the common up to Henlow Wood to run his deer. He had looked out one morning and found the village an offense to his eyes. There were only five squat houses in the way of his plans for a fine new vista in the Italian manner.

He told them they must move away to the other side of his land, out of sight of his house, there being better houses, emptied by smallpox long since and safe now, but only wanting cleaning and a little daub. Charity feared for Lazarus, for he had known no other place and now would never leave it. His family had lived in that place for who knows how long a lost time, long before my father had husbanded his paternity in one pack and come to Henlow.

All my birthday night I was awake and questioned hard the father that he had placed in my heart and that I had respected and loved all my life. It was not the same man that could do such a thing. My father had been so treated, so run over as if he counted for nothing when he was a child, and showed it still in his pride and his silences and his bandy legs. Had that man he had become and that I knew not forgot that he could do so to other men?

I watched the moon that night until it set, cold in my window. The cold fingered my skin, and my nightshirt huddled to me, all skinny and scrawny in the window. What I had to do did keep showing itself to me, and I did not like it. I felt a fool and afeard and thought great words like "choice between covenant and grace" and such to cover the nakedness I felt with everything I had took for granted stripped away.

So fool I was, my heart quakes still worse than battle to bring it back. A dark morning came, and I did take the shears to my curls that reached half down my arms and were my pride and joy and crop my hair. I did clip away the small lace from my collar and from my sleeves. I did set my hat foursquare upon my head and, clad so, walked up to my father at the morning prayer and did not kneel before him for the first time in my life and am empty still from the bravery of the act. I spoke to him as "thee," my equal as were all men in the sight of God, and called him "my friend in Christ" and that before Charity and my mother and all.

I still flinch from the striking of my father's hand

across my face. Not the fall of the rod I was used to, but the touch of his hand's flesh; I feel it still. Only for that second did he respect me enough to strike me. Then, ashamed, he looked around him, grew red of face, and fell to his prayers. I sat bolted to a chair in the corner and watched the sunlight from the new windows crawl up his back while he knelt, leading his people and preparing himself for me.

He locked me in my chamber.

All through the day he came again to me. I'd hear the key turn in the lock, and he would stand there, and all he ever said that day was "Doff thy hat." I stood there all day long, my hat foursquare upon my head and hearing no small voice of grace within, only his "Doff thy hat."

What he went through I know not. All he said was "Doff thy hat," as if the whole matter between us hung on the tilting of my hat and the length of my hair.

At evening he opened wide the door, and I knew from his eyes that I had lost him. I passed so close I could hear the creaking of his chest under his leathern jerkin. It made me try to touch him, but he shrank from me and would not let me.

I walked down through the long stone corridors and heard my mother whisper from the light of a door, "Didst doff thy hat?"

I shook my head and said, "I cannot other than this."

"Fool," she called after me, her voice rang along the stones, " 'twas only after all the doffing of a hat." I saw nothing of her but her hand raised yellow in the torchlight.

"Fool" into the night court followed me.

I still go, and they still call "fool" and "doff thy hat."

We must accept as hallowed the unblessings of our fathers.

I could not leave my horse Nell, for after all, I'd reared her and broke her and she was mine.

When had he given orders to saddle her? I still

wonder and still see her standing tethered in the courtyard; no one there, no sound, the silence of cold and
evening, when all men are gathering by the fire and
no man should be alone.

I am so far from Henlow now, yet there is that in
me that is always turning at the gate, always ashamed.
How strong the shame that comfort, habit, and the rod
breeds in a man, as I have bred a short turn into Nell
by the touching of her ribs. I sat there, huddled in the
dark, Nell waiting under me and sighing and champing
at her bit.

There is no sound so final as the clanking of a gate.

How many words for "dark" my Oxford tutor made
me write, for he said it was a vulgar thing to declaim
always in repetitions. No. Dark it was when the gate
clanged, dark dark of cold, sensitive dark to the first
stars.

I crossed the dark of Henlow Wood and kept away
from the woodfolk, who would have stripped me clean
without a sir or by your leave. I could see their fires
away in the distance and could not help from smiling,
for my father thought to own Henlow Woods up to the
hanging tree. I rode toward Lacy House for the first
time since the war began. Where else was there to go?

That night there was no sound of chaffing and fellowship. It was so still when I knocked and waited that
I thought it all deserted and all fled. I pushed open the
door to the great hall and stood within listening. Then
my aunt came toward me down the stairs, crying fit to
kill, and held me to her.

And holds me now, and I still whisper, "What's
amiss, madame?"

She whispered back as if the dead hall were listening, " 'Tis Sir Valentine, my love. I fear he's adying."

She smelled of lemons, her hair, her hands. I held
back from her with all my muscles and touched her
only with my cheek and the tips of my fingers, for I
have longed too much for the touch of another since
waiting alone all night for a sign.

"He fell over and his face went red and he could

not breathe and now one side of him is all frozen. Peregrine's gone for the physician, but 'twill be a terrible time before he comes." She led me up the stairs, and I heard her say, "How did you know and come here so quickly? 'Tis so like you to do that." She did not see how I was dressed or changed or grown. She was intent upon her husband.

I went toward him, propped up on the pillows, grinning a great one-sided grin, and I smiled back until I saw it was the illness that had ricked his face. Could I have ever been afeard of the bawling of that mouth, the stamp of his feet, the smell of sweat and spilled wine of him, the clanging of his spurs upon the stones when he'd throw off his boots? That mouth that ripped the air with oaths and yet could whisper something to her when she kissed him that made her smile was like a hollow cavern.

But he could say "Damme," as always, and his eyes were as alive as ever. He held me by my coat and rattled the words.

"Why are you dressed like a cobbler?"

I could not answer. I could see her in the shadow beyond him across the bed. He jogged my coat and made me say, "I have left my father's house," as if that were all.

"That all? No wonder. Old skinflint. Wife's brother-in-law, not mine. I reckon he never gave you a groat to bless yourself with on the road. Old skinflint. Went Presbyterian to save money from giving cross and candles to his parish church." He fell amumbling, lost in his old neighbor's quarrel between them, and she came to him and wiped his head with her handkerchee.

When his voice came again, it was as clear as if he were well. "I reckon now you are going to join the army."

Why, I had then only a niggle and ne'er a notion as the young boy said to the whore of what I was to do, for I had thought behind me all the way through Henlow Wood and not before. I like to believe it was a noble step of mine, thought out and persevered, that made me go to war, but to tell the truth, I had hardly thought of it, but said to him, "Yes," in a little pee-pee voice that shamed me.

I heard her stir, her skirt move, and the rustle of her sleeve.

He said, "King or conscience?"

I whispered, "Conscience."

It was not that I hadn't thought of going to war—I had, and dreamed; all boys do, but it was another place, another time, great things, not this standing by the bed and this admission, first on one foot and then on the other.

"Speak up," he said, through his ricked mouth.

"Conscience," I said, and felt the spit bubbling in my throat.

"Damme, all God, gruel and marrowbones, eh? The Parliament army don't even have women with them, they tell me. Give him some money, Nellie. Kin and neighbors are a damn sight closer than politics." He forgot me then and clutched her hand. "Honey, I hoped to get another son on you, too young for the wars." She fell acrying again and kissing of his purple face.

"Draw in the horns," he kept muttering, "and forget the damned thing. We're all level, all fellows now, all cobblers, tinkers, chimney sweeps now, all freeborn, all fellows, down-diddles, king's stripped, bishop's stripped, all gone. No more witty fellows and drinking into the morning. Might as well die. They say we are to be ruled over by poor people and barrel makers. Damme. Draw in the horns. Governin's not about people. 'Tis treaties and borders and such like things." Oh, he rambled much there while she wiped his chin, and he cried, "Get a son within thee before I die. I drank too much and did forget to mount thee."

And she whispered, "Never mind, my baby."

I am ashamed to say I was offended by his muttering, for no man likes the sound of the grinding of any ax but one like his own.

"I'll go," I said, but she ran to me and held my hand.

"No such thing," she told me, and waved her hand to a servant to watch by the bed, and put her finger to her lips, for he had fallen into some kind of sleep.

"Come, let's put up Nell." She was already smiling, and the tears for him still streaked her face.

I followed her out through the courtyard, and it was she who led her namesake clattering after her across the stones. Under the dim light from the windows, it made my heart cry to see her, so delicate a lady, leading Nell. She brought her to the stable herself and lit a flambeau. It drew the stableman running, but she dismissed him, and we loosened Nell's saddle together.

"I do believe you named her for me, did you?" she teased, and her words were as palpable as if I held them in my hands.

She knelt down like a lass and opened the saddlebags and spoke as to herself. "You did never pack these, my Johnny." She took out my leathern pocket book, the only thing I had put in myself. "Oh, you are a fool and need a guardian," but she said "fool" as a honey word, not damning as my mother did, pointing her yellow hand. "Aye, a change of shirt and small drawers, stockings, a Bible, a thimble, a knife," and then she drew out the Book of Martyrs and a piece of dried beef and laughed. "There's your paternity," she said, squatting there. "No money, as he thought. These saints that make themselves God in their houses and will not let their children free. Now hark it, my Johnny, money is freedom." She looked old to me then, for a second.

"Freedom's more than that." I did not like to hear such words from her lips.

"Aie, money's the oil of it, though. Let's see." She rocked back on her heels and fell aplanning and looked a child, playing at wife. "A breastplate, and a pot, and better boots"—she read the list by holding up her fingers—"and a leathern jerkin, and pistols and a sword, and money, and . . ." and could not say more but would have to fall acrying again, and I picked her up, and all of me came toward her and encompassed her, rose on her. Oh, Jesus, she led me in among the hay, where the pigeons moaned and the grass smelled sweet and molded with her soft hands the body I had forgot I had and knew and knew me, and I knew her, ungirdled her, rolled toward her, entered into her belly, forever home in her, and filled her with myself, and she filled me with her softness and we said never a word.

Remembering her now does not make me rise as other, grosser memories would, for 'twas the wholeness of us as one making love to air and darkness. We were in a place where there was no brute lust, no shame, no mounting, for we did lie side by side, and faced each other, and looked at each other, and entered at that moment eyes, bodies, and all, and then fell tenderly acomforting each other and petting as if 'twould never leave off until she shivered and said, "Oh, God, I must within, my Johnny. Come."

I lay all the rest of the night in a chamber in the tower and watched the pattern the moon made through the mullioned windows as it moved along the polished floor and hoped for her, but her duty and her heart were with the dying.

At dawn she came to wake me and fall again on me; this time our thirst had grown a lifetime in the night, and we slaked hard on each other. I could see her in the dawn light and run my hands on her as if my hands had eyes and saw her all, and she on me as if her hands had mouths and molded me all and licked and kissed me like a mare a foal.

She turned and came away from me. Oh, Jesus, I am still like one flayed of her.

"He has fallen into a coma, and Peregrine is with him, and the physicians have put the leeches on him, and he has said his prayers with the vicar." Like the good wife of another kind of fondness, she fell sad again, dressing me as if it were a duty as she did when

I was three and wetting of my breeks. I see her still there kneeling, her tears mingling for him and me.

When I was up on Nell to go, she clung to the saddle as one grown there and murmured, "Oh, Jesus, what am I to do? I do love my old man more than life itself." Peregrine took her shoulders and led her away. Her tears were wet on Nell's wither and my boot.

And there I was that morning, already shedding her. It was Peregrine who acoltered me and waved me from the gate and sent me with a smile to fight against him.

I rode along the road that morning with my boot still wet from her tears, through first May light and mist toward Northampton town as one led by angels, new sixteen and blessed by God and women, all decisions made for the moment whether to fight or kneel or simply ride along. 'Twas more relief than ever I had felt in my life before. At the edge of Henlow Wood —how could I have forgot this until this moment?— my setting dog, Jubal, who had waited there all night, did bound out to follow me and I did have to speak stern to him and send him home. That made me cry there in the road as prayer or death or love or father had not, and I let Nell carry me all blinded with tears down the misty road, all the necessities, all the decisions, and even love behind me, toward what I knew not, a motley prince, a cuckold of politics, a lover, a fool, but in the fear and coldness of that going forth, all I knew was I could not let them decide for me.

No, not father, lover, general, priest, or judge, or who takes the mantle of decision away from a man and seeks to wear it for him; I had heard something stronger, the voice of going forth, though in truth, that was being drowned by my noisy sobbing.

"Whither goest thou awhickering and sniveling for thy dam?" I heard a voice, and someone took the reins and stopped Nell.

I thought he was to rob me, but I only said, "No, for my dog," and sniffled a sniffle, ashamed of being caught so like a baby, even by a thief. Then I opened my eyes.

Gideon MacKarkle, you have a soul as sweet as a lark within you, but on the surface of you, you are the ugliest man I ever saw. You had naught to cover you but a huge pair of striped taffety breeks such as some of the Frenchmen wear. Your hair hung down in wet gray tatters on your skeleton, for you were so skinny you sank into yourself. Your face, Jesus love you, Gideon, I wonder if you have ever seen it. You outnose Cromwell; your eyes are like a spannel's and droop at the edges. You have a fine, big mouth that could grace an emperor's head, but your bones are hard put to hold it up sometimes, my honey, you do, you leave it open as one who has forgot to close a drawer. Your age? How could I know? You were as creased and gaunt as the old man of the sea, but had no fading in your eyes.

I thought, This old man hungers, and my newfound sanctity made me reach for my bag to give him food.

His spannel ears cocked, and he moved more graceful than a lass, snake silent; he dragged me from Nell's back into the woods, shoved me down into the wet leaves, and shushed Nell to the quietness of a doe, all as fast as lightning. His hand clamped across my mouth, as strong a hand as ever I felt, and I heard him whisper, "Harkee."

I heard then, against the ground, as he would teach me to listen later, the distant thud of many horses, very far away. We stayed so, his sack of bones pinning me down, as a party of king's dragoons tantivied past along the road. Oh, the music of their going, I thought it a fine sight and wished for a second there that I had not been converted. Their feathers floated; their armor caught the new sun. He kept us so animal still that no one looked our way.

"They would have stripped thee of thy raiment and wounded thee and departed, leaving thee for dead, for thou art a goddamned ninny and asking to be plucked, ablubbering along with that fine armor tied to thy saddle." He spoke with the tone of one who was born to the Scottish tongue.

I had forgot I was crying. In truth, with Lazarus leading me forth, and now this ugly man, I thought, God sends me jack-o'-lanterns for my guiding angels.

"Will you pluck me?" I asked, and hurt him by it.

"I am a man of God," he said.

As we sat upon the ground, and he gnawed and growled over the bread and meat, for he had not ate for three days since he escaped the king's garrison, he told me all, how he had been pressed by the Covenanters from his Highland croft, how then he had been took and pressed by the king, then took again and pressed by the Parliament, and took again and pressed by the king's men at Newbury, then Parliament and king until I seesawed to hear the telling of it.

" 'Tis the way of the Lord," he said, "but I reckoned there was times when He kept achanging of His mind about me." I could see then that his talk of God was more his learning of the English tongue than conversion. He had learned from the Saints and from the king's men, and he switched from God to goddamn without a pause for breath.

"Now I go to join up with the Parliament again. The men eat good and look after their horses."

So we set out together for the army. I would have been stripped by the king's men, for they infested all that part since they escaped north from the siege at Oxford, if I had rode on to Northampton, but we rode south instead, and kept to the great forests for hiding, as he instructed me the first I learned of how to be a soldier.

Gideon still rides the horse he stole, though he called it confiscating from malignants and seemed comforted by the words. I watched him slide forward on his belly in the grass to where the king's men sat lolling in the sun at noontide, and crooning as soft as a baby in his native tongue, he crawled beneath a fine gray hobbled a little apart from the other horses they had let out to grass. He charmed the animal so that it wandered as he did slink along beside it into the woods, and we spurred on and were gone before they looked around.

"God hath vouchsafed unto me many talents," he said when it was safe to speak, and patted the gray's withers. "He had to, or my family would have starved in the Highlands."

"Have you a wife then?" I had to ask if such an ugly man could have a wife.

"Aie, and nine sons, all alive, who serve the Parliament, and seven grandchildren, all brought to Newcastle across the border with their dams. We liked the country thereabouts when we saw it with the army. Jesus, I had not saw such grass grow over all. It was a disgusting thing for one used to cleaner rock. We had to bring them below the border, for without men in the Highlands they would have starved, as many do." He spoke easily of God and took starving for granted.

A ragged dynasty of a man, he rode like a prince in the saddle. By the third day he had used his God-given talent to transform himself, cast off his mountebank breeks, plucked here and there under cover of night in one-man raids of king's men who never once heard him, back and breast, pot, sword, pistols, fine leathern breeks and boots of Spanish leather.

Stealing and learning, praying and camping, I moved with him through the forests under the great trees. We ate with woodfolk some, and I was proud of that, for they would have hid from me in Henlow Wood. Sometimes we came too near the road and would be trapped there.

We hid, watching while the king's men passed or his soldiers drove slow wagons south toward Oxford, with the spoils of towns, laden and groaning through the spring mud, with fowls, pigs, linen, kegs of beer and brandy, sullen ragged dolls. One wagon bled Brussels lace into the road behind it as it creaked along, another a sleeve of some lady's blue patterned dress, and one was hung about with kettles and pans and blacksmith's tools, and one well nigh toppling with worn shoes. The patient stolen cattle nuzzled at our faces as they grazed along the road. Gideon whispered it was but the way the king did pay his soldiers, by

giving them the towns. To me they move forever, lurch-
ing in the deep ruts. I will hear them always, the sound
of them in my heart's fear.

It was as unconscious as breathing for Gideon to
teach me, for he taught as he acted and still does. I
watch him with recruits, and he guides them so, with
the rough affection he would his grandchildren. I
learned to read the grass, the trees, the open downs
for cover, drainage, fodder, and how to ride, and how
to bind Nell's hoofs for silence. I think that poacher
wins over Oxford tutor in how to survive in this wicked
world.

It was only when we rode out of the woods near
Islip that we saw troops of Parliament men and Gideon
said we could leave the cover of the woods and night.
It had been four days since we plunged headfirst onto
the forest floor, and we rode out of the wood that dawn
helmeted and armed and looking two fine Saints indeed. Hungry as wolves, we fell into a tavern where I
saw the soldiers and drank first with them, though it
was the Sabbath.

Spilled ale and strong tobacco and the talk of soldiers heart-filled me then, and I could but stare upon
them who had raided all through the west country with
Oliver Cromwell and routed the king's soldiers out of
Islip. They told Gideon, who had had no news, how
many were drowned in the river and how many run
away of the mercenary damned crew and how they
took the queen's colors from her very regiment. A man
said it was a royal white banner with a broidered crown
and all set with flower-de-luce and did have a crown
of real gold upon the top of it. I have seen many banners now, trampled and torn and blooded, God knows,
but the one in that man's mind that morning was fine
and silk and clean.

I heard no name of General Cromwell then. It was
all Oliver and Oliver among them. Why, they never
could leave off the ringing of his name. He lodged in
them, as many Olivers as they had eyes to see. One
had him making bawdy jokes with them; another saw

him as he prayed with them before a battle. One told
how he stood by and yelled, "Thump him!" and,
"Thump" again when one was beat for not caring for
his horse, another how he picked two soldiers from
the ranks of a troop that looted a farmhouse and had
them hanged at Wallop, and one of them a pressed
lad who had newly come from London, and had another's tongue burned through with a hot iron for
blasphemy, for he brooked no evil ways with them.

"He let the Sodomite escape from Oxford," one said
from a corner, weary of the brag.

Another said he had not enough men but to sting
the Oxford garrison, much less attack the king.

"He must bite the king then, not only sting him."
They all seemed to know much of how it should be
done. They were all fed to the very teeth with the small
raids and the riding and could see no end to it and no
victory so they could return to their homes and plant
their summer crops.

Gideon asked where we should go to join, and they
told us to ride on to Marston, where the generals lay.
It was a hard thing I did to seduce Gideon from the
tavern, for God knows he had weakness for the drink.
He melted into such an abyss of it as I never saw before. By the time we rode across the great meadows
toward Marston he was hanging to his horse like a rag,
and as soon as we were in first sight of the town, he
slid from his back and fell upon the ground with the
reins still in his hands, though it was only then nine
o'clock of the Sabbath morning.

All around us there seemed to be no army, only the
quiet fields and the vaulted sky. I knew not what to do.
I stood there like a sniveling Johnny and stared at
him, until one in a great bald voice roared out, "Woe
unto them that rise up early in the morning that they
may follow strong drink. Gideon MacKarkle, you have
backslid again, and on the Sabbath, too."

I had heard none behind me, for the tall grass muffled the horses' hoofs, and the voice made me jump.
Not so Gideon. He lifted his head with much slow dig-

nity and said, "The Sabbath was made for man, not
man for the Sabbath. Now you know that, Oliver,"
and fell to resting sweetly again in the grass.

I saw him then, mighty Cromwell, setting his horse
high above me, followed by only a few officers. He
had dirty linen, and his hands and face were streaked
with mud from hard riding. He was smiling down on
Gideon. It was a sweet smile that belied the stern lines
of his face. His eyes looked as a man's who falls into
secret melancholies, apologetic, sodden eyes, with much
need in them. I would have said a drunkard from them
and from his swollen face, but it is not so—not for so
common a lover as strong drink.

"You quote Scripture to your purpose," he told
Gideon. "Stand up!"

Gideon did pull himself up by his horse. "Not no
more than you," he told him; " 'twas the voice of my
very conscience. 'Give strong drink unto him that is
ready to perish, and wine unto those who be of heavy
hearts. Let him drink, and forget his poverty, and remember his misery no more,' Proverbs Thirty-one,
six–seven."

Oliver laughed then, a great round laugh full of wind
and spirit, and bit the laugh off of a sudden, for his
mind was ever occupied with his task. "Where hast
come from?"

"Northampton. I ran from the king's garrison there."

"Where captured, for shame of you?"

"At Faringdon, sir."

"Come to me at noontide and tell me what you saw
along the way here. Ask for the house of Uncton Coke
at Marston. Damme, I must have more intelligence.
There is not a fart let by me but is presently carried to
Oxford, and I, in turn, know nothing."

He wheeled, impatient as always to be moving, and
suddenly, he turned his horse again.

"You, boy, what's your name?"

"Jonathan Church, sir."

"What troop?"

"None yet, sir."

"Go to Whalley. Whalley needs men." He wheeled away and was gone.

He seemed to take Gideon's drunkenness with him as he rode with his company away across the meadow and set pace up the far hill out of sight. Oh, Oliver, now turned great Cromwell, who knew first names and spoke among us as friends do, did you not know how much one boy had fell in love with you as you rode there, forgetting us, your back crouched in the saddle, your head down, as one listening for an inner answer he cannot hear?

We followed through the deep grass and up the hill at a walk, for we had already rode hard that morning and Nell was skittish out in so much space after the woods. At the top, we reined in and stood there. My Christ Jesus, 'twas a fine miracle, a drunken madness of sober men. There below us were rows of white tents, close to Marston church and spreading out as far as man could fathom among the copses, across the meadows, in the distant woods. There were no bells. All had been silenced for purity's sake and been melted down for cannon at Marston church and in the parishes around long since. Faint as wind over the grass we could hear the bells of Oxford, but where we were there was only the still blessing of the sky upon the ground. Down among the tents and under the trees were clusters of men fallen to their prayers, and never a sound but here and there the whinny and sigh of a horse, the creaking of my leathern jerkin against my breastplate, and still I remember the silken smell of my new yellow sash.

Cromwell had not rode so hard to battle council, but to prayers.

Ten thousand men, some gentlemen, some captured of the king, some pressed out of the taverns, apprentices, leathern aprons, clouted shoes, country lads from the north, the midlands and the fens, the poor and contemptible and the county rich, were for that moment as equal as blades of English grass, an English army kneeling in the meadows at their prayers. Oh,

Jesus, that they had stayed so. There was no sound of
sword, no clatter of armor, and I believed for that
moment that I was indeed joining an army of Saints,
new Israelites, new-grown out of the filthiness of poverty and streets and patient, irrevocable country anger,
as flowers from dunghills.

There was, for that moment, a streaming out of love
as if all brothers, unknown to one another, had met
in some vasty dream. 'Tis only words for it that fade
away in time, and the places of the moments cross and
meld within and become as one single lifetime.

Nellie, as I ride here on your namesake, your hands
are on my belly, and your hair touches my face, and I
taste your mouth and live the English army that moment at their prayers. All one needs at sixteen is the
possibility of all those free-choosing, God-struck men,
one moment when it is so and possible to be so and is
not a dream, a spacious glimpse of it, and one is
marked for life.

The moment was over, and the hymns and psalms
began, and here and there a shout of amen and amen
again in the distance, and I began to ride down among
them, hoping I'd be took for a soldier and not a raw
recruit. I clicked at Nell then and whispered, "Come,
my old heart, let's go to war," so Gideon would not
hear and walked down the hill through the meadow
grass and army-trampled flowers. Nearer, the camp
seemed smaller, flat and exposed under heaven which
was high that Sabbath morning. I felt diminished by
the rolling downs after the shelter of the forest. I rode
into a sailcloth village of tents with men around them
now that prayers were over, doing of such women's
tasks an army spends so much time withal, patching
and washing their clouts and renailing of their shoes.

I saw an old man, sitting in a tree shade, patching
breeks, and with him only a boy, I took him for twelve
years or so, holding a great leathern patch in place on
the breeks, his behind as naked as the day he was born.
The old man must have felt our shadows as we passed,
for he looked up and saw MacKarkle as one familiar

who he had drunk with not three weeks hence on his way to the army from Devon. We dismounted and hunkered down beside them. He spoke such a tongue I could hardly understand it, but I followed that they both had come from the west country, where they had been enclosed out of their village by a new Presbyter who had it for a grant of services to the Parliament. They had found the army on their way to London to find work. The boy was fourteen, though so small, but tough, the old man said, and pinched his bare skin. I could see that morning all of us, asking our way and meeting there from all over England.

We were halted over and over again on our way into Marston by the gatherings of men in the meadows; officers, hobnails, cropped heads, long hair, some with elegant white faces, some as brown as old honey, what a ribble-rabble it was, all cheek by jowl, listening around their preachers, soldiers like themselves, or mechanic horse preachers in plush jackets and red caps. They called out the word of God in loud voices from tree stumps, barrels, tubs, boxes, sutler's wagons, cannons, whatever they could find to lift them up above their gatherings to be heard. Some men clung astraddle of branches in the trees like Zacchaeus to hear and see better. 'Twas for all the world like barkers at some fair in New Jerusalem. One of the Fifth Monarchy, after the prophecies of the prophet Daniel, was thundering out warnings of the Second Coming enough to fling the world on its knees braying with fear.

He shouted, " 'And I looked, and lo, a Lamb stood on the mount of Sion, and with him a hundred forty and four thousand, having his Father's name written on their foreheads,' Revelation Fourteen one, and ten thousand of the saved are gathered in this field alone," and I saw an old and toothless man look shy to think he was a Saint and mutter amen and look around, hoping none had heard him. The preaching made Nell skitter, and I had to ride off from Gideon to calm her and did not find him again that day. I walked her apart from the noise, for she had begun to dance like one

taken with the word of God. Away then in the distance
I heard the dim words flung up toward heaven, Shiloh
I remember hearing then, and the hosts of Midian, and
away in the far reaches of the camp, a whisper brought
by the May breeze, "Babylon is fallen, is fallen, that
great city. . . ." I knew that they spoke of the war in
England, of London, and the Sodomitish king.

All along, as I calmed Nell on the verges in the un-
trodden grass, I passed men at work, although it was
the Sabbath, and helped everyone his neighbor as the
Bible says. The smithies' clanging was soft in that space.
Men held horses, quietly waiting to be shod. A car-
penter was planing staves, and down from the woods
a long line of men came carrying those they had cut.
I could hear only a faint tapping from where I was of
hammers driving iron points onto the planed pikes,
and in a field beside, men and boys were trying them,
as a lad tries a slingshot he has made before he lets
fly with it. I thought that they were moving like ants
from wood to carpenters to smiths and that my great
awakening in my father's house four days before was
only a wee drop in a vasty bucket.

'Twas then—no later, much later, for I had already
been told that Colonel Whalley's regiment was recruit-
ing and found my way to his headquarters in the church
at Marston—then I had been sent to Major Bethell's
troop down by the river. I had rubbed down Nell and
watered and fed her, and I was wandering around,
hoping to find Gideon again. I had cast off all but my
shirt, for the May sun was warm and sweet. The fires
were burning blue where some of the men were already
cooking of their suppers. I knew not a soul but one
rough and hungry-looking brown man called—what
now? His name is gone. He deserted soon after. No
matter. He told me to keep my money close, and I remember how strange it seemed to have to strap my
money belt on under my shirt in the army of the Saints
by the waters of Shiloh. I was hungry and knew not
yet how to buy food for myself, and I had not eaten

since the tavern at dawn and that was slops and ale. 'Tis hard to think I was so raw and green.

I heard his mild voice before I saw him. I thought he was alone, for I heard no sound but his reading and the hum of bees in the honeysuckle. Then I saw him on the riverbank, half-hidden by the profligate aspens and the white-blooming May trees. Around him divers heavy country men were gathered. Some lay upon their elbows, dappled by the shadow of the trembling leaves. One had rolled upon his back and snored in a patch of sun. Some had cast their clouts and washed them in the Cherwell, their strong backs all bowed there. A few were fishing upstream while they listened. It was as calm as a sigh.

He was perched upon a tree stump, his long legs drawn up, clad with zeal as with a cloak, reading to them that could not and telling of it as he went along while the May brown flood passed almost beneath his feet. 'Twas from his mild, sweet mouth that I first heard things even beyond my night whisperings at Oxford, and I envied him. I thought of the boy Jesus, how He expounded to the elders in the temple, but these were not great Pharisees, but plain and simple ignorant men, carved by wind and earth and work, and the sight made the tears come to my throat that had lurked all day trying to come into my eyes and shame me.

Thankful Perkins, oh, Christ, it does tickle me still to see you, all brown curls and pink cheeks and heifer's eyes and face like some hungry angel hovering over a fat man's tomb.

"The king," Thankful said, and startled me to stopping in the sun behind the men, "the king doth live," he said in the theeing and thouing of simple country speech and of family and childhood, and the quiet ones who make all equal before God and do not bear the stigma of false dignity and manners that sets one man apart from the other. I had tried to speak so for four days until Gideon in his drink said, "Why mockest thou me?" as if he were hurt, and made me feel more fool than ever I'd been called.

"Why, he doth still live in a great palace and sit upon a golden throne and eat off a golden plate with a golden spoon, and one wipes his face with a kerchief of finest linen when he doth dribble." He made it sound like one of the fairy stories women tell. "And he doth kneel before idols on a golden altar with seven heathen candles, and beside him sitteth the Whore of Babylon, the great whore"—and I knew he meant the Catholic queen—"and he takes into his mouth the Lamb of God, and he doth fast in the mornings, for he is a pious man," and then his voice rose treeward like a lark. "But the Lord saith unto him, 'wilt thou call this a fast, and an acceptable day to the Lord? Is this not the fast that I have chosen? to loose the bands of wickedness, to undo the heavy burdens, and to let the oppressed go free, and that ye break every yoke?' Isaiah Fifty-eight five–six; every yoke, brothers, the yoke of poverty, the yoke of one man bending down unto another, the yoke of one who labors for food and starves withal, while the other eats it and turns his lily-white hand to naught?"

"Amen," an old man said, and throwed a stone in the water, and one upstream called, "Quit. Thee scare the fish." He had a pile of fish already beside him.

What Thankful Perkins said was way beyond mild feuding between the Presbyters of Parliament and the prelates of the king, but the fartherest in independency that ever I heard in my life. This was no army to sit Parliament securely and only change the cut of the landlord's clothes. Why, there on the Cherwell bank the world was turned right upside down for me, as hungry as I was. I saw us as plants growing upward with the strength surging from below as we reached our arms toward heaven, not, as I had been led to believe always, that we were abysmal clods of clay, touched from the sky with being. We too had wings that day, creaking of leather like the swans.

I sank me down beneath a tree to listen and, in truth, in hopes I could partake of the fish. As twilight fell, some went apart and built a fire to cook, and I noticed that Thankful's voice was growing tired and was as soft as evening, and one near him said, "Give me leave to dip," and did close his eyes and let his finger wander and then stop on a Bible verse, letting God guide his finger, as they do seek guidance and tell fortunes among the Anabaptists and the country people. He read, "I will cause the arrogancy of the proud to cease, and will lay low the haughtiness of the terrible. I will make a man more precious than fine gold."

"It do say that now?" insisted the other, pleased. "Beshit me, for I never knowed that."

I thought then Thankful had chose it for him and only called it dipping. That was before I knew him.

Another wanted to dip then, and he read, "Thou shalt no more be termed Forsaken; neither shall thy land any more be termed Desolate: but thou shalt be called Hephzibah, and thy land Beulah: for the Lord delighteth in thee," and beamed at him as if he had read him a letter of his own.

Then Thankful fell to arguing, and God knows he can do that, with one rude Anabaptist fellow from Dorset about the baptism of infants, whether 'twas worthy in God's sight before one knew one's mind and soul. The men around them looked to one and then the other as if they played a game. Thankful got then to explaining the difference between the Arminians and the Antinomians, something of one early bishop, and indwelling grace versus justification by works. By the time he had run down I was laughing fit to kill, for all had drifted over to the fire away from him.

He looked sheepish then and said, "I told them as simple as I could."

One called, "Shut thy mouth, Perkins, and come and eat."

We did eat together on the ground as ones who had known each other all along. Can you know how it is for one set apart by birth to be allowed to sit upon the ground and eat with all the others?

Later we told each other about ourselves freely as

we walked to the tents. We talked until the night was black and the black fields were pointed with little fires. It was such talk as I was used to at Oxford, spinning words, but a new thing came out of it. Oh, I had known it with my ears before but never with my heart, the fear in it, the stepping forward into loss. 'Twas one thing to talk of liberty of conscience, a protected boy at Oxford, and another to speak where men meant it with their blood, how a man had a right to choose how he would worship, and civil magistrates should deal with civil things only and leave the worship of God to a man's self to do when and where he pleased, and all men should have a voice in the governing of themselves.

"Aie, and women too," Thankful said. Some man laughed who heard us, "And dogs, too . . ." he called.

I remember whispering in the dark, "Even the Catholics?" and Thankful answered then, not bothering to whisper, "Aie, even them misbegotten souls as well." It was as if we'd signed a pact to trust each other, for he spoke to my heart's core and strengthened me, and I stood once again mute before my father and said once again to my mother, "I cannot other than this," but stronger now the words than then.

I lay that first night under the trees at Marston as gentle and safe as if I had returned to a home I had not known was there, and I think that night I forgot all that had been before in my life. I could hear the breathing of men away beyond the campfire, and I did not know as I drifted off to sleep where I left off and all of them began. 'Twas not only new politics or being right or wrong in my conscience. 'Twas more than that, though what the more was I know not even yet, but I sensed to call it by all our Christian names.

M Y Christ in heaven, how new I was then! 'Tis no wonder recruits are called raw. These blackened boots that have been soled and soled again were new stiff leather then. This leathern jerkin that breathes now on my body wet and brackish with the rain and has a map on it of cuts smelled then of tanning and not of my own sweat, this old drooped hat, these pistols—no, not these. I picked these up from the field at Langport. I had forgot.

How all my new untried clothes creaked then, not yet a part of me, as Major Bethell trained the new recruits at Marston. I learned with Nell to ride close, knee to ham, to the man and horse beside me, to go at full trot, never passing the others. We wheeled and halted, wheeled again and halted under his voice. I stood to inspection, wrestled my new sword out of my new scabbard, and wobbled it in the air, copying the older soldiers. The men complained that nothing was ever to happen. Cromwell was ordered away with his regiment toward Ely for some business there we did not know.

Only nine days later we broke camp and marched north after the king. MacKarkle came to say good-bye. He had joined up with Grevis' regiment, and they were to ride west where the fighting was, not on some wild-goose chase north, as we were. We lay that night at Newport Pagnell, and in the fields around, the training went on until I wheeled and turned and charged at the trot in my sleep.

The older soldiers smelled a battle coming. I could tell so from their new, edgy silences, and the lowering of their voices, and the heightening of complaints and easy quarrels I would know later so well. Then I only caught it as excitement. Even Thankful Perkins, who had been in battle much before, spoke little of it. I had learned already to call him Perkins in the army way and was growing used to snapping to attention at the bark of the name Church.

When I tried to make Thankful speak, he turned his head away and spoke instead of God and other things. I felt left out of their waiting. There is, bone deep in every man, the hope of being a good soldier, the brave simplicity. It grew in me until I had almost forgot all else.

It was Friday the thirteenth that we came to Guilsborough and pitched camp. Rumors went through the troop. The king was still at Leicester. The king rode down on us and was four miles away. The king had turned tail and run to Scotland, always the king, the king of rumor, haunting us. The men liked it not, that it was the evil day of Friday and the thirteenth as well. They muttered against traveling on such a day. All their unspoken urgency they put upon it being a Friday.

In the long summer twilight, when no one could sleep, the rumor crept among the wakeful men around their fires that the king had been captured by our vanguard in an inn at the village of Naseby four or five miles to the north, and that he was drunk, and then that it was the king's watch found, all drunk, and took that night. We believed it or not, it was all rumor, as loud and impersonal as wind running among us, now of the king, now that a hare had crossed the road and brought us bad luck. I did not know then, as I know now, that it was playing on the worried, heightened senses of soldiers smelling battle, as wild animals smell salt far, far away, and it keens their senses and draws them toward it.

But the sound of many horses that I heard, ear to the ground late that night, was no rumor. My heart lurched. I thought it was the king's army come to find us. Then I heard in the distance a joyful noise, a shout, coming near until we were part of it. "Ironsides!" and "Oliver, come to lead us!"

It was Cromwell, and he rode near to us while the soldiers stood and called "Oliver!" Even I knew then that it was no ordinary meeting to bring him back from the east so soon to join us there.

At three o'clock on Saturday morning, at the first faint lifting of the dawn, word came to break camp and leave our baggage with the rear guard. Few had slept. They rose up, all around me, stretching and mumbling. " 'Tis an evil night for sleep; we may as well ride," Thankful said.

One called, "Think you we will flush out his majesty today?"

Another laughed in the dark.

Someone swore, "Odds fuck, my knapsack's been plucked."

The predawn was hollow and cold on my face.

The east opened up over the empty hills as we rode. When we came through Naseby village, it was first day. In the high morning wind the birds were wheeling. I thought, what a fine day for hawking, Peregrine and I, to loose the birds from our wrists into the wild air, and watch them pitch and glide upon the wind, and see them plunge straight down where Jubal stood on point and bring the partridge to our hands in their talons. I thought how Peregrine carried a peregrine falcon, his namesake, on his wrist and I a garefowl, and how we wagered and argued their merits.

A few men were already working in the fields beyond the village, but as we came to view, they dropped their hoes and ran, like ungainly kitchen fowl, into their houses.

It was seven o'clock by the sun. We waited on a hill northeast of the village. Downhill, beyond the sharp drop in front of us, the spring rain had soaked the ground among the furze and rabbit warrens. I thought myself a fine soldier, judging the spongy ground as too

soft for a charge, 'til Thankful said, "Johnny, are you
poorly? Your face is white."

I realized then that I was shivering and thought that
I had caught an ague from sleeping on the ground. I
never felt so young and foolish in my life, no falconer
now, but a youngster of new sixteen, with pistols I had
never fired, a heavy sword that had a quivering life of
its own in my hand, a poleax tied to my wrist with
Nellie's ribbon. I knew then that I was going to die. I
knew it. The tears came to my eyes that this should
happen. All that wide field west of us in the distance
swam before my eyes. I looked at it, and the new corn,
the new grass, my new friends, for the last time. I was
like a fledgling that had been kicked from the nest and
left to shift for itself with comic naked wings.

Thankful's voice was calm, though it had changed,
too, I could tell. He kept repeating, "Keep your knees
to the hams of the men to left and right of you. Break
not your trot. Keep your mind on your horse's forefeet
only, only that. Hold your fire. Keep each step separate,
one at a time, and you'll not flow into fear. Many a man
catches flight by going too fast too soon. Break not
your trot. One step at a time. One at a time."

All through that long wait he kept saying it until he
had dwindled my whole vision to a little space, flank to
flank, knee to ham. It was not fear he was putting into
me. That he was drawing out, as a surgeon draws a
boil. The flowing and weakening were going. Now
there was a wariness, as a fox cocks his head. A whole
cocked army stood waiting on that hill in the cold
morning wind, out of all the secrets and whisperings
and murmurs of my life. It was so clean and simple.

We stood there forever under a tilted sun, pale and
translucent in the early morning. There was a smell
of gorse and corn. Thankful sneezed, and someone said,
"Christ bless." The northwest wind blew the horses'
manes. There was a stillness a thousand times more
urgent than hunting, but like it, the edge of waiting
before a plunge that seemed never to come. In that long

holding of breath, I heard the water pouring over rocks, whispering down the hill into the soggy bottom.

Down below us, two men conferred, and others gathered listening to them. We all knew every move of those two men, as if each of our lives grew in long tendrils from them. It was Ironsides and Black Tom, Cromwell and Sir Thomas Fairfax, with their officers around them. They, too, were judging the soggy ground. One pointed west. It was Cromwell. The foot soldiers were marching in double file down the road toward them. I heard his voice calling from so far away it was a faint whisper. Horses wheeled from the center the two men made and fanned out toward us. I heard faint orders called, and the soldiers on the road turned about and filed up the slope in front of us. I thought they were retreating from whatever lay in front of us, hidden in the silence and the space.

The order to move to the left came through our ranks. We turned west, in two long lines, parallel to the foot soldiers, and rode into the wind.

I had seen nothing moving in that fallow field that spread below us, a great shallow blank bowl that rose in the north, half a mile away—a few trees, meadow grass, a few corn patches, some cover for wild birds, and nothing else, nothing that moved as far as I could see.

Thankful whispered, "Lookee." He saw it first, a long line like our own, a tiny shadow that crawled along the opposite hill. Sweat spurted from my hair. I had not known I was so hot.

"They move west to get the wind of us. We will have to fight upwind," Thankful said, but to himself then.

It was nine o'clock. We had been six hours in the saddle. Nothing was to happen, nothing but that waiting. For a mile along the back of the ridge, hidden by its crest, our foot soldiers had took up their positions and leaned upon their pikes. Away to the left of us and moving out of sight, I could see tiny colors flying. Thankful said it was the colors of Ireton moving to the left flank. We seemed to be left alone by the rest of the army, up there in the naked wind.

Down the crest, a hundred feet away, the forlorn hope of pikemen and musketeers were huddled together, dwarfed by the space. Their colors flapped, down out of the wind.

Full in the sun now, here and there a faint glitter of gold like a distant signal, the king's army, like toy soldiers, was spread out for a mile along the opposite ridge, so high in the wind that it brought us their voices calling and their laughter. I could hear them shout, "Roundhead!" and "Tapsters" and "Clouted shoes." Even my new sword and my new breastplate looked dim to me. We were so drab, standing there. Not even our colors flowed like theirs. We crouched behind our hill crest, waiting dumbly to receive their anger and their grace.

Two or three cannon shot bloomed in the air and fell short of our forlorn. The wind carried the smoke up to us, and I tasted salt and sulphur in my mouth. Then, as slow as in a dream, the long line of their foot soldiers was walking down the hill and through the valley, their forlorn ahead of them, moving to the bright sound of pipes and the thud of drums. The gold armor of their mounted officers shone in the sun, and patches of bright scarlet from the banners. I was not there. Such an outrage could not happen to me. One step at a time. Break not your trot. They turned as they came on below, to individual men in close order, their pikes ported, a long line of iron teeth. It was past ten by the sun.

At first I heard a murmur from our ranks; then it rose full-throated to a shout, "GOD OUR STRENGTH!" and "G . . . o . . . d," drawn out into a shriek not human, and our foot soldiers rose up over their hiding hill crest and began their slow walk down to meet them. They had been held back until the two forlorns met, all abstracted from where I was, as some vast game with toys. All together we could hear them fire, and men began to fall. We could feel them jar the ground, those two lines coming to the shock. Black smoke obscured them, and when the wind cleared it, there were no more straight fine ranks, but a tangled web of men and colors. No fine insulting yells and slogans then, but a single scream ripped and tore, all so far away, over some huge, yet tiny game of football on a village green in purgatory.

Our soldiers were pushed back, and now they fought near enough below us for me to see their faces; I saw no anger, not even any fear between them. They had thrown down their pikes, and hacked with swords, and clubbed with their musket butts. Some had only their hands to use. They fought with their own weight and thrust, concentrated on their lives. They did not seem to kill, only to fight. Then I saw that the ground under them on the hillside was slowly turning red. It came to me as the hitting of a wall: Those men are killing each other. I saw an officer ride among our men, using the flat of his sword on their backs, goading them back into battle as a man drives animals. The creek below ran with blood.

Still we waited there on the high hill above them, knee to ham. From time to time, a horseman rode along the ranks behind us. We could hear his voice, "Hold, my lads, stand fast there," and such other murmured comfortings as I would whisper to my dog Jubal to keep him from breaking point and flushing game too soon. It was Cromwell, comforting and holding us, a nerveless, calm, familiar country voice.

Thankful caught my arm. "Johnny, Christ be with you." I looked where he was gazing. Straight ahead of us, so far away, the line opposite us had begun to move.

"Who is there?" someone whispered.

"Sir Marmaduke Langdale's colors," another answered.

I heard, "Prime your pistols." My fingers would not work. Someone took my pistol and primed it for me.

Sir Marmaduke Langdale's horse swept down the far slope, colors flying. Through the patchy smoke they looked a river of flowing horses. I thought: Can I do it? That was all. Will I turn tail? That was all in my mind. Will I meet their shock or will I turn tail? In truth, that is the deepest thought a man can have, though I knew not then that any others thought this. They seemed, on either side of me, so still, so controlled. I was comforted by the pressure of Thankful's leg against mine and the unknown man's body against me on my left.

The charging horses were riding a career, opened wide apart, not moving slow and together. They looked so fine and gay, galloping now as hunters in the field, looking then all I had dreamed as a boy that fine battle should look. They reached the flat bowl of the valley. I could see their faces. Some of the horses stumbled in the rabbit warrens, and they turned away from the soggy ground and started up the hill.

The stranger on my left grinned and said, "Too far apart. Too fast."

It did not look so to me.

Then I was moving with the others, as if we were a single body, close ordered, down the steep slope to meet their charge. I had heard no orders, no trumpets. I could hear only the hoofs of our horses strike rocks and our men breathing. All I could think was to keep Nell's head up so she would not stumble. I locked my whole soul within that concentration.

Somewhere I heard a voice call, "Hold your fire!"

I thought that we would never fire. We had to. They were trying to kill us. A bullet caught Thankful's coat sleeve, and he cringed but did not drop his pistol. His lips were moving, but he said no words. I knew that he was praying. Someone was swearing quietly as if that, too, were prayer.

We were firing. We must have been. The pistol was smoking in my hand. I saw men wilting off their horses. It was so slow. There was no wide field spread out, but a hemmed-in space of ground that had been growing corn. I threw my pistol, and he, that other did, at the same time. We caught each other on the side of the head and fell together under the horses' rumps, the flailing hoofs, the animals screaming, the flying shit and blood of them. We were trapped there. I had to get out, get through this man and find Nell. We clung together. I tried to pry him loose, but he clung to my breastplate and was tearing it away. His rage of fear made him grab then at my hair, and I grabbed his, a better hold than my shacked hair. The poleax was all I had to use to chop him out of the way. I flung back his head by his long curls and chopped and chopped at his throat to get free of him. I felt him loosen from me, and we stood in the middle of that boiling mass of horses and men. His eyes were surprised only. His throat opened wide and drenched me. His blood ran down my coat, a gout of blood I still wear, faintly, after so long. That loosening ragged death after the urgency of his strong muscles, that body's giving up, as one after the pitch of love, was too foul to tell of, that awful second of the same satisfaction, the same. No, if I do tell of this war, I will not tell this to any man and God knows never to any woman. Soldiers do not. They tell of their dangers, and their escapes, and their weariness, and even of their fear, but not of this. It is too foul.

I could not get rid of him. His hand that clutched my coat would not die with him. I had to pry it off, and when I dropped him, I saw him for a second that never ends, his face stupid with its new surprise, his eyes that questioned me. He was as young as me. His hair dripped rainbows of lady's ribbons. There was that arrogance I hated left in his wide, slack mouth. I reached down and closed his eyes. He lay flung out there, his curls tangled. I forgot where I was. Two horses, locked together, backed over him and burst him. He sent up a foul stink from his bowels. Someone grabbed me, and I turned to fight again; but it was Thankful who jerked me up behind him.

Before God, we were still trotting in some kind of order, pushing them in front of us. What horses they still rode in that half-unmounted field they turned, as a tide turns. I saw Nell ahead, trotting after them. We caught up with her. As I had done, she was following, mindless, her coat running wet with panic, but too hemmed in to cut and run. I did not realize until I had mounted her and we were sweeping after them up the valley road that we had broken their charge and were chasing them off the field. I had lost my sword, my breastplate, and my pistols. I had only my bloody poleax, still tied to my wrist. There was in me a new surge cleaner than fury, a new strength. Running away and running after are the difference between strength and weakness, as natural and as terrible as a dog that knows it has won and bounds for the kill. As we rode after them, we made small bouncing shadows on the dirt of the valley road. It was near noon.

I saw Major Bethell ride ahead to turn us, but that must have been later. We were out of sight or sound of the battle. We rode back toward our rendezvous. In the flat hilltop away behind where the king's army had stood so long ago in the clean morning, our men were plundering the sutler's wagons, deserted in the sun, abandoned, some turned over, with their wares and odd domestic loot flung out along the ground.

One of our soldiers handed bread and a piece of dried meat up to me. " 'Tis the loot from Leicester," he said; "there is nary a body on the field that has not at least fifty shillings in its pockets. They must have cleaned the town."

Two men had climbed up on the side of an over-turned carriage, a fine one with a crest upon the door. One brown-looking man, all bloody, carried a long taffety sash over his arm and was turning a jeweled necklace, catching the sunlight on the jewels and gawking at something as fine as that in his country hand. Beyond the carriage a woman, richly dressed, lay sprawled. Women lay faceup around the wagons, the now-faint wind tugging at their torn skirts, their faces hacked and slashed so that I could tell only by their clothes that they were women. There must have been a hundred of them or more. They were all over the field, as abandond as the wagons, our soldiers moving among them, searching for pay.

I leaned my head on the pummel of my saddle and puked down Nell's body.

One man looked up. "Whores," he said, disgusted. "Filthy Irish whores. They will not be used again in so foul a sin, praise God."

That night we lay near Leicester. What had happened in other parts of the field, the charge of Prince Rupert, the wounding of Ireton, all the single acts that made our victory, I heard in drifting dreams as I tried to sleep.

Thankful's arm throbbed from his wound, but he said nothing, only lay against a tree, staring into the fire, his face chalk white.

All night long the soldiers of that broken army filed past through the dark, and when at last I slept, near morning, I was at Naseby, only it was Armageddon where I fought. I heard myself cry, "Hold, boy, hold. Style is all. What are you doing in my mother's room?" When he turned, it was Thankful standing there, crying and vomiting, with blood run down his shirt and paddling at it with his hands and crying, "Oh, I am undone. I have seen things not to be seen and know things not to be knowed." Oh, my Jesus, the gray-green of his face!

I saw him ride through the field of Naseby and rein in like an avenging saint. There came one of the Four Horsemen of Armageddon, the horse that is red out of the clouds, and Thankful was astraddle of it, his little gallant face aglow with battle among the green and yellow banners, and he held one before him, PREPARE YE THE WAY OF THE LORD.

At last I was awake and on the ground again. The fire had gone out, and Thankful was asleep.

I had been two weeks at war.

I SEE two lines of horses, one moving slowly, the other reflected under it, across a sheet of spring flooding like an enormous lake. We slosh across it, following the safety of the horse ahead, feeling our way through what might be hidden creeks under the deceptive flatness of the shallow water.

Now that the fog is lifted I can see, at last, the men I ride with. There is Little Will, only fifteen, riding alongside MacKarkle. I see John Roper and his brother Simeon ahead of them, west country men, who ride together always and have little to say to the others. There's ugly Johnny Cantloe, and Pinky, whose name is Panck but none call him that, though he is forever telling us how it is said.

The farmhouse of a flooded farm in the distance is mirrored in the water; a grove of trees still holds some lingering fog. The sun is trying to break through the high flat cloud and makes a milky light there in the west.

To travel through that time after Naseby was like this; what seemed a flat morass held hidden current we could not yet fathom. Looking back now, I can see that there were streams, barely perceptible, as some that move the water here as we cross it.

The victory had been too simple, and it settled nothing for us. We had won the old tired war against the king. Those who had not been there clung to it as a solution to all our ills—to kill other men was all to them. In truth, battles must be seen from far away, with men as small as pawns upon a table of green earth. They make so fine a pattern. Only such people as those who lined the London streets to jeer and shout at the prisoners as we rode them in triumph through the town care for such easy climaxes. Their questions, in the taverns and the alehouses that night as they welcomed us as heroes, were as urgent as the virgins who would question a whore, curious at her secrets.

There are no secrets, only a passing in experience beyond what they still dream, not even grotesque, but as dull as work unchosen.

We rode on from Naseby and London's triumph all that summer. There was no more testing. That came once. I knew that that moment, the trying of a man, was like a wall before, but, once passed, like a cloud barrier behind. Before Naseby our raw, untried men had been called better Christians than soldiers. Now we were turning, God help us, into better soldiers than Christians. Slowly we became like mercenary troops; the ease of it, the ever-growing ease of obedience, the thoughtless relief.

Then the old man, the preacher Baxter, was sent among us. I think it was the trying of our minds that woke us from that long sleep of what we were becoming. How much we owe to our dislike of one old man, who was sent among us to point out to us the error of our ways, but brought only a change in the wind from far away!

My God in heaven, that old man did weary us. We could not sit and smoke our pipes and argue as we would without he came and sat down in the middle of us to root out heresy and what he saw as anarchic distemper with his long nose! When I looked around the campfire, I would see men I knew, and most of us scarce more than boys, but he saw in the same faces plotting, subverting disputers. He followed us as an ewe a ram to speak against church democracy and state democracy and, what he hated most, liberty of conscience. His voice would rise, preacherlike, and he

would declaim to boys and trees. He was a very Praise
God Barebones.

"To let men serve God according to their conscience," he thundered, "is to cast out one devil that
seven more might enter." He said that God had spoke
to him directly to come among us for fear of our souls,
but Thankful allowed his God had very much the face
of Parliament. I had never heard him speak so of religious things before.

'Tis strange to think now that our secret meetings
began so innocently, to hide away from that old man
and speak in peace together as we had done before. It
was out of those meetings that our certainty grew that
we were fighting harder battles than ever we had fought
against the king's soldiers.

If Baxter was indeed sent among us to wean us
from what we had hardly yet become, he pushed us,
by his intemperate orthodoxy, toward what we became.
I see now that we owe the old man much for saving
our souls from becoming what the powers would mold
us into being. In truth, God does work in mysterious
ways His wonders to perform.

Oh, my Jesus, we had begun to lose, not to win.
How could we know that all the fine cheering of the
people and all the pretty speeches were over? The
Parliament was finished with us, and we became, for
them, a raggle-taggle nuisance. How could we know
still riding, still fighting all that summer and into the
winter that the army of the Saints was already no
crown of laurel but a thorn in their fat flesh? We had
fought for liberties they hated, those men who thought
and spoke like my father. But that had been only what
we fought for. What we had done was win for them
the greatest thieving of the land since the Normans
came. They parceled out the lands among themselves,
and we went on ariding.

At first we thought that this was happening only in
our regiment and by the accident of one old man among
us, but it was not. A whole army had been courted
into service, but unlike such as Lazarus, we were no

longer simple. The orthodox Baxter argued that such things as liberty of conscience were never understood by common men. He saw them with minds like children, to be used and cared for. What he could not see was that there were no longer such common men as he had hoped, for the swords that were the prerogative of gentlemen had been put into their hands and the meanest of them were turning tiger to defend their rights. We had entered into men's society and done men's work, and such impudence had long been put into us that we grew gallant spirits from the arts of arms and the speaking of our minds and, God knows, the friendship we had in what we saw as the right.

Events may try to temper us or break us, but 'tis our friends who strengthen or weaken our metal. If I would tell of two years of changing illusive civil war after Naseby and how the new spirit grew among us, it would be of friends I would speak, how some came near and then were ripped away by orders, changed plans, or were seduced into preferment; we were caught in the change that reached all the way down to us from far away in London.

Some I will tell of, as there all of a sudden, as Thankful who sprang into my ken preaching on the riverbank before Oxford and has not left it. Some came seeking a cause as one seeks a game to play, some because it was a fashion among us, others lancing old angers of their own. There was much of ancient sick grievance finding its first words; some who met with us had no place else to go and warmed themselves at our passions.

I remember in those days how I would look among them, around the fire or leaning against the trees, the old and young of them, their faces shining as at a prayer meeting. Such meetings moved so subtly from prayer to politics we hardly noticed the change. I thought then, in the woods among the disaffected and the bitter, is it with them we seek to build a democratical England? Is it these men they fear so in the Parliament that they already seek to pass laws to stop

our mouths? In truth, at first we built a house with
windfall branches instead of oak. When I remember
our first meetings then, I smile.

We could not know then, cut off from all but rumor-
ing and whispering, that such angry gatherings of men
were springing up all over England, in taverns, in the
woods. As I look back now, there never was a time
like it, when every man had so much to say in his own
destiny. It was like early spring, when the frail shoots
seem so isolated in the first flow of mud and dark, dark
earth.

But Robbie Lokyar is my other name for tears.

He came toward us gradually, ever watchful and
weighing all in his grave way, from the back walls of
taverns, where he listened and said nothing. He was
there, then closer to us; then all quietly, as one who is
strong is quiet, he began to inform us and help us shape
ourselves, until he seemed always to have been among
us. He was twenty then, as I am now who God help
me must somehow fill his place, though his face was
pocked with old smallpox that made him look somewhat older.

Aie, I see him now, moving his head and hand forward across a dirty table, with a finger crooking and a
smile that came seldom. He did little, with all his re-
fining passion that had not a kind of hard, not hard,
stripping wit about it.

"You," he said, "think yourselves too high and
mighty poets and preachers to weave your way through
politics. I tell you this"—he always began so—"we
may speak the language of religion, but politics informs it." How often he returned to that refrain: "I
tell you this, political religion is the weapon of our
enemies, religious politics our strength.

"It is not," he would say, "arguing with old men that
we must do and leave all acts to them and then mewl
and whine of what they do; we must take action of our
own."

There was hardly a tract by Lilburne or Walwyn,
who trumpeted the new democracy in London, a letter

printed and flung out upon the London streets, a petition by the people to the surly Parliament he did not
have in his hands in days after it was printed. He was
learning and teaching us a new language to fit our ten-
uous hopes. He made us see ourselves, not neglected
and forgot, but men with a single shining purpose. I
think he cared little for religion. What he called reason
instead was the blood that warmed and moved him.
He was a man who cared not for conversion. He distrusted it, but he loved the word "reason" and spoke
it with the same kind of passion that Thankful spoke
of God.

What did he look like? Christ help me, the dead face
fades from the mind of a friend as a soul from the body
and leaves not visions but qualities instilled by them.
He leaves within me that watchfulness and wit, that
impassioned hatred of all forms of neglect of men.
He was liable to sudden unfair angers. Like one stripped
too much to the elements, there were times he shivered
more than other men at such things as small neglects.
He had moments of a fine-honed gracefulness, but with
a boy's awkwardness still in his man's body that had
been four years at war. He would knock things over,
tankards, candlesticks, with his long arms, deep in talk,
and then would set his elbow in the spilled ale and not
notice it. He had a slim face that would have been
gaunt later in his life and eyes that seemed to see into
some hope of his own beyond our meetings in dirty alehouses.

The voice of religion can grow loud and wild on
waves of feeling, but the voice of politics is low and
has direction. He had such a voice. We must lean forward to hear him, as his long body arched over the
board toward us and he thrust his hand into his black
hair.

The old men of the Parliament had got what they
wanted, power over the king, and they had promised
much to get it. They had administered to him a stern
and sensible whipping. They wanted only peaceful
treaty, and all to be, not as it had been for them before,

but for those they had used. We had been the sword they could not wield. That we had passions, minds, and hopes angered them. I think it was the blind mediocrity of their anger that offended us most.

On a night in late September we heard that the Parliament had passed a law against liberty of conscience, a wild, unworkable law against the beliefs of many around us. It was punishable by death to deny the Trinity and life imprisonment to speak against infant baptism.

When Robbie heard it, he spoke not for so long we thought he had not understood. When he did this, his voice was softer than ever, but as if he spoke louder he would scream. He reached out for a candle on the table and broke it and began to break the pieces and break again until there was a little pile of fragments before him. He spoke not to us then, but to the white fragments on the table.

"Why, those old men detest and abhor us. They spit at what they call toleration and we call democracy. I tell you"—he looked up then from the candle fragments—"they will try to disband us and send these poor men who have fought so long back to the same forgotten lives they left in all their hope, to the same arbitrary power and oppression they have known all their lives. Now I tell you, it will be the same for us as it was, laws against our conscience, laws against the speaking and writing of what is in our minds."

Thankful reached over and began to gather the fragments Robbie's elbow had scattered.

He was right. One law after another came from the Parliament that was conjured up to crack our hopes. There was nothing we could do against them. We could not even know of their truth, for we were victims of ever-seething rumor, tap talk and words wasted in the night air like pipe smoke. Who could we trust? John Lilburne had left the army in one of his ever-public gestures, as dramatic as a player in his passion for public martyrdom. It was not that he did not speak the truth always, with a pure and furious integrity. It was that his acts were too public, too timely. He made himself into his own puppet. There was some high cockalorum about him we did not care for.

Cromwell? Why we'd as lief watch a seesaw as he was then. One day he sat in Parliament and promised he could curb us, as if we were horses and not men. We heard another day that he conspired with the king to be a peer of some newfangled realm. One swore at the same time that he lay near death from a fever in his brain brought on by long fatigue and age and disappointment, and that was nearer truth. Then it was rumored that he was gathering some favored soldiers around him to leave England and fight for the Protestant kings in Germany. I see now that he must have been drifting as we did in the changing winds of that time, for God knows that if he held a key to unlock our sorrows, he used it not.

I know now that new leaders were growing in all that rich soil of disaffection, men like Colonel Rainsborough, but how could we know then? We were expediently scattered, put away in small garrisons throughout the country. We despaired of God's hand upon us, who had been so fine and such believing men. The rewards of God then seemed showered on more ambitious men. Oh, they prayed much, great public rumbling prayers and fast days, and when they thought of us at all, it was as men preoccupied with finer things than single, simple men. If we troubled their prayers, it was only with an itch.

We, who had been called the Saints, disintegrated into thieving, some into rioting, some to desertion, all into bitter, bitter disappointment. I saw in those days many a godly man walk away with his head down, leading his horse, all that was left to him, saying not even a farewell, going back into the anonymous life he came from. Every desertion was treated as an answer to a problem.

Colonel Whalley no longer paid us. He seemed to be trying to starve us out of the army as dangerous men, for he was an orthodox man and culled, in every way he could, the disaffected from his regiment. Many weak men or men with families left the army. He was glad to see them go. His orders were to cut out at least twenty from each troop of sixty men. Christ in heaven, how could we not read this in him? He was Cromwell's close cousin, hand in glove with him, and yet we clung to some hope still that Cromwell would come to lead us and leave off his sulking. The war had took a country man in him and forged a brilliant soldier, impatient of the soiled maneuvering that went on in London. Now a Presbyterian majority jostled into power; now the Independents, as they called themselves, jousted at them. There was the ever-constant treating with the broken king. First one faction, then another sought to use him as a symbol of their power. There was more and more parceling out of Cavalier lands among the new landowners of England. Even Cromwell accepted a huge tract from Parliament, a fine parcel, and a rich pension.

Aie, such grabbing of spoils touches me to the quick, for I had heard, after two years of silence, word of home. I met an old servant from Lacy House in an alehouse in Banbury. He had wandered off to join the army, a man of sixty years with no place else to go. I hardly remembered his face, but when he told me he had dragged me from the river once when I was small, I remembered red strong arms that plucked me out of that wet fear, a big red-faced country man. Now he was shriveled, his face mapped and creased by time's weight upon him.

Peregrine had died in the siege of Bristol, and for a long time, Nellie had been there almost alone, with only himself and his wife to watch over her when she carried so rare a burden, Sir Valentine's posthumous child within her. Then the soldiers came to take Lacy House that had been granted to a parliamentary man. They used the chapel for their stable, beheaded her image, and burned it. One pissed into the font and baptized his horse there.

She had been forced then to go to Henlow, to my

father's grim welcome, and there she stayed and grew my child within her, a son who would have been the heir to all the Lacy lands.

The beliefs that drive an army are great things, and she, nodding there in charity's prison, is so small. Oh, Nellie, you have to sit there unsmiled on and your hands not touched, in a blank room, grow old with no one coming there to comfort you. I long for you, you trapped within, and me without my father's house. My son is three years old now and must comfort you. I can see you squat and croon to him, "Come up, come up, my darling, my knight," but there are no castle steps for him to climb.

That day at Banbury I went and lay in the woods, blank as a fallen branch, and tried to see myself a father, but could feel nothing, only see Nellie, come full circle of her life, back to Henlow. It was the first moment, to my shame, in all that time that I had lain and thought of her and of myself alone. The comforting of comrades, the we of it all, was stripped away as a deception, and I was I again, flung down there on the leaves of the forest floor. I let my body roll over, and there, above me, the sun made a thousand drifting, dusty shafts of light that filtered down over me. I had not noticed such things in many months. My starved and private soul did hurt to come alive again.

Sickness for home engulfed me. I could see myself passing familiar fields, walking into my father's house, and holding Nellie close to me. But while I dreamed there under the trees, I knew that I would wake and go on waiting with the others, for it was not over, what we had come to do; there was no hope of any such future that was really something behind me, haunting and impossible to find again. Another, realer vision filled me, of my father's dogs set on me, of being thrust away like a beggar from his door, for I knew that there was no forgiveness in him for the man I had become.

And so I stayed, to steal my food or take to the woods, trapping to keep alive. In late summer it was good, for we helped with the harvest to pay for board and lodging. But in winter the villagers turned their backs on us when we passed in the street, for we had to pay for shelter in tickets that no one hoped would be redeemed. It was not their fault. Why, if the four Evangelists themselves had lain so at free quarter upon them, they would have been so treated. They had to live by the day, and the soldiers were to them, as they always are except at that foul entertainment of battles and banners, a nuisance and a burden.

Some of us had no place to go and owned nothing but our horses and our arms. Some feared to go back to their homes without any act of indemnity passed by the Parliament against acts of war, for many had gone home only to find themselves jailed for such offenses as they had been ordered to by their officers. Some simply, week after week, expected their back pay to help them set up their farms or crafts again. A few of us stayed, and God knows it was fewer every day, because what we had come to do had not yet been accomplished, but such hopes as we had grew cloudlike, weakened and spent in night talk without action. I know now that if the Parliament had not acted, we would have drifted apart, and such ideas become separated, empty dreams. But they had not the wit to wait. They acted.

Thankful has wakened. "Where are we, Johnny?" he asks as one roused from a dream. "I know not this land."

The white glow of the sun behind the gray sky lies at four o'clock in the west. We have been riding on this march all the long day from ten o'clock, northwest across the land.

"Before Christ, I am tired," he says, watching the soft ground. We have long since passed the flooding, and our horses' feet sink in new plowing. "You were far away in your eyes, Johnny. What thinking?"

"Oh, of where we are," for I must answer him. What I have been seeing is so far away now and has no words, even for Thankful.

"There are only three or four more hours of daylight. I think we must not stop tonight."

"Aie, I agree. We can hide among the Cotswolds, and keep on resting and riding slowly. It is better."

"Let me go forward and speak to the others." He waits for me to answer.

Nothing follows, not a horse or man or animal in the open space behind us. Ah, well, I worry more than is good for a man. I want him to ride forward and leave me, for he has interrupted my dreaming, and it is more real to me than this, this incessant beat of the hoofs. He must know this, for he leaves me without speaking and sets his horse to trot along the men where they have disappeared out of sight down a rolling hill to reappear way yonder up the other side of a shallow valley.

Where are we? Before Babylon? Aie, such fine talk is gone and has no place with us anymore. We ride now in daily dangerous fact. Ahead lie the Cotswolds and night to hide and rest and ride. We have done these slow, interminate rides so often, keeping the horses to a walk into the darkness and the light again, that slow-paced lulling treadmill that covers so much distance.

There is naught lulling of what I have been to within me this day, that following of another road of time and change; aie, mumbling of such things as Parliaments and this and that. What in hell did they mean to us, except as we were caught there waiting, waiting, and waiting to despair?

AH, yes, Parliament acted. We had assisted in their fatherly chastisement of the king. All was over but the brushing of us out of their beards. By their arrogant neglect of what we were, they had fed and watered what we became. Even their first decisive act, when it came, was stupid with certainty, and old, old as they were. We were given a choice—disband or go to Ireland. Poor Ireland! What would England do without it? If there is need to weed out the disaffected, turn the eyes of the land from troubles at home, send an army into Ireland, for there is always enough of the trouble we have planted among those poor folks to milk a needed crisis.

Thank God the order woke us into action, too, for we had been too long asitting and festering without direction. It seems a boy's game now that was to grow so big. I saw then grave Robbie become young again before our eyes. He laughed much and spoke little of great matters, but acted as a hungry man who is fed at last.

From regiment to regiment, the word was spread, and in those nights of late May, two years ago, 'twas a fine and goodly time when one rode secret and single to spread the word and meet. What we found out was like a smile from heaven itself. There were so many of us, not so few. All the coded letters and the messages delivered by the dark-cloaked riders spread like a strong vine among us. Out of the letters grew petitions, signed by the soldiers, and out of all our impotent complaints, demands.

It grew that spring, as plans for battle grow, a new simplicity out of our diffuse wrongs. In the fields men gathered near their quarters to elect their representatives, and we were fair, as men are fair who feel new strength in them. We elected two officers and two men from every regiment to meet and make petition to the Parliament. They were the first free elections without regard to rank or property ever held on English soil, and we knew it. We knew it in our mouths and in our backs and in the raising of our hands, every minute that we stood there. We had heard much of the secret election of God's grace upon a man, but this was no such private fearsome night matter, but the free election in the light of day of men by men.

The Battle of Naseby had been the end of an old quarrel for power that touched us little but to try us. 'Twas a headier thing by far than battle, to have a new answer, a stepping forth into the light of reason beyond that which was ever seen before, and the raising of men's hands, unafraid, to be counted.

Robbie Lokyar was so secure in the saddle of action he was like one reborn, and he conferred with me and Thankful so solemnly in his new part it made me smile. It was decided between us that we should desert from Whalley's regiment and join Grevis, for he was a strong Presbyterian man and death to liberty of conscience in all his speakings. We were needed among his men to cheer them into action.

It was easy to do. We rode to Holmby, where the regiment guarded the king, and were took on as replacements for deserters there. By then the orthodox officers were so far from our thinking that they saw only the old fatigue and what they judged was shallow-mindedness in the desertions and rejoining, and would take men if they had horse and arms, whether they fought for God, or the king, or the devil.

I had not seen MacKarkle for two years and had well nigh forgot him, nor had any hopes that he would still be of Grevis' regiment, for he changed his place so often. But he was there, God be thanked, and by

the second night of our coming among them he had
set us well among those who already had begun to
speak for the men, though we were strangers. When I
asked him why he had not gone home long since to
Newcastle, he answered, "I got bit with all this talk of
liberty, God damn me, and at my age too."

We had been among them only three days when
Cornet Thompson and Cornet Denne, the chaplain,
came to us to welcome us and discuss the plans for
election in the regiment. Cornet Thompson is a fine,
swashbuckling kind of man, a very child's view of a
soldier, a man of easy extremes, even of courage. He
has such a sanguine way he could have been a high-
wayman. Indeed, it is rumored that his more famous
brother has turned to that since he was cashiered for
disaffection. They belong to the night, as a cat does, as
Thankful belongs to the morning.

Cornet Denne could take a man and lift him up to
heaven with his voice and then plummet him down to
hell. Thankful was entranced with him, with his attentions and the serious way he spoke in discourse with
him. No one had paid him that attention in his religious
thought before in his life.

If I told all this to anyone, how we guarded the king
there, they would want to hear of that, and not our
planning, for "king's" a magic word. In truth, we saw
him little. Our minds were on other matters, and the
king had then no part in them. We distrusted vain preoccupations with him. He was but wool to pull over
our eyes. What fine plans he was making in his turn as
we saw him, from time to time, walking in the distance
back and forth across the privy garden, a little figure,
pacing and pacing in a prison that no one called a
prison, was far from our minds.

His only importance lay in his possession, to gamble
withal. With Grevis guarding him, he belonged to the
Parliament; that was all, and easy changed. When
Cornet Joyce came to take over the king's guard, we
expected him and threw wide the gates to him. Word
spread among us that he had come from Cromwell him-

self. It was the first word we had heard of Cromwell in many months. We were given a new colonel, Scrope, one more to our persuasion.

We escorted the king to Newmarket, where the regiments were to meet to draw up a petition. The king was little troubled with the change. He went on, pacing and pacing the privy garden of a new house.

Newmarket! It was as if the time had turned back to Naseby and all the bitterness between forgot. Even the action of Cromwell was the same, for he had a talent for timely entrances. I think there is something of the stage player in most good soldiers. The day before the meeting, just as at Naseby, the word and shout spread through the ranks that he had come to lead us again and had not chose the side of orthodoxy that we had feared.

'Twas his son-in-law Ireton, his voice, some said his very mind, who drew up the final petition when the Agitators met. The words were so fine they still ring in my ears, for they seemed to say all, and distill into mighty music what we had meant so long and could not say together.

June 14, 1647.

> We were not a mere mercenary army, hired to serve an arbitrary power of a state; but called forth and conjured by the several declarations of Parliament, to the defense of our own and the people's just rights and liberties, and so we took up arms in judgment and conscience to those ends, and have so continued them, and are resolved to assert and vindicate the just power and rights of this kingdom in Parliament, against all arbitrary power, violence and oppression. . . .

I should know the words, for we who could read read the petition over and over to the men, as Thankful had once read the Bible.

Aie, the mighty men had come once again to throw in their lot with us. Parliament was scoured of their enemies, and we were thrown upon the scales to weight them into power. How could we know then what they were? Such men and names you read of in newsletters and see, if at all, from afar, all grand with fame. We watched them as you watch a weather vane to see how it swings. Their legends grew among us greater than they were.

The regiments were separated after Newmarket into small groups to hear and approve the modified petition agreed on. Some said it was to prevent a mutiny if the troops did not agree. Already there was a new pattern if we could have seen it, but we were so blinded by success that most of us saw it not. The petition had been modified a little, but enough. There were to be two councils, one as we had hoped made up of two officers and two men from each regiment; the other, over it, a council of war, made up only of officers. Why could we not see then we had been courted and cozened? Only one man among the colonels stood out against the divided power that was to geld us. He was Colonel Rainsborough, a man we knew but little before that time.

Wishes and hopes were our blinders, aie, and memory too of what Cromwell had been to us. He sat our saddle. We were not broke first to have our purer spirits harnessed by the enemy, but by those who came among us already set apart with fame and ambition and changed and used us. There were no more comrades' orders and agreements rode through the free night. They came from above, from the officers who had at last heard us and danced to the tune we had made up and whistled so prettily among ourselves. When we saw how finely we had been cozened, we circulated new petitions among us. Petitions grew like flowers in those days. In truth, the real war was fought not at Edgehill or Marston Moor or Naseby, though the Parliament of old men would have us believe it, but at places that every Englishman will remember as if they were wrote on his hand—Newmarket and Putney.

When the gathering at Putney was called to debate among us all the new proposals, it silenced all but the most cynical.

Was there ever such a time and such a meeting? Why, it was like the first day that ever I saw the army. We were all drawed up before London and spread out through Putney town and into the late October fields. At the last minute, by some plan we knew not of, we were taken from the king's guard. He had been moved to Hampton Court and Cromwell's cousin Whalley and our old regiment put in charge of him. We hardly thought of the change, for there were greater things afoot than the old clothes of monarchy that no longer fitted us.

What could I tell of Putney? I was no Agitator then, and I never sat in council. I, with so many, gathered around the church to listen to the debates. As in the old days of preaching, we hung along the opened windows and in the trees that had changed their summer leaves to gold and red. I had climbed up a tree near the west window so high I could look out across the Thames and the boats upon it, as big a river as ever I had seen, strong and deep there, carrying boats like butterflies from where I was to all the countries of the world. Below me, through the window, were the tops of their heads who gathered there. There was a wind. I remember that, for I had to hold on with one hand and clap my hat to my head with the other.

When the first names were called out, Jesus love, they spoke Robbie's name! I did not know 'til then that he was there, elected Agitator of Whalley's regiment. Thankful, clinging to the branch below me, reached up and pinched my ham and so lost his hat. " 'Tis Robbie!" he called out, as if I had not heard.

First there was read the new proposals of the soldiers that had been spread among us and that we had signed, and it was a godly thing to hear the words read there, for unlike Newmarket, we had reached way beyond ourselves as soldiers to ourselves as freeborn Englishmen.

"Are they reading all?" Thankful asked, worried, for he had been troubling the soldiers below for his hat and missed much.

"Aie, of the new reforms of counties in elections and of new elections with every man of twenty-one to vote. . . ."

"Religion?"

"Aie, matters of religion not to be trusted to any human power." By then several of the men below who could not hear were calling up to find if they had read about the pressing of men into the army.

"Aie," I called down to them, "all of it, of not impressing us to serve in wars against our own freedom. All. And in all laws every person to be bound alike and no privilege of birth or estate to confer exemption."

"That will be the day when dogs piss wine," one old man grumbled.

The long reading of the proposals was nearly over, and he who read it raised his voice so that all might hear the ending. It could have been Robbie's very words that we had heard him say so often.

"These things we declare to be our native rights and therefore are agreed and resolved to maintain them with our utmost possibilities against all opposition whatsoever, being compelled thereunto not only by the examples of our ancestors, whose blood was often spent in vain for the recovery of their freedoms, suffering themselves, through fraudulent accommodations, to be still deluded of the fruit of their victories, but also by our own woeful experience, who, having long expected, and dearly earned, the establishment of these certain rules of government, are yet made to depend for the settlement of our peace and freedom upon him that intended our bondage and brought a cruel war upon us."

"That's the king," one man said below me, awed.

I could not hear more then, for there was much speaking and argument, and then Cromwell's voice rose beyond the rest. What he had been saying before I knew not.

"Would it not be confusion? Would it not be utter confusion?" There was angry fear in his voice.

All day long the voices drifted out to us, some so low that a soldier who had found a seat on the window ledge had to turn and tell what was said; some rose so loud they rang among us through the October air. Once I heard Robbie call out so clear and unafraid that I was proud that he spoke so among all those grand men.

"For the change of government which is so dangerous, I apprehend there may be dangers in it, and truly I apprehend that there be more dangers without it. For I conceive, if you keep the government as it is and bring in the king. . . ."

The very mention of the word brought forth a riot of argument, and I heard Ireton say when it had calmed a little, "For the king . . . I shall declare it again that I do not seek, or would not seek, nor will join with them that do seek the destruction either of Parliament or king!"

"I knowed they would draw fear of the king across our eyes," the old soldier below me fell agrumbling again.

"Aie, 'tis so," another answered him. "The king matters as much as they make him matter."

Then I heard one within the church say that all the debate of that first day was naught without they did repair to God for guidance, and they should call a prayer meeting before they met again in argument.

"Watch them buggers when they lay on to fast and pray, for they will smite us under the first rib!" the soldier perched in the window yelled into the church. Someone tilted him out, and he fell on the ground, and the window was shut in our faces so we could hear little more that day.

As I climbed down, there came an officer out of the church door so angry he could not see me, and I nearly fell on him.

"God damn me!" he said as if we had been talking a long time together. "They are but repairing an old house that when they lay the top stone, it will fall about their ears." We walked together along the common then, and when I looked around, Thankful had slipped away, too shy to speak with such a fine man.

Oh, Francis White, when I first saw him that day at Putney, there was not a gesture of his I did not want to ape. He walked beside me, his head up, his thighs arrogant in a fine pair of breeks, his hair still long and curled, unlike the others, his black hat slung at a rake-hell angle, his collar tweaked with fine lace. Yet he spoke to me with more passion and anger than ever Robbie had, though with it all he urged a judicious timing that set not well with his hat. He had the classic way of speaking I had not heard since Oxford, and I felt at home in a way I had not for so long in some forgotten part of me, listening to the familiar allusions and the Damascene edge of his wit.

He told me how timing must weigh words—even the timing of anger—and he smiled. Even Antigone, he said, sat quiet and played the pretty lass in the palace of Creon until the time had come, a fifteen-year-old girl of no import when she stood there holding a little dirt in her small hand, but when she turned her narrow wrist, she shook the state.

For days the debates flowed on at Putney church. Some pitched their voices so that we could hear; others, Cromwell and Ireton among them, mumbled a more judicious song. I still cannot think how it happened, and I myself in that place where every voice was heard, aie, heard and parried and thrust in those deceptively soft autumn days of our short season of liberty that had grown as goodly grain in a new season. Some there, as that tall man with the piercing voice, Colonel Rainsborough, tried to keep it growing; some, though most of us were loath to think of it, were harvesting it to use it, for themselves. We began to see two forces in one body there, as if a right hand and a left hand clashed in their own quarrel.

We could only watch by day and say nothing, but we argued it all out with our Agitators in the evenings and repeated and mulled over among ourselves all that had been said within in their seesaw of fine argument as we sat like birds among the trees and listened.

I can still hear Rainsborough's voice as one remembers all words that strike at the heart of one's agreement and forget others to my sorrow that wearied me with their niggling insistence on old forms and ways we thought we had shook off. Some men of Lilburne's and Rainsborough's party, and under Cromwell and Ireton, did scribble all day to print the words that night and cast them among us. I carry Rainsborough's speeches in my saddlebags, along with the Bible and my poor neglected pocket book. 'Twas a strange thing, the crossing of a barrier of dreams, when night thoughts among boys were spoke so and wrote down there and printed for all to see.

There were the passionate words of Rainsborough: "I think that the poorest he that is in England has a life to live, as the greatest he; and therefore truly, sir, I think it clear, that every man that is to live under a government ought first by his own consent to put himself under that government; and I do think that the poorest man in England is not at all bound in a strict sense to that government that he has not had a voice to put himself under. . . ."

Then, day by day, tap-tap like hammering, we heard the terse clipped answers of Ireton but could make out little that he said. Sometimes, in his zeal and some edge of fury in him, he did speak loud enough to hear: "All the main thing that I speak of is because I would have an eye to property," and his voice went low as if he remembered to seek what privacy from us he could.

He murmured long then, until Rainsborough shouted, "I wish you would not make the world believe we are for anarchy."

There was a murmur from Cromwell we could not hear.

One of the Agitators called out, "You but choose the rich to rule us as in the old days."

He made Ireton so furious that, forgetting us, his voice rose again. "The Law of God does not give me property, nor the Law of Nature, but property is of human constitution. I have a property, and this I shall enjoy. If either the thing itself that you press or the consequence of that you press do destroy property, I cannot give my heart and hand to it, because it is an evil thing to do and scandalous to the world."

The Agitator called again to him, "But it seems now, except a man has a fixed estate in this kingdom, but he has no right in this kingdom. I wonder we were so much deceived. If this thing be denied the poor that after so much pressing they have sought, it will be the greatest scandal. There was one thing spoke to this effect, that if the poor and those in low condition were given their birthright, it would be the destruction of this kingdom. Why, we have been the preservation of this kingdom! Their lives have not been held dear for purchasing the good of this kingdom, and now they demand the birthright for which they fought. Those that act to this end are as free from anarchy and confusion as those who oppose it. . . ."

There was a lowering of short November days. For more than a week they had debated in the church. It was too cold to stay without, and no house was opened to us who lived not in London. We gathered in the taverns to keep warm, unwelcome as we were who had not been paid in so long. Robbie found Thankful and me at last, huddled together by a smoky sullen fire, for the landlord wasted no fuel upon us. Winter fog blanketed the common, and all were silent ghosts that we had passed that night.

He came and sat down with us as if we had been together the night before and two years had not passed. He looked much older, gaunt with some constraint upon his face. We knew him too well to question him but waited for him to speak his mind. Once Thankful touched his hand in love and welcome, and he looked

up and smiled. Let his soul forgive me now, I pitied
him sitting there and thought his loss of joy was that
he longed perhaps for the freedom of our old secrecy,
as a boy when he must put away the imitations of manhood he calls play and be a man himself. He was too
familiar to us, who had such new idols as Denne and
Rainsborough and Francis, who came among us as if
there were no longer officers and men only, but behind
that free men of England and all born with equal
rights.

"How was it today?" I finally had to ask. "The windows were closed against the cold. We could hear
nothing."

"The same," he said, and bent to warm his hands by
the paltry fire. "Why, those grandees there are offended
to sit cheek by jowl with us."

"Why do they do it then?" I wanted him to stop,
for I was in love with what was happening there and
could not bear to hear speaking against it.

"Because we are the only force in England ready to
hand. They have need of us today, but they would as
lief shed us tomorrow. I tell you, these men have never
intended aught but to wrest their own power and safety
out of this."

"I do not believe you, Robbie." I told him that, and
once it would have drawn his passion, but no longer.
He only watched his hands, turning and turning them
before the fire.

"I have heard them," he finally said. "It is the old
fight dressed in the new fine words they took from us
and Lilburne and such others. Oh, they have gleaned
some and censored some. I have stood day after day
and heard them tear at the hope of equal right of election and justice like dogs, and so judicious and so godly
they do it! There is too much talk of God among
them."

"You hear only with your ears, Robbie."

"What other do I have? Rainsborough at least speaks
for us."

Thankful said so little I thought he understood not.

Robbie waited for an answer. He was demanding something, perhaps intelligence, from us after those days of complicated debating by clever, unscrupulous men, and we denied it him. He tried once more to reach us.

"True election is a jump they cannot make. 'Tis either/or with them. When they but sniff the hope of a new liberty, their minds draw back in fear to touch it. Aie, Ireton is subtle. He would cozen every man with a shilling in his pocket into fearing that it be took from him if all men voted without regard to property. They bank on that fear and blind us with vain preoccupations with the king. Oh, Christ, we could have been the pride of all Europe in our fairness, and they are turning back." I think he had begun to cry, but I could not see his face.

"What of Oliver? I heard not this in him." Thankful spoke at last.

"Cromwell! What hopes we had in him. That man is neither cunning nor subtle, as some think. That's his priest Ireton. He is worse than that. He is as pre-occupied with his own direction as a hardheaded dog. He cannot hear us. He only waits. There is one thing perfected in him, his entrances. Even they grow now as professional as a mountebank's. From one side to the other, now upright, now arsy-versy, he knows when to change."

"He is treating with us. What more would you have?" I was furious with him to speak so. I loved Oliver then and could not bear Robbie's blind disappointment. I liked him not at that moment for the first time, that he should bring clouds into my eighteen-year-old days of such sunshine. "Why, he took us broken and frustrated and has drawn us up to unity and strength. He treats with us as the fairest-minded man in England."

"He does not treat." Robbie's voice was so low I would have leaned close to hear him better had I not been in such a fury. "He courts. He does not treat,"

I think he said. "He knows not what it means. If he wins not in this debate, he'll take another way."

What was there to say? I did not believe him.

He got up and walked away through the dirty room, crowded with soldiers. He was crying, and I never followed him. From that time I never saw him more, except at a distance through the church window. I never saw him speak another word.

"Eh, my lads," one spoke above us. It was Francis White. He had left off his hat and had no doublet, though the night was cold. He stretched himself across a chair, familiar and easy, and called for ale for us.

"Now," he said, "we have begun to find a way to unity. What think you?"

"Sir, I thought you had been thrown out of the council," Thankful said.

"Aie, and at the right time, too." I think he was already somewhat drunk and was pleased that he had found us. He began to tell the story of Antigone again, forgetting he had spoke of it before, but Thankful, for reasons of his own, called a halt.

"I can find all I need for guidance from the Bible," he told Francis.

Francis changed his speech to please him. "I meant only the wisdom of serpents and the guilelessness of doves." He smiled. "By Christ's bowels we will need both before this work is done. Where will you sleep tonight?"

"On Putney common."

"I must into London for to see my family." He stared long at the fire. I think that he considered taking us with him to lie within a house, but he said naught. "Aie, I am fatigued to the teeth."

He went away and left more ale to warm us. I was warmed already by his attention. He had asked us what we thought. He had said, "What think you?"

On the last day at Putney we missed Rainsborough. Rumor came among us that he had been sent off on orders to the navy. Some disgruntled men said it was to silence him, but I did not believe that then.

Was it accident as well that a week after Putney the king was let to slip his leash and escape out of our hands to the Isle of Wight? Cromwell had him guarded by his own close friend. There were many in the army who said that he had done it to save the king's life from those who were beginning to call for his execution as a traitor and a man of blood. Would Cromwell have so broke faith with us as to throw the country back to civil war to have his way? No, in the hot and cold and change in his actions and his loyalties he never did do that. Hard he has been, God knows. He rode a crooked way as a man wheels his horse in battle, and the route he followed seemed ever to mark our defeat; but there were reasons. There were always reasons. My shame must outweigh my doubts in his work after Putney, for doubt can be a burden and a luxury in these delicate times.

I think that we were too stunned by what had happened finally there at Putney, and after, to act. We had lost, our proposals compromised into defeat and all in mighty language to pull the wool across simple eyes. The new constitution that would spring from the vote of all men was struck out. Freedom to worship as a man pleased was gone. The pressing of men into the army "to keep the peace" was sanctioned, though by God's grace they did forbid the pressing of men to fight abroad. For the rest, all of our hopes were drowned in much murky talk of God's will.

It took time to understand how we stood, and by then we had to hear it from rumor, for the army was once again divided, this time to keep the king from rallying new forces to himself. There was reason for that, too; as in all Cromwell's veering, there was reason. He and the grandees and the Parliament in their pockets had piped the tune of anarchy too loud. Many jumped back in fear all the way to the king again, and fighting broke out in Wales, in Kent, and with the Scottish army in the north. I cannot think that Cromwell foresaw this. They had only meant to discredit us in the army and to sow fear in the people of our party in London, for many had gathered around Lilburne there. They, too, elected agents in imitation of our election of Agitators. The doors of the Commons were besieged by their petitions. As we had hung our hopes upon their words, so they hung theirs on our way of organizing.

Our troop took up quarters in Blandford, and all those maneuverings were a far cry from us. It was only in stories that drifted to us along the roads and through deserters that we heard of the mutiny that broke out in the army at Ware among men who refused to accept the compromises of Putney. One soldier was shot in the field as an example to the others, and other leaders of the revolt made to run the gauntlet and be disgraced before the regiment by having their swords broke over their heads and rode in disgrace backwards on their horses.

We thought them fools to mutiny when a new civil war was breaking in upon us. The raising of new rebellion by the escaped king brought even Rainsborough to be reconciled with Cromwell.

Day by day, and gradually, we were took down again and silenced with war as an excuse. First the right to petition was took away. We were once again "soldiers in time of war." There were no more Agitators to be heard except when they were called up by the council of the officers. If we acted against that council, it was mutiny. What a double-faced Janus it was for a simple soldier to understand. Thankful and I found it hard to ravel out for the others. One day we were an army and subject to military law; on another we were free men with a right to speak. Which acts of ours were which we found out only after they were done. Some of the Agitators we had elected were silenced by preferment as officers. How could I not see that it was but a new and subtle way to milk us of our strength? Then the day came when it was death to petition or even to speak of freedom in the expediency of the second war. The presses were stopped, Lilburne in prison, Rainsborough fighting far away in the north.

All was gone. We were, as we had been before in New-market, under old masters with new names and patents.

We well nigh perished of the cold that winter. There was little food, and that evilly got, for the harvest had been the worst in years. The town huddled under weeks of ice and rime frost without even snow to gentle all with its illusion of comfort and white stillness. Our greatest battle in the new civil war that had so conveniently drawn our teeth was with the local minister, who used the prayer book in his service. So much for our great principles, chasing an old man through the town as he clutched the little book to his scrawny chest. We were hungry and took out our impartial fury by a bloody banging of the heads of poor people with prayer book for excuse who did riot for their stomachs more than for their souls.

At last the spring came. Thankful was eighteen, and I nineteen. We used to slip into the woods where a company of Ranters kept vigil, hiding from the new ordinances. At first we went for the food they shared with us, and then for better reasons.

Thankful loved a Ranter lass, who was as red and round as any cherry. We used to watch, night after night, as they kept up their constant dance in honor of the Second Coming. All lamplit by torches in the trees, they jigged in turn, around and around after the Scripture: "Rejoice ye, for the day of the Lord is at hand." There were two I saw there, a brother and sister, ajigging half-exhausted in and out of the light. They looked as fine and thin as knights or ladies who lie on tombs and rest from ancient times and wars, but I could see that their eyes, set so royally, were mad. She looked on nothing as she bobbed there, and he but shambled and darted furious rat's eyes around him.

But when Thankful's dolly danced, she played the pretty wanton, even with God. Sometimes, when it was not her turn to keep that jigging vigil, they would walk together, looking safe and touching each other. She was lamb soft, and what none of us dared tell him was that she would tip over for the asking and nestle like the animal she was in the arms of any who petted her, and if they'd leave a coin in her petticoat to get along with, she'd count it as a gift of God for such a little favor and the scratching of her ears. It was only a part of spring, and a sweet thing to see, but Denne and Thompson treated it as a new invasion upon us. They had no more than that to spend their zeal upon. Denne preached to Thankful long and thoughtfully upon his duty to our cause, but Thompson took the short, swift way. He tumbled the little lass to teach Thankful and to part him from her. They said they could not trust even Thankful not to betray us guilelessly into her ear that could be bought as easy as her quim.

He ran across into the woods when Thompson told him, and there I found him sobbing against a tree as if his heart would break. Why, his love had fallen on her without respect of persons as rain upon a field flower. I touched him, and he hid his face behind his hair and jerked his shoulder. How strange to think of her now. 'Twas only the betrayal of a slut. Not even that. But he gave Christian love, unquestioning. . . .

Thankful finds things out so desperately.

In the late fall we heard that Rainsborough had been murdered. How it happened we could not know. Some said that Cromwell had had it done, some said the king's faction disguised as Cromwell's men. Each faction used his death to accuse the other and finally blackened his name. Ireton's execution of two royalist officers after the siege of Colchester was laid to Rainsborough, who had been but a member of the council. In truth, judicious whisperings were as strong a weapon then as print had been before.

All we knew was that he was murdered in his lodgings. The sea-green ribbon of his regiment no longer waved so brave among us. His mouth was closed at a convenient time. Did Cromwell order it? A man can go with the tide, not rule it. I wish I had not fell apondering such evil thoughts. It makes me ashamed when he has given his word so gallantly to us.

But I cannot banish from my mind what a ripe time

it was for Rainsborough to die. Without one to speak for us, without our Agitators, we were, of a sudden, gathered again to London. If Cromwell could not see his way to grant a freedom to us, he would give the disaffected the king's head instead. He would put out our flame with the king's blood as one who splits an ox and draws its carcass before a forest fire.

T HE sun has broken through. The birds sing praise that the gray day is over, nesting and busy. The horses ahead are disappearing down an avenue of poplars planted by men in olden times. How peaceful it is and domestic here after the space. There is more rise and fall of the land around us. Cattle are grazing across the rolling wastelands. I can see a village, the tops of the houses, and the squat tower of the church. The sun has drifted through the last of the clouds there and touches the roofs with one of those distant shafts of light like dim Godshine, and then the clouds obscure it, and it is gone. That must be Bampton, but I would have thought we had rode farther than that. By the sun it must be later than I thought. At last I am under the sheltering trees. How peaceful it is. I remember such deceptive peace.

On the morning that the king was to die, for a few hours in the first dawn I was fooled by trees and such a peace. I had wandered around London all the night before. Who could sleep then when we were about the killing of the king? I walked all through St. James's Fields through the bitter cold night, and as I came to a frozen pond there, not knowing where I was, the birds filled the air with their chorus, a bird-dawn cry of women chittering and screaming as if the dawn had run among them, scaring and scattering. I would have thought it too cold for their cry, but they sang as if it were the spring and not cold January.

London was alive all night with the human beasts that ever prowl cities, though then their marauding was blamed on the new time, as every man caught in his back the fear of what we were to do. I walked beyond St. James's Palace and down the path the king would take, past the tilt yard, and around the Abbey into Westminster Yard. I remember my own footsteps sounded on the deserted stones as if they followed me.

A London drab ran toward me through the fag end of the night, her mouth all wide, a hollow chasm, a screeching bird, the laughter following her, pounding after her. When the men caught her at the corner of the yard, I tried to stop them, but they thrust me back among them and held me. She crouched against the wall of Westminster; then two of them held her up there spread-eagle under the carving of some indifferent saint, and they flicked out their stiffened weapons. One spread her legs and dived and pumped into her, moaned his quick pleasure as his body melted against her, while the others jostled and played with their pricks and called, "Be quick, be nimble there!"

Two knaves, then three men, then four, they thrust their cods within their breeks and waited for one another, holding her to silence, and the sound of their short ecstasy, and one said, "Come, boy, hast no manhood in thee?" and I was ashamed because I was big and hard against my breeks.

Dying down from fire to satisfaction and the night, they ran away, and she was left like a rag there on the stones. Her defiant bird shriek was silenced; she stumbled up the wall then, whimpering, and when I tried to touch her in some stupidity of comforting, she made a little childish jerk of her shoulder as Thankful had when I had tried to comfort him and wandered off along a narrow street. A tiny litter of semen and blood drops followed her, falling from her, her only *nunc dimittis*. A man rode by with lace upon his boots, not seeing her, but she, seeing the Quality, tried with little bird gestures to hide the shame she had cried down with scratching of her foot.

Later in the morning we rode through icy silent streets. There was no joy, no sorrow, but an almighty holding of breath as in a dream when what could not happen is coming to pass. The ancient wild edge of men that ever lurks beyond the sun of reason waited there to sacrifice that petulant man and make a king at last of him.

It was a cold, cold day. There was ice on the river, and our horses slipped in ice along the street, and our hearts and our faces were stunned by cold; the cold and the time brought tears, although we tried to look not toward him for a kind of embarrassment. I looked; I had to. I saw her there below me in the crowd, the woman of the night. Her face was hateful, blaming all the indifference and dirt of her life on him who stood there, stripped down at last to a dignity and grace that still stay in my eyes. I heard her calling out there, not bird shriek now, but part of a moan as if it came from earth as he stretched out his arms, controlling his own death as he had not his life, and the head of him fell. When it was lifted up, it was very small and the hair was wispy gray. He cried down blood as she had and stared so as she had, a dumb surprise, and now his blood in me has mingled with hers, his bird woman, the least of all his subjects.

We should not have killed him. It was a mistake. But to have let him live would have been too cruel. Martyrdom at our cost was all the victory left him, and I fear we will pay dear. We made him too important, and he lives on in the crooking of men's knees. I fear the knees of slaves more than the gray ghost of the king.

How am I to tell who made the roads and why they turn so? But I can tell, as most men, where I have been and what the markings were to guide me. I know not what went on behind the closed doors of Westminster or in men's minds. I only know that within days after the king's killing we, who waited for such doors to open to know where we stood, were served up with an old warmed-over portion.

Why, with the changing of their hats, the old council of the officers had become a new council of state and, much trumped among us as a new thing, a commonwealth. To us they were the familiar names, the colonels, the generals, in a new guise.

They even made new crisis of the old convenient danger of Ireland. They would put it to us that armies there who had not come before to the king's service in two wars would come among us now. As before, at Newmarket and Putney, the army was divided, some stationed in London to keep the new peace, so many others, we among them, sent to the north, the west, out of the reach of meetings, to await our lot.

Thank God they went too far. Within a month of the king's death, the law was passed that we could petition only through our officers and not as free citizens direct to the Parliament. Lilburne and Walwyn and others of our persuasion in London were flung from their beds at night and sent into the Tower for treason. If they had thought to cleanse the land of the king, now they set about cleansing minds of all dissent against them.

By mid-April we were given the choice to be disbanded or go into Ireland. In a week we heard that London was a city in more turmoil than there had ever been through all the years of war. The soldiers rioted and flung down their arms to join the people. In the midst of it all, the new council met and put the names of all the regiments into a hat and had a little child draw out those regiments designed for Ireland. 'Tis said, though, the little child drew many times before God vouchsafed unto Cromwell the most disaffected, to bleed them out of England.

We were in Salisbury, safe away from the catching of revolt, when we were told that we had been chosen, along with Lambert's, Horton's, and Ireton's regiments to go there. I think it could have succeeded with us, I fear so, for we were numbed by then by hearing of events we could take no part in, the petitioning, the excitement, the urgency of those thousands in London streets who marched against the betrayals of our hopes, the silencing of our mouths, the overturning of the presses, the jailing of their leaders.

We were stunned by a new turn. Cromwell himself was to take us into Ireland, he who two years before had thrown his weight to upset the balance of the old state and Parliament over the same decision. What in God's name is in his mind to allow himself to take such part in this? Like a fighting dog, does he taste still the king's blood on his teeth and move as instinctively into new battle against so puny a foe?

We heard that one soldier on the news had stood upon the high porch of an inn, and they say he spoke with such great eloquence and passion there that when the loyal troops arrested him, for before God there are always men who will obey orders no matter what they are, even the women tried to pull them from their horses.

Then we heard that the soldier was Robbie Lokyar. I could not fathom it. He, who had ever warned us to move within legality, caught in a mutinous act—why, what a waste of passion! Despair has passion of its own.

He was took out into Westminster Yard, where Prynne and Burton and Bastwick had stood so long ago and where in the night the bird shriek of the woman had pounded its walls. When they stood him against the wall there and shot out of him all that longing and despair, did the birds fly up and shriek so?

Well, mighty Cromwell, can you hear it now? Do you still count in your sleep the thousands upon thousands that followed at Robbie's funeral? I fear the killing meant more to them than the soldier killed. The symbol of the body obscured the sweetness of the man. Of all the deaths his primed what he had lost hope in. The color he despaired of seeing again, Rainsborough's sea-green, was carried there to his burial. His horse followed his coffin carrying sea-green rosemary to remember him, dipped in his blood. They said it was the greatest funeral ever held in London.

In two days after that single funeral that's set us all aflame, the regiments have begun to elect new Agitators to demand a new meeting, as we did at Newmarket and Putney. But this time we cannot be muted by arguments of the danger of the king—they've used that pawn. We cannot be fooled again by threats of Ireland when those who try to lead us there once spoke so fine against it and cannot wipe their words from our memories. Third time's a charm, Oliver. You have whipped us out of innocence and despair by the firing of the shots into our Robbie.

Election! What a thing of God's grace was that, that all the regiment should stand on Salisbury Plain and choose Thankful and me their Agitators to represent them against the murderous plans to transport us into Ireland lest we speak out and open up the prisons they are trying to make of England where men are being thrust into the Tower for their opinions or shot like lovely Robbie. What time is there for poems now? Though they say that Robbie wrote poems on the night before he was shot, but the guards tore them up in his face.

It was a far greater May Day only two weeks ago in Salisbury Plain than ever I had before, when I did sneak to see the dancers around the maypole and pay for it with my father's whipping. Aie, he'd whip me unto death for this May Day's work. Now the regiments are all aflame with conscience. Elected! Not in the darkness of memory and desire and loss where God is planted that he may rise in a man like the sudden sun so that he knows election among the Saints, but in another light, the light of choice, although to tell the truth, we were soaked with rain that day as if the sky wept for Robbie. The sea-green ribbons dripped from our hats, the tracts were too soggy to read, but the wet hands of the men went high in the air for us. That's hope indeed, a hand held high to be counted. Henry Denne and Thompson were the only officers to throw in their lot with us. The others fled to Cromwell. It was as if the thousands upon thousands that marched behind the funeral of Robbie and wore the sea-green ribbon two days before had marched on toward us.

In a dark room that night with the fire glowing late we met for the first time as Agitators. We worked through the night, and there was such zeal, such spirit, such an urgency and passion in that room at Salisbury where we writ the first letter to send out to the soldiers.

Denne flung gestures in and out of the firelight that made his shadow hands as big as the hand that writ upon the wall at the feast of Belshazzar and said, "Why not begin so? 'Fellow soldiers, it has pleased the Lord to open our eyes, and to let us see the wretched conditions we are brought under and our crying sins, which cry aloud into the ears of God. Oh, the ocean of blood that we are guilty of, oh, the intolerable oppression!'"

Thankful was trying to set down what he said, but had to interrupt him, though he loved everything of Henry Denne too much to speak out to him. "Cornet Denne, sir, I cannot take it down so fast."

Denne stopped and said, in his sweetest way, "Thankful, thee must call me Harry; are we not all equal in the sight of God?"

Thankful said, "Yes, sir," forgetting already.

Denne began to ponder for more fine words, when Cornet Thompson interrupted and said, "Leave off, Harry. What about the wages? We will never move the soldiery with your holy drivel."

Thankful fought then, as he was wont to do when Denne was attacked. "I think, sir, that we should tell less what's been done to us and more of what we have done and are being ordered to do, though we are not a mercenary army, but have took arms as freeborn Englishmen for our rights and liberties."

I saw the soldiers tearing at the faces of the Irish whores at Naseby and could say nothing.

Thompson paid him no mind but to say, "Take this, Thankful, and set it in," and then to me, "You put it in your fine Oxford words, Johnny"—he flung that at me always. "Tell how Cromwell has abused and scorned and kicked us like dogs and forced us to get our bread by force and rapine and how we have been used to fetch in taxes in these hard times when we did never join for such foul bailiff's work, violently taking all from poor people and ruining them with our wasteful riot. Then write how they do but plan to get the disaffected regiments over into Ireland for a trumped-up war to stop our mouths of democracy and liberty of conscience by the cutting of our throats."

I insisted that we had a right, and a legal right as soldiers, to elect two officers and two rankers to sit in council together and debate these matters, even as we did at Putney two years gone.

Thompson laughed at me and made me ashamed until I caught myself; he said I was forever rolling legality around my tongue and that the generals cared naught for all this; now that they had might on their side, right could go to the devil.

Thankful went on as if he had not heard us, and I watched him write, "What have we to do in Ireland, to fight and murder a people and nation who have done us no harm, only deeper to put our hands in blood? We have waded too far in that crimson stream already of innocent and Christian blood. . . ." Then he writ, "We poor and simple men," and God forgive me I thought he was diminishing himself in his own eyes.

He saw me watching then. "This is the center of what we must say. We are only courting, Johnny, with our talk of wages and what we have been forced to do," he said under the harangue of the others. "If we but honor men by telling them true, we need not court them so. You must needs see MacKarkle hearing this, or Little Will, or Panck, to know that. It is sinful to do other."

Thompson interrupted him and ranted the Salisbury room and made the shadows twitch and flow. Thankful writ faster now as he took down all Thompson preached into the night. "Say this . . . now have become the greatest tyrants over their brethren themselves, which when they can refrain from sighing"— and Denne took up from the corner when he paused— "and sobbing. Put down 'sobbing,' in their broken and rustic language," and Thankful cried, "Enough. Slower. Slower."

We sent the letter to Bristol to be printed, for it is there we will meet with the regiments picked for Ireland in rendezvous. But we have sent fine official letters to Lord Fairfax and Cromwell.

Every day more men have joined us. Colonel Eyre rides here who was cashiered at Ware, and Thompson's brother, so outspoken in his regiment he had to be weeded out on trumped-up charges. Cromwell knows he must treat with us and fairly, else why, now that we ride to meet the other regiments, does he send word that he will not follow hard upon our heels but meet and treat with us as in the old days at Newmarket and Putney? Before God, he has picked the one man whom we can trust beyond the others as his envoy to us. When I saw Francis White ride up to us this morning, I knew that Robbie had despaired too soon to his death.

NOW Thankful comes back, riding a prancing career past the men. He must show off that horse when he feels happy. I think the sun has touched him. He reins in and falls awalking beside me.

"We are near to Burford. They say we should rest there this night."

"I like it not," I tell him. "I thought we were to ride slow all the night and meet the other regiments at dawn."

"They think that there is time enough. The dawn comes at three o'clock. The horses need rest. Only a few hours of night there. Then we will be within the Cotswolds." Thankful is persuading himself and me.

I wish I could trust more. It is an abiding fault caught from the times. Cromwell has never broke his word, for he is a man of God. Before God, the old man will try us to the quick, but he'll not cheat. Even Robbie he did not cheat, but caught fair in mutiny and riot.

"What thinking now, Johnny?" Thankful has caught my worry.

"Why, of Robbie. Ever him. It fills me with blood rage."

"No sin in storms," he says, "God sends them."

I will shake off the past that has dogged my day and be as buoyant as Little Will there ahead, riding into the evening beside MacKarkle. He holds his pot under his arm so the girls can see his yellow curls.

Come, Johnny, you know you ride in miracle. Shake off this lack of trust. Here are twelve hundred men who refuse to fight in Ireland strung along this road, and as many more await us near Bristol to treat with the general as freeborn men, not the mercenaries and Turkish Jansenaries he would have us be. We are the forlorn hope.

It is our duty to ride heads up and feathers flying to give the others courage. Did ever such pride ride here, though in truth 'tis hard to ride so when your ribbons are wet and dragging in your eyes and jerkins still laden with water from all the rain and fog we've passed through? All the way from fording the river we have rid in mud, weighed down in spirit by dirty, sullen clouds. Now, in the sun, the ribbons are drying. The late light makes the sea green of them almost yellow.

The men's backs are straightening as they wake and know they come toward the town. I think the word must have been spread among them that we will rest.

Oh, Oliver, you grew us into this and now do hate your harvest. Did you not know how much we loved you, who now have taken the lives of two poor gentlemen soldiers and cashiered many and broke their swords upon their heads, and made them ride the wooden horse and be bastinadoed for the speaking of their minds?

How still the fields are this evening. Aie, there's an exile of many a poor family in this reading of the miles of Windrush Valley greensward, all fenced into the new enclosed pastures. I can still see the hummocks under the thick grass where once the fields were tilled and fed men. Now there, along a new path of the hill field, a shepherd drives his snowy flocks toward the town at evening. Here is another such place where the sheep have ate the men, though they make not hedges but stone fences here, some still raw, some weathered, so they must have enclosed long ago. No, not so long; this Cotswold stone weathers fast and changes to the color of centuries in a few years. I have seen it in Oxford. 'Tis not like my own country in the north, where still there are great forests, and when the fields are made, they are hedged in hawthorn that the women will not bring into the house in this month of May for fear of witches. They even call it witch thorn, but I miss the ghost May bloom of it as I miss home.

The moon is out today to meet the sun. The men will read much in it, that we are blessed today, for they call the sun Christ and the moon the Holy Ghost. For all their courage there is that in them that drives me to despair of our cause, when I would have us reason together as the Scripture says. Despair of our cause. Let me not catch that from Robbie. A cause can only succeed when it has already been despaired of. He did not live to find that out. 'Tis like the trimming of branches from a tree to shape and help its growth to trim a cause of hope.

My Christ, I am suddenly ashiver as if someone walked across my grave, and now I will face what I fear, although I am ashamed even to think it, as I have faced all the rest today. My inner voice says that Cromwell and Fairfax will not keep covenant with us, though they have promised to treat with us, and we have half the regiments behind us and more to come. All my hopes cry out against my voice. Can trust be a decision? Must I forever ask this question while the others trot on and now fall to singing of hymns as they have always done to show they are the Parliament's army and no paid mercenaries of the king? I fear that if I choose trust, I will not enjoy it for long, for I scent a bloody business.

Ah, well, the column has begun to trot up ahead. Put your head up, Johnny; you're a soldier of the Commonwealth. All you have left of the poet you once thought you might be is your melancholy drivel, for you've writ not one since you turned politician, but tracts in service of democracy and conscience and left dactyls and iambics for a kinder time.

Oh, Jesus, I see it now, the spire of Burford church, rising beyond yonder hill, like a beacon of safety, a finger pointing up toward God. Why does it promise that they will give me safety there who have traveled so far, to rest a little while? Johnny, you weaken too easily into need. You know that church spires rise as high as the church's fines for sinning or as the brag of men for their pious fortune. I have already read from the lack of tilled fields along the river and the hills beyond that the townsmen must be rich and fat, so there is no surprise that they have divided all the land among their sheep. How could it be else? I remember now where I have heard of this place! We are moving through the new granted land of the great saint William Lenthall, the Speaker of the House, Saint Master of the Rolls, Saint Lawyer, Saint Land Grabber, even Saint Chancellor of the Lancaster; why, the fervent prayers he spits into his hands make land deeds stick to his fingers more than any man in Parliament. He's sat at

my father's table more than once and prayed the joint
cold and then talked his rich new talk of my this and
my that. We are indeed marching straight into the
sheep's mouth.

I can still see the officers up at the head of the
column, riding behind the colors, Denne and Thompson.
Francis rides there too as Cromwell's envoy. I have
learned to fear his irony. It makes me ashamed of
myself. Is he your envoy, Cromwell, or your spy?
This is a thought so foul to me I sicken at it. I know
he does not come out for us but tries to treat honestly
between us and the general because he waits for the
time to ripen what we have planted and watered. I wish
he would ride from the head of the column and talk
with me. I can see far away his head high and his
helmet in the light from the west. They must have
reached the first houses. The men behind him are all
donning their pots and unfurling the colors. How the
breeze whips them aloft in this new sun.

Francis' helmet has disappeared around the river
road. Their hymn floats back as light as the air that
carries it, the old one hundredth. . . .

"Make a joyful noise unto the Lord, all ye lands,
serve the Lord with gladness. . . ."

Now the spire is higher as we ride the wide curve,
so still and safe even the sky seems to circle around it.
There a heron rises from the hill meadow and flies
toward it, and a white flutter of little birds follows it.
Oh, let me not fall into this illusion of safety. How
God-inspired it looks when even the birds fly toward
it. How easy it is for a tired man to read signs as if
the child in his eyes does not tire as he does. There
must be woods beyond the town that they fly toward
to their nests.

The sun streams down now like a benediction on
our cold shoulders. Seven swans run along the water
and spread their great white wings and rise from the
river. The heavy strong leathern creak and thrust as
they climb the air—I can hear the strength of them.
The seven Angels of the Revelation must sound like

that. I cannot keep the God voice out, for even the seven angels fly toward the spire, so great a sign over the soldiers that they stop singing to watch them and then begin again softly, as befits this soft time of evening. They ride like boys now, with that certainty and tenderness that long for home and see its promise everywhere as if every ride at sundown were toward it. The psalm ripples among them. They follow the swans and the white birds blindly, but I am twenty today and beyond all that, although I wish to God I were not.

I should ride down along the soldiers and cry out to them, "There is no reward. If you do this, that does not follow. But do this anyhow." Why, Robbie, they could be your own words; must you ever goad me so?

The still turning air is pink now, the rose of human flesh and not of roses. I think of the rosy skin of young girls.

I think of one girl and I wish to God I did not. They told me that when she came out of the bull yard to let the soldiers through the gate, all grace and daring with her mother screaming from the door, they were so panicked, clogged there in the road between the high hedges before the gate and followed by the mercenaries of the king, they overran her, and that flesh was not rose, the rose of this sky. After the soldiers had passed and we followed slowly, having fought behind them, it was like a slaughtered hog in the road; a horse's hoof had gone through the bone of her jaw and made her eye spurt from her head. Her mother sat beside her in the road, still fondling her child in what lay there, as we see God in earth scraps, sun scraps, hope there, hope again, in the neutrality of the earth we tread. She told what had happened over and over to who would listen, thinking we lingered to hear and comfort her, not seeing that we paused at the gate because we were no longer followed, and our enemy was dead.

Oh, my loving Jesus, that spire looks so safe, my knees ache to kneel before it and receive its blessing.

I ride between these stone walls as if they led me there
—oh, that it were true, the safety and cave of it.

The column is moving faster, flowing now, filling
the gray town street with horses. You would not have
thought twelve hundred breathing, sighing horses could
be so quiet. Not even a dog barks. There is only the
hollow clatter of horseshoes on the cobbles. These
stone houses are shut to us, and waiting. We turn into
the village green now, and no one sings. We are moving,
after all the bravado of our entry, ashamed before this
pent-up stillness. The men speak so softly, not as men
taking a town for quarter for the night, but as if they
might disturb the men who listen behind closed doors
and the beating of wife hearts in the closed rooms
where they pray to be protected from the phantoms
their minds make of us, not the tired men we are, only
wanting shelter now, not them, not their bird pulse or
their fear.

Ah, well, a soldier is a soldier to them. They have
been quartered upon and robbed and ate out of house
and home for many a righteous cause.

Beyond the green, the road dips down to the river
again. The men ahead are riding up the bridge back
and now, across it, turn into the water meadows beyond.

Now at last I know how tired I am. Oh, Christ, do
lack of food and the cold of this soaked jerkin and
the nervous clank of armor and the loose bits of horses
that set my teeth on edge and too long, too many miles,
too many hours, too much weight of loss break a man?
Does it then break faith and hope and decision of the
mind as eggs break, as a horse lies down and dies beside the road, and nothing matter until there is sleep?
Faith in Christ Himself needs food and shelter. My
mind cannot bite this decision but go along with it,
running like this soft river purling in the direction of
the spire, and I, faint, follow, cannot help that, want
to go home. No sound comes from the church it rises
from, though it is the time for evening prayers. There
is instead the whinny and sigh of the animals in this

stunned village under the rose sky. How sweet to think of tethering to this spire—rest the night against the wall of her.

Nell, my old sweetheart, your head is down, and you've begun to limp. 'Tis you decides at last for me, no woods tonight. I'll soak your hocks in the mud along the river and give you good shelter, and not the damp of the night meadow.

Thankful has rode up and dismounted by Francis. Denne is lifting both his palms, for they will confer with God before they decide what they will do. Come, raggle-taggle Saint, care for your horse before your soul. She must carry both you and your soul to Bristol tomorrow. Does God persuade the heart or the heart God?

Aie, Nell, your hocks look sore. Stand here in this welling of the stream, and let the mud heal you. Your smell of sweat and hide comforts me. Far behind me across the meadow the sound of men is like the purling of the weir and could be nature. They look as tired men do who have let themselves be convinced against the scent of danger. I do not like it, Nell, but you cannot travel with this hock.

Here comes Thankful, looking to convince me as he does when he needs himself to be convinced. Look at him there. He stops with little knots of troopers, to tell them all, and in the wake of his walking they loose their sheepskin saddles and let them fall and slap their mounts, untethered, out to grass. The horses smell the water and wander toward it. All down this still, dark stream under the willows, they slowly bend their heavy heads and drink so delicately they scarce disturb its surface.

Already some men are fishing their supper away beyond the weir.

There is the scent of evening and moss and water. Up there through the trees, beyond the other bank, the manor house sleeps and catches the light of the last sun in its high windows. It still has the saint's niche above the door as old religious houses do. Are they all

so alike then, these priories with walls so old they are
sunk into the ground as if they grew there, not built
by men, but with the new fine windows as high as the
rooms within, the mark and pride of new owners like
my father and Speaker Lenthall? There on the bank
are ancient walls, covered so quickly with ivy as if the
earth were ashamed as Eve of what men had done,
small foundations of what were once monk's cells or
cottages that were in the way of Lenthall's staring. Now
he can see across this land, this little river, and dream
of some empty purity of his own, some grace represented in the fall of the leaves and the grazing of the
does and little fawns I see under the water oaks. They
are sweeter than the women who shriek at him outside
the House of Commons or the men who have fists.
Here is only space for animals, space for sweet water,
this new Eden where men play Angel Michael and all
are excluded Adams for the sin of being born at the
wrong time in the wrong place.

Why, with those neglected potential hands we could
lay great keels and grow food and feed each other with
our fingers, and live together—but no. Here is a place
that deceives us with its peace, where the red deer and
the peacocks are loved more than the men, and the
love of cattle passeth the love of women, and for these
lovely fields, to walk alone over them, booted and
demanding, the few, always the few, only the few. The
whys of it are more than the mind can suffer, this indifference to the fall of man, this passion for the raising
of a tree in his place.

Thankful has hunkered down beside me and says
nothing. We are too tired to speak. We let the water
calm us and the coming night, but we must go soon
if we are to find lodging. Already the troopers are
streaming over the bridge into the town again.

"Major White has promised . . ." he murmurs to the
water and to himself, letting me hear.

I know what Francis promises, that they will treat
with us as they told him, for he promises it to himself
as well. Francis, you speak of future well but not of

the present, here, now, the decision of this moment and in Burford, which is the only true decision to be made, the solid ground between past dreams and future promises.

"Come, Thankful, we'll find some shelter. I must needs put Nell in a stable this night." Our boots sink in the mud, and Nell, behind us, sinks in the muddy grass.

"Will we sleep within?" Thankful sounds as excited as the boy he is so often.

"Aie, within, though I would sleep in the woods." Already I can see, on yonder hill, men tenting down under the trees.

"I do not condone free quarter," Thankful announces, as he does every time we stop. He throws his leg up over the gate top and slides across it.

"Now is the time to use the money. What about Elijah?"

"He is not even sweating after this hard day's ride. He's out to grass." Ever since he captured his fine horse from a king's officer, he has glowed so when he speaks of the big bay gelding that he sits proud as a child astraddle of his father's mount.

WHEN soldiers come, the town opens like a whore, services rendered but the heart's door shut. Where there was silence, now, ahead of us, the taverns roar, already full of men. The clanging laughter of a drab cuts air, then stops, as if she had seen Thankful's solemn, disapproving little face. They will provide all, preacher or pander, for this is a market town, until the night comes and the money's spent, the shutters pulled down in our faces, the fires lit, the profits counted, and they forget us and sleep. They were not praying when we rode in an hour ago, but preparing of their goods. It is too easy to misread the blank doors, the blank streets, the blank faces of a strange town. On such blankness we write our own longings and fears.

Already the quartermaster's men are chalking of the doors. Up ahead, one after another, the pitch-pine flambeaus are being lit to draw the men with money to the inns. If they but knew how little money we had, they'd put them out again and damn and sink us here. We were given two weeks' pay to quiet us, who were owed for a year's service. Even that two weeks' sop came too late and too little to stop the men's mouths.

There is the sign of the horseshoe. Where there is a blacksmith, there will be a good stable. Nell has stopped limping, but her head is still hanging. No matter, my sweetheart, I'll bed you soon. Damn, across the green Francis is waving from an inn door. If we go, we will talk and talk, and she will have to stand in this new evening cold.

"Thankful, go and see."

He weaves across the green, aclog with soldiers searching for lodging. This entry is only wide enough for one horse to pass. It must be older than the others, built into the innyards wide enough for a carriage or cart. The troopers have not found it yet. There will be fewer horses here. I can watch her, hidden here beyond this passage like the entry to a cave. Who would notice us? Here is a place to be gentle and quiet within.

"Major White says to rest here, so he can find us if he needs us to confer." I did not know Thankful was beside me again until he touched my arm. How shy his touch is.

Thankful's new office has given him a new language —confer, condone. He is important with it. We have conferred enough and, God my witness, condoned enough and writ enough circumspect letters to the general.

How loud Nell's shoes clatter in this little passage. This stableyard is so still and stretches so empty through the new dark you would not dream the town had swelled by twelve hundred men. The forge is empty for the night, but its firelight breathes on the walls. It casts a pretty glow across the cobbles and lights the well house in the center. The stalls beyond are empty, undiscovered, good.

Or it would be still here but for the little flurry at the dark corner of the yard. The candlelight from her window touches a fat old wife and one of the quartermaster's men. She will not let his arm go. He is embarrassed and dares not cast her off. We sit down on the stoop by the well and watch and wait. There will be some sport here.

"Leave off achalking of my door," she rails at him.

"You'll be paid." He is trying to pick her off him.

"In money?" She has let go enough at the thought for him to shake her loose.

"In scrip," he admits, who is one of the Saints and cannot lie to her for fear of hellfire.

"God damn your scrip and scrippage." She leeches onto his arm again. "I've done been chalked and scripped by king and Parliament and democratical men. 'Tis naught but the old free quarter writ a new way." With each political persuasion she gives his coat a tweak. "They're all the same, eat me out of house and home, steal my plate, clobber up my floors, and me a poor old widow."

She must have railed her man to death. She has a glass window, and beyond it, in the candlelight, her pewter and her blue Holland plates shine. God help me, I've been a soldier for four years now and seen much, yet quick tears blot my eyes, even through my laughter, at the sight of Holland plates.

The quartermaster's man hears us laughing and turns. It is MacKarkle, who could fell her with the shaking of his arm, caught so.

"Aie, Johnny, 'tis a foul task. This lady is unmannerly with me."

"Unmannerly you say." She fetches him a clout. "Look at them, free quarterers," she spits at us.

This stings Thankful to his feet.

"We are not that, mother," he calls.

Now she does drop MacKarkle's arm, and he runs through the passage before she can clout him again.

"Aie," I tell her, for Thankful is not good at huckling. "Four shillings for both and the stabling of my horse."

"Six." She waddles toward us across the cobbles.

"Five," which is what I intended all the time to pay.

"Done," she says, smiling now.

"And supper." I stop her.

She thinks and then says, "Aie."

The bargain's made, the stable is clean and dry, and in the darkness, rubbing Nell down as she feeds, there is the smell of fresh hay here, and goodly, clean fodder. I pray we have fallen into a night's safety.

Thankful is fooled by the hope of food which he takes for sanctity. I see him, smiling his sweet smile at her, there within her kitchen. He sees her mother fat and comforting. He sees her as he wants to see her, I as I fear she is. She welcomes us because we can pay and she must placate us. Come, Johnny, leave off your mumbling and enter your Palm Sunday of acceptance through her little door. We do not live Christ's life. He lived ours, our every day, when one gesture is our Palm Sunday and another our crucifixion, and they can be an hour apart and form us, etch us, kill and resurrect us day after day.

She has given us only scumming from the pot and bread and whey and cried poor like a prayer as we ate. No matter. It is good here among the plates, the shining trestle table, the heavy scent of beeswax candles, and if she would but shut her mouth, we could fall into such dear illusion of her mothering. Thankful has indeed fell adreaming and will fall asleep with his head on the table in the warmth and dry and safety of it all.

The fatigue of this makes me see too well tonight, see through air and shadows, stumble up this ladder through dreams that will not wait for sleep. I am almost become what I see, the old woman ahead, lugging her huge, bag body up the ladder. Sisyphus-like, she drags her weight slowly, and her candlelight dances up the stone wall, not plastered yet for show as the room we are passing, her sleep room, sometime whelp room, where her spinning wheel and distaff glow in the firelight. But she is taking us beyond, into the loft. The dim tallow candle she carries spurts smoke and tiny anger. Will the old woman never move up the ladder?

SHE did not even leave the candle stump for us, for fear we'd fire the place. We can see only by the light that comes from the fire below through the trapdoor she has fastened open lest we get into some mischief she cannot hear. I can hear her below, grumping and sighing and shifting her weight. Ah, Thankful, we've found a fine lodging in this pigeon loft. There is enough white dove dung here to breed from the boards, five shillings' worth of scummings and pigeon loft, dung and darkness to stretch in at last under the mother beam of the roof. It is so thick and black it must have grown with Druids' blood in ancient times.

The beldam has took our shoes and left them at the house door so we will not track mud and stored us here as she stores her feed that will become beast or doves, neck wrung, throat cut by her, then eat. She saves her dung to feed the earth, then clover grows, and so thence into the loft again like the old bawd's story. But here in time, this Monday evening, it is fresh clover that we lie upon.

You, Thankful, at your prayers? Canst pray alike for me? The spirit does not move me. Would that sweet God you see there under your closed lids that makes your face shine like a child's when you speak with Him know one such as I?

I can see a fragment of the full moon, rising beyond the pigeon holes. Thankful, dost know how far away the moon is? As far as London.

Now he is asleep, all loose. The moon has found his face. I wish he had not left me so soon for sleep. My body will not plunge down. My mind's a millrace. The dung-white floor is my slow clock. The moon shines through the pigeon holes and makes longer and then longer bars across the floor.

When we lay down here, it had not even fingered through the holes, my windows. Why not sleep as he can? Look at the bawdy boy. He smiles and touches his hand to his leather breeks and in this dark loft, all smell of our horse sweat, bird dung, clover, tang of old woodsmoke from below, scents of night riding, of secrets of men, turns in his dream as in his bed at home in rhythm to the breath of some sweet girl who smells of buttermilk and apples.

Why do I elect myself the watchman of the night and cannot cry all's well? I still do wish we had slept in the woods. We are too far from water, and the Delilah below has took our shoes instead of cut our hair so we are impotent. My Christ, I could not be afeared to go to sleep. Damn, this is womanly. A soldier slings himself down, forgets, and sleeps when he can, all sleep to him the last before his death. He carries this knowledge in his bowels, not skittering in his head.

There, the moonlight has passed Thankful's face. He turns, flings out his hand to it as if he were to hold it. How alive it is, the hand of my younger brother in God. Its movement stirs the hidden doves. They gossip

quietly there, bubble and purl as softly as if I were
forgiven and blessed by them. I wish we had thought to
bring water.

I've had nights like this before, when, too tired to
sleep, a wakefulness lingers at the edge of sleep, dips
into timeless dreaming, and then draws back. The hours
stretch like the moonlit bars across the floor. Such
nights take the spirit from my muscles and ready me
for haunting.

I know you, my first kill at Naseby, I know you are
coming to bring this nightmare down; form yourself,
damn you, and watch me as I watch Thankful there,
left out of life as I am left out of sleep, expecting something, needing something more than I can ever give.
You do not accuse. You wait, with that enormity of
your surprise in your dead face.

Why? Why do you come to me in the dark? Thankful has killed, aie, sweet Thankful there, like an avenging saint, he is in the field, and Robin too, and Jarcey,
and old Josiah, Nathan, Zachery, they have killed in
full attack, sure of their strokes, killed in Christ's name,
forgot, and gone on. They sleep sound. Why not I?

What do you want to hear—my confession, as if
you were a priest from the old times? Would you shrive
me then? Well, I was as bawdy gaudy a boy as you,
profligate as you, flinging my days behind me, rich
with countless days. My pocket book was new leather.
I could smell the newness of it; the words in it were
new. Did you know that pages written on can die, grow
dusty, lifeless, but not so quickly as your hand that
clutched my doublet did? I tried to pry you loose. I
was afeared, and so were you. I saw it in your eyes.
What did you see in mine that froze you so—ten talents, the arrogance of new light, or simply fear as
yours? I thought 'til then a prick could kill, but it takes
a long time, forever, to slice a human throat.

The embrace you fall from still exists still; we are
in it, you and me. You in me can stop my mouth and
set my boat toward icy water just when I touch the
shore of a woman, or friend, or country evening. I

find, with you, the icy water more my home than all the hearths behind me.

I could not let you go. You would have killed me instead and left me forgot as I cannot you, old bird whose neck will never wrench. How long it took you, all my life it will take you. Not the lullaby of doves or Thankful's sweet breath or sleep can interrupt your ever, ever dying.

She throws a log on the fire below. The light flings hard against the roof beams, then dims to softness. Her bones and chair creak together. She sits waiting for something to happen, for us to steal her geese or the virginity she's grown into again, life over, fire dimmed.

She's listening at the foot of the ladder for our breathing. Go to sleep, beldam. You demand to be remembered all the night long. Your old life galls me when I am with the young dead.

I envy your folly most, boy, you my judicious act, for you would be alive now and not I had you been more judicious. I saved my life on you and must live now at the other side of wisdom. The mark of Cain is not upon the forehead as some think who do not know it, but reflected in the eye. We who have it know each other and are quieter than the others. We bear the understanding that once we did that act. Obedience to the convenient moment yoked us once, and we know forever which way we did step then under the goad of decision. On nights like this, late nights, when the moon is full and high and white and sleep is beyond us in the shadows, we who are marked so can go back to this side of the moment, but we can never cross it. For we did this instead of that. It is Creon who writes about Antigone at night. He has the old crone of convenience in his loins, and she has not.

Now I am condemned to understand even the old woman down there below, whose whole life is lived in the raised arm of Cain and between Peter's cockcrows. She knows no other moments; all's chore of surviving with her. She has never glimpsed, whiffed, caught a hint of time lost, profligate, flung, stolen, shrugged time.

Why has she put another log on her fire so soon? She is part of the waking night. The sparks fly up and light the opened trap. She champs and sucks her gums and settles down amid her fartings.

Aie, brother, too, to me, as Thankful there, I'll say it—for you had in your face what I thought to have drove out of mine by a new motley of clothings, habits, words, all to disguise the nakedness of nights such as these. Leather and lace, crucifix and kiss curl, both can cover, lie and strut. . . .

I have fought my way here from such as you, from the solemn league and covenant my father keeps and will not share, toward this new way I pick to assuage myself. I know that if we honor each other even in death, this democracy of men will work, but courtship will kill it. My father did not honor Lazarus when he sent him off to war. He courted him, and all hope ceases at that act. Even when the old man in the tavern told me Lazarus was dead, such news was blotted out then by what I heard of Nellie and my son. Must he forever take a humble place, even in his dying? Why, he had walked into the new lake one night and drowned himself, perhaps doing a thing as simple as looking for his tame deer or his front door. Lazarus had come forth when he was needed. Now he's flooded over, and the deer move lightly in the deer park.

It is the difference between seduction and love, between using and honoring him, but he had no ears to hear, no voice to speak. I must lend mine, that is all. Will it wipe out my laughter? There is no shame in facing this small thing, this little careless wound, for it has pitched me here and made me see. Ones like Lazarus and Charity will sit long in rooms like this and cry tears down, dumb tears louder than any howling and crocodile weeping for policy, and they will change the world. But those of us who hear them must be quiet to listen, for they sound as faint as the chirling of these doves, the rustling of the mice in the straw, the creak of the wainscot in the fire warmth that makes us prick our ears and shrug and say it is nothing.

What will rouse them? What will make them stay at pitch point? I have seen them plundered and stripped, moved as pawns, damned and sunk, violently used, their innocence raped, their spirits dashed and broken, all in the name of one right or another high in the air above them, and yet they do not speak! They are broken to their crying as a colt is broken. They call to someone else's pure stone God, letting their hope drift upward. Oh, Jesus' blood, if I could save them from their hope!

Why am I lying here awake with the moon in my face, apicking at the straw wisps off the floor as a dying man picks at the sheets as if they would hold him back on earth from dying, clutching of the straw of Lazarus' forgiving, and the boy's?

How the past goads us! We move toward tomorrow, but the past informs us. These civil acts we do, these oaths we take, are but recognitions of something that's already happened, the whip already cracked, the door slammed, the hurt healed to livid scar. Some lash again in turn, some turn their other cheek, and some do turn the wrist. A string of such moments brought me here, and each I termed conversion when 'twas more the flickering of a thing already there and deeper, deep as earth pulse, the hopeless necessity to see to light my way.

When I am gone from here and peace has come to England, I will live on a farm, not such a farm as takes the bread from others and lords over them, but a farm as Virgil had when he rested from the wars and city streets and duty, and for my flying mind, the will-o'-the-wisp of me, I will eat the hearts of large patient beasts and avoid conversion. I will have a wife whose shoulder I can touch as I pass and say nothing, and me and my friends will drink small beer and sugar under the fruit trees and speak as we like in fear of no expedient men or no knock at the door in the name of the king or general or Christ or other. The tears sit in my eyes. I long for future, past-sick over that which has not even happened. No. If we fail now, I will go to Virginia away from this. For England will be over, sun set and great minds diminished to fawning by their fear. She will have been a terrible mistress, the most unfaithful to her word of all, but her sweet tongue we could take with us to another place. . . .

And yet, need not . . . what is it? The moon is higher, whiter in the sky. The fire's down almost to darkness, and the chimney's growing cold, and she, snoring down there, has walked into her own spacious dreams, where she washes our severed heads like sheep's heads at the well, wasting nothing that comes her way.

The moon rays through the pigeon holes stretch like prison bars; I must crawl to the wall and look through one and not feel so confined. I can see the priory roof far beyond the forge and fields and tree shadows, all paled and shadowed with moonlight. Not a dog turns in its bed, it's all so quiet.

There's the clock now. One two Christ sees you, three four Gospels more. How can I stop my wits baying and greeting like this? Eleven. Twelve o'clock. Three hours I've lingered here, acourting sleep that flirts with me. But I must have slept and not knowed it, for I still am caught in dreams. I hear the sounds of battle and horses like waterfalls coming nearer and nearer; riding nearer, they fill the night streets. They have no faces. I cannot see their faces to strike at them. Run. Run. There's crack of burning branch.

N O, 'tis the clock strikes twelve, oh, Christ, 'tis shooting and the clock together. I must have slept; I am tangled in it and must push through to what those sounds are.

Out west, the cocks are crowing; the cocks in the east answer. Now a donkey brays; now one nearer whinnies; now Nell is whickering in answer. Jesus, wake me. Thankful moves like a dark ghost and kneels against the wall to hear and motions me to watch at the back over the stableyard. Damn all, I knew we should have slept in the woods. We are surrounded.

They flow now, the horsemen from the west through Sheep Street from the east down the Oxford road, from the south across the river to dam us up here, a shoal of men and horses. Thankful picks and scrabbles at the thatch to make a spyhole. He wastes no time on surprise.

Listen to the sound of men running in the priory lane. The priory grounds are black with horses under the moon. "Can you see aught, Thankful?"

"Reynolds' colors and Okey's. They ride a career to charge the street."

"They sound so tall, the horses."

"The noise is greater when it slaps the stone of the houses." Thankful's voice is so small there in the dark. "We can take to the roofs when it dies down, for there's no safety here. They will soon start beating up our quarters."

I can almost hear the old woman beat her heart

against her ribs down there for fear. Thankful slips like a shadow and closes the trapdoor and piles straw upon it. Time's gone awry. We've been betrayed while the clock is still striking. Christ, thou knowest it takes little time. No. It is the bell in the spire that someone rings too late to warn us all. How have they kept that bell from being melted? Paid well into the right pockets.

There's pistols firing very thick. From the smell it's close, in the stableyard. There comes Will Pentecost up the lane, running without his breeks, an ugly sight indeed, the skinny thee-thou Pentecostal quaker! Oh, run, Will, hide; he's seen you. I must have whispered. Thankful whispers, "Who?"

"Will Pentecost arunning with a dragoon from the general's regiment hard after him. He's caught Will and strips him of the shirt his wife made him and puts pistol to his head to drive him naked into the street." The dragoon's boots are loud in the passage below us, but there's no sound of Will's bare feet. Where is the old woman? God stop her mouth from calling out. " 'Ware market towns," an old man told me, "they'll buy and sell all. 'Tis how God made them."

The firing's all around us now. These are our fellow soldiers who, two weeks gone, followed Robbie's body and wore the sea-green ribbon. No wonder we see hell as fire and brimstone and the stink of sulphur and the thirst of salt unslaked, for it is the smell and taste of murdering men.

"Thankful, what can you see on the street side?"

"The flash of guns. Northamptonshire colors. They mean to break our necks here before we can speak our minds, Johnny."

"Our minds are done spoken, over and over, since these wars began."

"There is Major White running in his night slippers, trying to catch first one horse and then another as if he alone could stem this tide." Aie, Francis, it is too late now to stop the troops once paid for by my father. Those pots, that armor comes from Henlow's yield,

and Lazarus wore it once. My father sends a heavy rod
of iron to change and chasten his boy's stammering
tongue, but he is too late to do aught but kill me.

"They drive so furiously. Some of the foot are set
to pulling men out of the houses to strip and pillage
them and fall apicking of their pockets; they're scunning of their own fellows. Why, Cromwell must have
drove after us all our way, who said he would not
follow hard upon our heels." Thankful sounds awe-
struck. Strange things surprise him still.

Who then betrayed us? Who appealed to our ex-
haustion and told us it was safe? Here is no accident,
and we know it, but a guileful, subtle meeting. Was it
Denne? How I mistrust the passion and persuasion
that rape our silence with easy God words. All the
time he persuaded us here, did he know them to be
following with force upon us?

Who's running there? A country man and long since
a soldier or a poacher by the way he uses the shadows
of the yard. He seems to take the shadows with him
a little, then part from one and melt into the next.
Now he is part of the well house, now the wall. He is
nearly to the orchard. It is Gideon MacKarkle! Don't
move. Don't move. Yonder's a horseman stepping up
the lane from the priory, such a silent hunt in the
midst of so much noise and riot. He must hear the
horseman. Now he flushes out of the shadow of the
forge, toward the apple trees. The moonlight has betrayed him. Even the shot sounds quiet, under the bawl
and crack of all. He's down to hide; no, hit. He does
not rise. The other dismounts and bends over him to
strip him, picking and picking like a black bird of prey,
and mounts horse again. Now he clatters through the
passage under us. MacKarkle lies there under the moon.

Was it you, Francis, who played the decoy duck to
draw that half-naked body to lie in yonder orchard?
God knows I have unweaved and unraveled you since
I sensed the change in you after you spoke so for us
at Putney two years gone, and yet I find no fault in
you except you did not speak for us again. Is that all?

That you spoke not? Come, Francis, I pray you, tell
me who you are. Under your much vaunted timing did
you too, as so many, prefer losing to the danger of
winning? Had you had enough of courage? Was it no
longer in the mind's fashion?

Do we embarrass you who use the democratical
words you spoke so in the fashion at Putney? Do we
speak so in the wrong time and at the wrong season,
as a ragtag whore still drags her dirty summer flounces
in the velvet time of winter because she has no other?
You spoke then at Putney as one inspired, when there
was a threat to disband us, and we purged Parliament
and took the king. I saw you cast out of the great council for your brave speaking, away in democratical
notions beyond the grandees. The sharp, intelligent
edge of you, your thinness, your precision, why, all
were at our service then. You were an officer and lost
no honor by how you threw the dice at Putney. Was
it but gambling on future and career that made you
speak so that we trusted you and laid up trust in us
then for Cromwell to spend on this work tonight? No.
No gamble—not knowing it. I credit your emptiness
with guile you do not have.

God damn you, Francis, you weaned the poet and
fed the politician in me and never did deceive me, yet
I die of you. I saw you once playing at ball with your
three daughters in St. James's Park. You had left your
coat and hat on the grass and looked like a boy flying
among them as blond as they. One most like you stood
apart and judged the game with your fine cool gray
eyes and yet looked sad to be apart from all the
running, though when you tried to throw the ball to
her, she shook her head and smiled, and you smiled
with her, understanding all. You have smiled so with
me, too, when I have said something of wit to your
liking. Do you agree with all and smile with all?
Francis, get out, you have not earned this loft with us.

"Johnny, come and look. 'Tis not to be thought,
what I see," Thankful still whispers, though 'tis not
needed here under the volleys, the storm and shot in

heaven that lights the High Street and fouls the night. He pulls me down beside him, and huddled together underneath the eaves, we can watch through the thatch the saddest triumph an army ever had, the triumph of betrayal of its brothers. They move so slowly, clotted in the wide green, color after color, now the old country regiments of the earlier war, now the mercenaries of the new state. Oh, Oliver, how have you triumphed here? Why, it is even over your own dreams. From every door along High Street, the foot soldiers are routing out unwanted men, half-naked in their shirts, all timid there, all shrunken as the bravest shrink who are left with vulnerable faces among faceless men.

"In all my time of serving I never saw soldiers such as these—not in the New Model." Perkins speaks now and disdains to whisper. Does he not remember how, with saintly zeal, they slashed the faces of the Irish whores at Naseby? What you have done, you will do.

"Oh, Thankful, I must tell you. We are like birds so joyful in their twittering that they think they fill the world with sound, but when the beasts bawl, they cannot be heard."

"No. 'Tis a fact that they take up and pass sound and that the message of the owl in Putney can reach Land's End as fast as sound."

"Were you thinking then of Putney, too?"

"Aie, of all of it, all of those bright mornings."

What bobtails we are now, crouched in the eaves here who were so brave at sundown and carried all our spirit west. There is anger still in the bodies of the men down there. One struggles and is silenced by the thump of a gun butt on his chest, so loud we can hear it. Men who are shivering with cold are not so brave a sight. Now come the colors of our own colonel, and he, riding there in his stubborn triumph, looks neither left nor right at these men who have made his name immortal by voting against his dumb demand to fight in Ireland, where we have no quarrel, and leave all here unchanged. Why does he not look at us? Why, but for us he would die as nameless as a discarded shoe.

" 'And the brother shall deliver up the brother to death,' Matthew Ten twenty-one. Why, 'tis the Scripture fulfilled before our very eyes," Thankful says, awed.

Now Cromwell rides below. No man calls "Oliver!" and "Oliver!" and no man loves him now. He's chosen other and rides ruling the ground his horse treads with iron horseshoes. Oh, Oliver, how have a little time and success changed the honest shape of you? You chased us here like truant children to break our heads for disobedience, you who said at Putney, and many times, for you have the habit of repeating words and thoughts so as not to waste them, "It is an act of duty to break an unrighteous engagement; he that keeps it does a double sin."

I have spoke aloud, for Thankful answers, "I stand upon the bottom of my conscience in this matter." We laugh, but only for relief, for it was an old game we played at Putney, to mock your repetitions, because we loved you.

Look up, Oliver, that is the army shivering there who put you where you are. Your head is down; you look defeated, not a conqueror, as you ride between them, standing so cold and diminished.

Do you charge us blackmail for your sadness? Do you stop our mouths with bullets so we will not say what you know to be true, that you used us politic, and politic you agreed with us, and politic you climbed us, Oliver. When you fast now, men hide from what you call the will of God, and when you pray, property lodges safer in the hands of those that use you, and when you weep, for tears are your hardest weapon, men die of them. No two ways about it, eh, Oliver, you have buffed off the democratical mud you had to wallow in to get to that street below and play the Caesar in dirty linen. Why, you have brought order to England, and the law is safe with you, and all is as before, Priest is Presbyter or rich Sectary, and I will die of this quarrel between my father and Sir Valentine over the hanging tree in Henlow Wood. Was it never more than that?

Why does Thankful sob so when he sees the old man? There is that in me that knows all this within, but he can be betrayed as I cannot but for a little while. But in that little while my heart breaks, not from surprise as he, but that it is ever so and does not change.

"Thankful, leave off your sniveling. We are betrayed enough from without."

"Oh, Johnny, we were never all as I thought. Our zeal had only lit the faces of these neutral men. I thought it was their own shining."

"It was, for a little while it was." I cannot say other, remembering that first day at Marston fields.

We can do nothing but watch them strip and march our own, who were free men, down the High Street, goading them, riding them forward, clearing the rabble from the street for Cromwell. The shooting is nearly over, a pattering in the distance, and the green is massy with slow-moving men and horses. Even the shouting is weak under the moon now. A few soldiers are left, kicking open the doors along the street to search and seize and rout us from our quarters. But no one comes here, no, not from the stableyard either. The wood creaks like more shots when I tiptoe across the floor. The stableyard is empty. MacKarkle is gone. He must have crawled or been took away.

The clock strikes one. In one hour is all our cause ceased, and, Thankful, you and I are dead, for we are the Agitators, and he will make example of us. He will hold all against us; our stumblings and our bravado, our hopes, our fumblings, and our nonsense will make up our indictment and our winding sheet.

"Johnny, come here." Thankful's voice is calm as if it were all one, and in the dark I see him struggling with the bales. "Now we can get out." Why did I not think of this? My dumb habit of melancholy shames me.

We've cleared the trapdoor with so little sound we

might be mice or pigeons feeding on the straw and grain. How quiet it is. Lift softly. "Here, let me," he whispers. "It must be stuck. Lift with me."

"We have paid with our lives for shelter this night, Thankful. She's latched it from below."

"Why, Johnny, what could she have against us?" he says softly, and he is gone back into the corner of the loft.

There is nothing to say. When betrayal comes, it is such a dumb thing, a getting quit of men. She treats us as she treats all in the way of her tyrant habits. Why should this be the straw that breaks us—an old woman latching a door? To her who huddles there below us and prays protection to the small God of her own making, we are enemies, and the death of a man for her liberty is broken crockery and blood upon her floor. She sees us all alike, and God a self of her own sky-shine.

I hear the drums in the distance fading toward the church, and over in the priory there are lights. The sobs of Thankful are stifled in the dark there because he does not want me to know he is crying again. It is not from fear with him. I know him too well—there is one thing only that drives him, like a child, to make such sounds of darkness and loss. 'Tis when he sees betrayal of the heart. An hour of war among three thousand men, the shutting of the loft, would strike him the same, as a cold thing.

His voice comes now calm as a stone. "But it is the way it is done, Johnny." He echoes something of his own.

AS if there had been aught happen, the clock strikes the half hour. The birds have shuttered themselves again beneath their wings and sleep, though our two worlds are changed and will be blotted out. Now I can see the empty orchard, and the priory and the steep village roofs under the high moon, and the slow shift and slide of the river. She will open the trap. I see how we can go. Through the orchard over the priory wall, follow it to the willow, the hawthorn bank, the river. The hawthorn's a ghost this night. Nell, I will have to leave you, for Thankful's horse is stolen, and you cannot carry both.

There's the sounds of drums still, or do I hear it faint within me?

How dumb to wait here until she opens the trap. Here am I crouched, and Thankful waiting on the other side, adrift on his own islands, his rivers, his lands which are not my lands.

The fight is over. The lights are blown out. Only there in the great hall of the priory does a light burn still where Cromwell plans on and gives orders. I wish I could stop the dim sound of the drums within me. Can I see from here a shadow pass the window? Only the window of my own mind; it is too far away. I can see him sitting there, as I have seen my father, and see him stare at the wall, and when he dips his head with decision, I see the quill scratch change and power over the lives of the bashful and silent, and he recasts, rejects the lives of men he does not know or care for.

Cromwell, you have no right to invade my last night.

Or will you wait and have us killed a Wednesday or a
Thursday for politic reasons? How many tears will it
take you, how many prayers, before you have put a
balm of Gilead on a decision you have already made?

Now you get up and cross into the night. I hear your
son was married Thursday last. Was the bride with
child, and were there many acres? Will you rest after
this work at Oxford or at Bath? They're goodly places.
You can tuck our deaths between wedding and banquet. You piss and watch the stars like any other man
and shake and tuck yourself and sign our death warrant. I think Thankful has caught my vision of you,
for he scrambles up and laughs and whispers, "Do it
this way, Johnny. If we use the floor, she'll call the
soldiers," and he digs a hole in the hay and thrusts
his prick there and pisses silently into a bale. I do it, too.
It's good, the feeling.

That release releases all. Oh, Thankful, we've caught
sorrow like a blow and cry in each other's arms. Who
would have thought that dying was a noble thing? They
write that who survive to write so. Why, 'tis to cease
to be, never to touch other forever. I cannot believe a
man of twenty should shiver and cry so. Where are the
people I would have loved? There's nothing else; all
else is false, a shame and waste, a shoring up of walls
against nothing. Why, I went to a fool's war and killed
men, and it has come to this. I wonder if they are all
so, all only paths to death's blind kingdom.

'Tis three now of the clock, and nothing moves.
Thankful sleeps curled there by the trap and will spring
out of sleep to action. The doves nestle and sigh and
moan a little. I fear—no, not fear—but something of
it, to be this while alone. I want to creep down beside
Thankful there for comfort and hide with him in sleep
as the Disciples did when Jesus prayed that night, but
I cannot do it. To move forward, even now across this
floor, is to lose my life. If I avoid this night, this three
of the clock, expecting the footfall on the ladder, parting the fear from the warning, making towers of their
neutralities, I will have lost the life I must measure

out now in these moments and the last sighing of the doves. There is not much time. Ah, the urgency of it. When the trap opens, it will not open the way I do expect it to. All hope and all control by hope are false, a false thing. How the real astonishes which is not weighted and blind with expectation.

Whatever I am to know to help me die—and 'tis the reason for all of it, the wonder and the fear—must be seen now, run to ground here in this prison loft, for the wall I stare at is the wall I die against, and you, too, Oliver, and you, old woman, and you, arrogant, innocent, pious, mincing king who lit his death with the insistence of gold candlesticks and famine. There is forever no more time. It is this, this silence pigeon-dunged that I am given to find my heaven and hell in. Compared to this perpetual taking place of the thing, the old temptations and the night horrors seem small now, and they twitter. I would have asked for angels, or at least devils, to save me from this drift and starshine, this abandonment.

I must grow senile before the morning comes, for this is all my life. What do I hear? Only the neutrality of night, as every night. There is nothing, nothing to fear, no thing to fear, no thing to bind to, run from, only an every night that follows every day. My heart howls for the security of hell, for the attention of damnation.

How still it is. How holy it surrounds me. How real the ground, the air, the sighing of the trees, the dark of moondown and the cold brightness of the new stars that take its place, the faint mist that rises from the river and clings among the willows. Soft, soft, miss nothing, Johnny; all sleep within as many million worlds of dream as there are stars above us while the water drips and the pump settles and the mice skitter, and I am here adying as best I can.

Why did I waste time on gaudy visions when this was what was real and waiting for me? It is the real that saves us from all the seductions of the others, in love or hate or politics or redemption, that will reflect their

stunned Narcissus faces and keep them safe awhile. I
do not even want to pray, that call to air for the protection of habit. I did not know that to pray was only
to listen, clear and indifferent. Was it this I came to,
only and all, in this beshitted loft?

No cry of "Take me not away in the midst of my
days." No, I sing indifference, a thing old men should
fear who die of cold and nameless pale longing, not I,
twenty years old and muscles hard. They say that loneliness grows greater when age comes. 'Tis not so. When
I was only twenty, an hour or two ago, 'twas most my
fear. Now it is the only face of God that I will see, and
I am grown within it. No one will come to me, no
matter how I bleat and crawl—Nellie, my son, father,
Thankful, all, all sleep, and the priory light is blotted
out. I seek silence and abandonment and the stars that
circle earth and night.

I had thought that one who loved Christ would see
Him and be comforted. Oh, Christ, it makes my heart
plead for thy love. Why, it is not thee we see and thy
hand's touch we feel. Thy vision is a greater thing. 'Tis
what thee saw. That's awe enough, an awesome glimpse
to try to cover over with gold or visions to hide it from
our faces, as an old saint's skull in a gold mask. That's
thy miracle, not a face imposed for comfort's sake on
the reality of stone or gold or treading neutral sky all
full of light and judgment. It is all men who die of
other men's acts, of the cold steel of the world, who
partake of thee, all shot, all betrayed, all ignored.
Ministers of grace and promises, take your Gospel
words that any man can use and take your images and
give me mine. Let me sing to this night and the doves
and Thankful's sleep of the length and depth of things.
God love thee so and I and all, that we may say amen.
Heaven's so little and hell's so mean a thing compared
to this, my newness, my onlyness and thine.

And I will die, dear God, I will rot, and I will never
touch my dear Nellie again. That never, and never is
an endless black space. My stomach sends up gorge. I
am going to take a vomit. There is two of me, one was

adrift in peace, and now the other fights from below, full of stink and vomit and fear. Oh, Jesus, I am afeared. Were thee? Did thy traitorous body begin to stink and cringe and cry up at thyself, "What have I done?"

Thankful's voice behind me is sensible to the trouble and calm. "Well, my Johnny, here is retribution enough for a fire-and-brimstone Ranter, and all for a few mistakes in the way we have been." His dear solemnity comforts me as if he touched me across the trap.

"Now what we done." He is cozy and gossips in the dark, and I hear him scrunch himself about to be more comfortable against the hay while I am trying to wipe up my shame with straw. 'Tis all domestic between us, voice and act. "We must set the saddle on the right horse, for something's amiss. I think that we did stoop to our fellow creatures when we writ the letter to the soldiers. We tried to seduce them to our way of thinking by appealing to their anger over pay more than to their free spirit. We will be shot for our politic ways, though they think 'tis for our politics."

I have never in four years heard Thankful play at wit before. He could have all the time of sunny afternoons from the way he speaks now in the dark.

"Stand up, stand up," Thankful whispers in my ear and answers my cry that went out to him. "Take your hands from my shoulders and stand alone." And then it comes again, a gust of wonder like the first night at Marston, wonder and joy of being a man.

"We'll jig now," Thankful whispers, very practical. " 'Twill keep us from growing stiff and cold, for when the old woman opens the trap, we must be ready."

Like ghosts in the strips of moonlight, first slowly and then faster and faster, we two jig and dance around the loft and sing the only tune we can remember who've sung so many psalms. "One knave, two knaves, three too old, and through her bush the wind grows cold." 'Twill draw the old woman, the creaking of the boards. We jig between her curiosity and her fear; with a one knave two knaves three too old we dance around the loft as the Ranters did to wait the Second Coming.

We've waked the birds. Ah, 'tis good to pant so; I know I will travel now. Who can hold us? We hunker down on both sides of the trap to conjure her hand to the bolt. Boom boom boom the wind blows cold come come now, come old lady, slip hand to hasp.

We can wait the rest of our lives here for her movements, hers and his at the priory. How are they alike? I think they've felt no wonder. Do they fear the abyss of it or do they envy? Locking us in won't stop that old sickness. Betrayal is a small thing, not a blow but a flick, not arm to arm in battle, but the turn of a head, the shrug of shoulders, a half-finished sentence, a quill scratch, a hasp, and Johnny is no more, and Thankful Perkins dies. Stand not in the way of the certainties of the fearful, for they will blot you out, my boy. Oh, leave me to my last night of peace, go someplace else to squat and assure yourselves, and summon up a king's dignity to play with your own privates, and mew, " 'Twas ever so. I had to do it for the good of all," or whatever song you sing for self-abyss to protect you from the wind that blows around us as we haunt you with the faces of boys who never finished life.

But when we hear a step upon the ladder, we flick into place beside the trap. She is as close as the boards, listening. We could be breathing each other's breath. No one moves; we try to will her fat hand to the latch, will and will.

Another step. She's moved down from the ladder.

"I am very near to lose my patience," Thankful whispers.

I cannot help it. Up like the vomit from my belly, the laughter comes, gusts of it, gusts, and Thankful catches it. She knocks on the trapdoor with a stick and calls out. "Be quiet. I'm trying to sleep."

To sleep. Oh, Jesus, help us, 'tis not guile that traps us, or malice. 'Tis the desert of stupidity she lives in, grumbling and maunching. She does not fathom our prison or our sorrow. She only kept the soldiers so she could court uneasy sleep. This old, dumb, neutral woman that I made villain of and Thankful mother does seek sleep only; that's her great matter, and if we're caught in it, 'tis no concern of hers. "Lady, what reason had you for the murder of this stranger?"

"I have trouble sleeping."

"Oh, dear heart," says Thankful, and digs his fist across his eyes to wipe the tears from his laughter. "What old fart's catched us here? Must we needs die of a joke?" and stopping. I think almost that he sleeps again, but he says, "Johnny, not one thing made us ready for this night in all our lives."

He has been on his road, too, through the hours of silence, when I thought he slept. He is ashiver with cold. If even tallow candle were lit and blowed out again, we'd be plunged into darkness, but now the withdrawn moon yawning over the floor or our own night sight lets us see each other, and I cannot ask him why he is shivering there, as he would not say aught of the vomit I took, or my tears, or his. No matter.

"Here, Thankful, I am cold. Let me hug you for warmth, and we will lie against the hay. I'll listen for her moving and wake you."

Thankful mutters, "I must needs stay awake," and promptly, like the mixture of child and soldier that he is, falls asleep upon my shoulder. I love you, Thankful, as soldiers love, or brothers, for I would die for you and who would die for passion of a woman?

I wanted—what is it? The tailoring of my dreams. I wanted God. I've trudged toward that and listened and thought of heavens opened for me and all of that, but here it is, my revelation comes and moves into me sweetly, softly, this boy who puts his head down on my shoulder and trusts and sleeps a little. Sleep's a greater act of trust than passion, for that's wary. Wary, weary, this boat on the blue water, ah, I knew 'twas water that I sought. From the sky float down the prettiest country flowers that e'er I saw, gentle as rain and softer, float; it is air and words distilled into the flowers, and they drop on through silence. I fight for, fought for . . . keep awake. The danger of the democratical way is that men are courted, instead of being honored, one by another. Is that what Thankful said? Or I? Or someone. Mother, you do not understand. 'Twas for release of honor, one by another, that I left your house and came all this way. . . .

What is it? The doves are moving. I have been drifting and thought I was in some boat upon the water and would slip to the well and drink. Thankful's sleep is deep, as after recognition when there is no more need or hope in being watchful. Yet I cannot stop it, even now. What I wait for comes toward me. There is no need for aught but patience. Oh, it is so empty here, away out beyond war and beliefs. At the moment of nothing in the cold air, I hear Thankful's heart abeating. Sweet Thankful, I would give my life to keep your sweet heart beating in you for many mornings, that's all, and as for great sides taken—one cannot take sides in the beat of a heart.

The heartbeat grows, the yes and no of it, the life and death, the savage thump of it. Thankful's and mine and hers and all grows, the beat systaltic diastaltic of the whole of the town, and animals and tiny, timid, fluttering hearts of doves and silly rabbits and lurking cats and old men in their houses. Under fear and longing and demand, there's the beat of the heart, and now here's fear of the throbbing, it grows so great around me. Thankful moans and turns. I must have clutched too tight upon his shoulders.

I dare not move. It is all around me, is the buoyancy of the night grown yellow with some great strength. If I move the cramped muscle of my arm, Thankful will wake, and it will be gone. How every day it sounds.

In all my life I have never been so calm. Malice toward the old woman is too heavy a burden for me to bear now. There is, after all, only neutrality in her. She cannot see us, and she does not care. I hear her turn in her sleep into crisis of her own, another day or a dream, what matters which? What I hear is nothing of what the dumb preachers say of great angels and the heavens parting and all. 'Tis beyond awe, beyond tears, beyond sorrow, for that's a luxury too for the trapped and numb.

She locks us here because she wants to sleep. Am I meant to love her? Is she the evil I am bound not to resist? The only question worth asking now is why. Oh, dress it not in reason. Are we to submit and be as birds are and Christ is and all, holy boys? But here's my dirt and sweat and weight of longing and bitter gall of disappointment, and how am I to carry that? Bravely, eh, or screaming? Can this great heart I hear guide me?

It fades, and lofted high here twixt night and morning, I, Johnny Church the fool, have had a kind of vision. I suppose, and 'twas no fine faraway thing to glimpse. Why have I pushed my heaven and hell beyond the house roofs or into the caves of earth or past or future time? This loft holds all of it—all, all there is, the God who walks through the middle of things as through a street. And now, no more.

I would have lived a different life now, had I lived, but I did not, and 'twas only for the turning of a wrist. With a one knave, two knaves, three too old, and Thankful turns and cries, starts up, and settles down again thick with dreams. Have off them, there's no time for that now. There's three of the clock. It is the last sweet stillness before the dawn intrudes and I give up my life as men do every day, but this time, for me, the last. I am thirsty. If I could only get to the water.

There's the first faint lift of darkness. Let the hay cuddle you, Thankful. How he sleeps. I must to a pigeon hole to see the dawn if I can lay him down without waking him.

The cocks map the town with their crowing and answering, back and forth, and the pigeons call their incessant moaning and swoop and wheel and turn and lift to meet the new faint light as if life begins each day high in the air and they must lower it down and down to the ground; gray dawn now, and the roofs are dark against the paler sky, etched black, waiting.

There's a dog. The first dog of Creation trots his

busy nose along the path through the first ghost-colored dawn. So here is my vision of Zion, my seven gates, a cold yard at dawn, a lane where a dog wanders in the stone cold morning.

If only I could keep this room, only this space to stay in until I begin to face these flicks of miracle that pass my eyes like the pigeons' wings, always nearly gone. I live within the coldness of this moment. Now's my luxury. I have none other.

Now the dawn is white, and the drift of wing waves is at the level of my eyes, and they fly back and forth, bubbling at one another in and out of the pigeon holes, look in and see me, turn and float away. Thankful's hand is white now against the boards, and the dunged floor draws whiteness from the dawn. The forge loses its light to the day.

The first sun strikes. How often I have seen it and not seen it, the first faint brush of color. The blacksmith is at his door, looks left and right and does not see, and stretches himself. Nothing but sleep and every morning shows in his face. He takes the air for granted. He mumbles something, turns, and goes within, scratching and yawning and yapping. Was I like that? Yesterday I might have trusted to call out to him. I can hear Nell moving in her stall.

Now, there, from the oaken door beside the orchard, one bent, too old for easy sleep, moves slowly, as we would have moved, from tree to tree, inspecting them as if they spoke together, and now beyond them, he bends only a little more under the new sun to begin the weeding of his corn. When he hears the shots that end me, perhaps he will look up, as a laborer does when he hears bird shot, and go on bending then, for he must reap and harvest.

How long has she been standing at her door, her shoulders drawn down heavy on her body, her head drawn down between them? She, shading her weak eyes, rises into the day as alone as one of the pale turning stars that kept my night with me. The very air comes not close to her. She cringes against it, unloved, unwatched, forgotten. Does she calculate our rent against our slops and the trouble we have been by our living? What's your neat gain, lady?

She does not even glance up to where we are but listens for nothing while men in their still-dark houses turn to their good wives, spurt life out of their slumber hardly knowing, not delicate or piercing with sweet pleasure, but only dumb and comforting, man turned boy turned man again, almost before they wake and stir the fire and sink into their life, beginning again without questioning. They invade me, their warmth, their comfort. Those rare visions I have had this night, these visitations, are not enough. God send me mother comfort too, and someone eye to eye, and someone's hand.

How pitiful she is in the dawn, and yet I must not pity her, for pity of her dumb neutrality is false and saps my strength of the anger God comforts me withal. She drags her rump across the yard and sits down by the well. Christ, I thirst.

There's movement now of shadows jostling under the trees at the priory. All my muscles know that calm movement, the feeding and watering and rubbing down of cavalry horses, the first act of the day.

That boy of twenty years within me cries at the sight. I want to get to the river. I want to feed my horse. All I've seen this night and all I've thought—I'd trade it now for one touch of my love and the fondling of my son. Don't you know, who set us here, Thankful and I are unused, oh, all written on already, but nothing yet read? Oh, Jesus, turn thy eyes from thy perpetual martyrdom and save us from being blotted out here, with only the muteness of the old woman to bless us and the huge breathing of the smith's bellows. Why, even that ragged hag running and screeching like a bird through Westminster Yard was more of miracle than you down there, old woman, for she at least cried out and let the world hear her cry. I end here loving her, the mad screech owl who took not her rape for granted, more than you who gather all your fat around you to protect you from surprise.

"What's she adoing of?" Thankful whispers in my ear, and his hand rests on my back, an answered prayer. As we hang on every movement of her who holds our lives in her hands, she raises herself on one ham and satisfies herself with the first fart of the day, so loud it jostles the birds. Is that what she's been waiting for all along? The bellows breathe, and she sinks down to scratching of her head and staring at the cobbles. Some decision is reaching the daylight of her mind, inevitable as birth.

"Move, old woman." Thankful begs the air for only that.

Decision reaches her shoulders, and she lumbers up, walks toward us with never a glance, and disappears below. I cannot see. There's a great hissing. She comes into sight again, as calm as if the goose she holds by its neck were not beating and flailing at her body with its white wings. She holds its body under her left arm, its head in her right hand. So supple is her killing wrist that she has flung the body over the mounting block and severed its head all in one twist. Now she watches, weary-eyed, as the headless goose flings itself about the dawn yard slower and slower, stops, its dead wings flung across the cobbles, flecked with blood. Now the day is all its colors. The goose blood's red upon the stones, and there's a beginning of hurly-burly in the town.

She brings a sack and squats there plucking, plucking, in clouds of goose feathers, wasting not a feather, as she will waste naught of us.

She has assured herself, for her weak eyes are as certain as stones. She is going to bring us water, let us try to run, give us up, or cook her goose, or hide the carcass more like until the soldiers go, for the smell of cooking will draw them like cats. It's all the same to her, same energy, same shrug, and always for the same reason, her own survival. She will live so long and so long and never live at all. Even if Thankful and

I die, we will live, and live more in a day than her in all her life, and that's the difference between us. So much for my greeting and pleading for a longer time. What's that?

We are in her power so dumbly because of chance and place. The ground where she hounds and betrays us is low, is bog ground; reason and humanity hover in the air unseeing, innocent of her there, pluck, pluck, plucking, without what we more delicately angry call a conscience.

There's naught to do but piss again into the straw, albeit we'd like to shower her from our nest.

"Here they come again," Thankful whispers from his peephole to the street. We listen to the horses thunder through the passage below us in their morning search to cull out the strays of us. There are only two of them. They rein in over her, and she only glances up at them and shakes her head and falls aplucking.

"What miracle!" Thankful whispers. "She shook her head." The sudden hope hurts my body.

They are ready to wheel and go, already tired of seeking us out, when one turns back his horse and reaches down to grab the goose from her. She tucks the carcass tight under her arm and takes to running around and around the well house with the soldiers after her. Their laughter spills over her as they try to corner her. The blacksmith comes to his door to watch, that big, simple man, gentle with horses. He laughs with them to see the cooking of her goose, and, aie, my belly's aripple, too. I cannot help it.

Now she screams, "They made me do it," and they rein in and listen. She's pointing up toward us. They wheel and dismount, tether and begin to run, all in one flowing action, and behind them she, triumphant, pets the naked stump of the goose neck, for she's saved her goose by cooking ours.

"So that's the way it was to be done," Thankful says. His hand has fell from my back. There is, for the first and last time in my life, nothing, nothing to be done. I could not see their faces for their helmets, but

they rid like old soldiers, and those sent for this spite-
ful task against their fellows would not be easy to
persuade.

We watch the trap lift at last, slowly, as if there
were twenty of us, desperate to spring, and here am I,
as empty and limp as a flung stocking, and Thankful
only leans against the chimney and stares at the floor.

Why, the boy is but sixteen and swallows hard as he
calls below, all afeard in his voice. "I've cornered two
of them," he calls, and his jack-in-a-box head disappears.

"Stand by. Come down, you clot!" The other calls.
There's stumbling of armor on the ladder, and one
other coming closer, and the clatter of the boy as he
slips and falls.

When the trooper sees us, Thankful is so deep in
giggling that he cannot stop even when that man of
father forty slaps him to the floor and says, "I'll teach
you laughing, you fine Jesuit!"

He jostles us toward the ladder as if we were a
crowd to be controlled and not two hungry, thirsty men
who have no defense against the flat of his sword that
keeps flogging at our backs, but I do not feel it, and
Thankful moves lightly as it were his own decision,
down the ladder first.

The boy, all fierce now, is guarding the door, with
thunder in his little pimple face, and flourishes his
sword as we find our feet, the other coming down behind us. Thankful walks to him, and the sun falls on
his head from the crone's fine window. "Why, brother,
thou are but a boy. What in Christ's name hast thou
against us?" The boy, all fear now, thrusts to keep him
and his words away. Thankful claps hand to arm as if
he'd been bee-stung, and when his hand comes away,
'tis soaked with blood.

"Aie, brother, no need of that," he says, mild. "I
have no quarrel with thee, nor any arms."

"Come, tie them," the trooper says behind me, and
I turn and see his face so close it swells into my eyes
as he jerks the leathern bonds he carries close around

my chest and arms and thence to my hands, and will tie me to the saddle as I have tied many a prisoner, God forgive me. The boy ties Thankful now. He bleeds harder; his sleeve is soaked.

"Not in here." The old woman screams at the door and pounds at it. "Get from here. 'Tis unlucky for a stranger's blood to be upon my hearth." So has the mocking of the old law of charity lodged in her mind. It's a deeper fear with her than the losing of her goose was. It makes her so brave she runs in among us and grabs the besom from the hearth and falls to ridding herself of all of us.

How piercing is the sun. I can smell the water in the well. God give Thankful and me to drink, I pray thee, just that simple prayer.

"Lookee," the pimpled soldier calls, and points to Nell, who looks with her round soft eyes on all alike from the stall beside the smithy.

"Watch here," the other says, and leaves the boy and us tethered to the saddles so near the well, and strides across the yard.

The smithy puts his great hand gentle on Nell's flank, and I see it ripple as it does when she's comforted. "This here is my mare," he says, and stands before her.

"Is it so?" the trooper calls to the old woman, who has come up behind us, still carrying her besom.

"No," she squeals, " 'tis mine. He's. . . ."

"Mother!" The smith tells her much in his speaking, for he holds her there all silent with one word. In a little while he says, "Tell them whose horse."

I fear so what she will say that I call, " 'Tis his horse. I seen her yesternight. He calls her Nell. I seen them." Nell needs more rest, and the trooper is too heavy for her and is used to riding with a heavy curb. He would run her to death.

The old woman says, sullen, "Aie, 'tis his"—and brightens—"but I own the saddle hanging there. He borried it of me."

We have been forgot in the division of the spoils.

The trooper shrugs. " 'Tis naught to me. We can only have the scunning of the rebels for our pay. 'Tis the general's orders."

The smithy walks now across the yard. "These men have had no water," he tells them, and so, for the gift of Nell, he sinks the dipper and holds it to my mouth.

"Bless you, brother," I whisper, "use her not on heavy loads, for she founders easy, and walk her some before you let her out. She's hunter-trained."

"Bless you, brother," Thankful says loud to hide my voice, and drinks. The water spills down my throat, another prayer answered.

"Oh, I sicken at this task," the trooper is grumbling. "Culling boys out of attics is no fit employment for a soldier. Come, you little clot," he says to the ranker, and they ride us off. We paddle along behind like tethered colts, trot down beside the smithy, now the oaken door, now the long path, and all along beside us is the orchard I have watched in the night. We turn along the priory wall. The boy grins down at Thankful and clicks his horse to a canter, and Thankful must needs run, but he is too faint and falls, and the boy drags him.

"For love of God, stop," I call out.

The trooper sees what's happening. "God damn you, have your sport another time. There's work to do," and cows the boy, not out of mercy, but impatience. They wait for Thankful to stagger to his feet.

So we walk into the crowded priory grounds and one calls I do not know, bound there before us, " 'Tis the two elected Agitators that led us into this," and lunges toward me, but one stops him with a blow. 'Tis Francis White. He does not meet our eyes. It is humiliating and a naked thing to stand here all forlorn and dirty, tethered to a saddle while no one seems to see us.

Francis speaks to one there, a heavy back that I know well enough, who carries his head lowered, one of middling height. I thought him taller. I realize I have not seen the bull of Ely unmounted. "Aie, 'tis them, sir. Will you speak with them now as was your word?"

"Aie," Cromwell growls, "I will speak but not treat. For where would it stop then, Francis? Must I quarrel with every dog in the street that barks at me?" He turns and looks us up and down. Cromwell's eyes are mild and dogged with lack of sleep, his face is petulant, preoccupied, and what? My life depends on it—there is a softness in the look he makes so stern, and the most feared nose in England is a silly sot-colored thing.

"This was a dangerous game for boys to play," he says, but not to us, then, "Bind that boy's arm," and turns again and stumps into the priory, grumbling to Francis, who he signals to walk beside him, "I would have healed Babylon and now must treat and play with boys?" He goes within, and Francis does not look at us.

It is true, we have grown younger in the night when I meant to grow so old.

W E have sat here above three hours like islands in a sea of waiting, long since ceased speaking, except in little words. How dear a May morning they have picked for this trial of us. This room we sit in, Thankful and I alone here, with the back of a soldier leaning against the window and, I suppose, beyond the door, from the sound of hard boots to the floor, this room is so like my father's as to be a dream of my father's house. Aie, Englishmen brag by letting slip connections and building houses, oblique and borrowing of sheltering style as hermit crabs. There is the same fine new carved chimney piece that the Quality must touch to know who they are, the same chairs of leather, tooled in Spain or some such place. I have heard my father speak long of this but have forgot all. This shining floor of wood that reflects us covers the old stone of the priory where many a papist monk has knelt. 'Tis hard for me not to hear the sand shifting over it to polish and polish as when the room is dim with the sound of busy housemaids. Speaker Lenthall can look through his polished windows that reach from floor to ceiling and see himself in them, and beyond his own image, if he cares to look so, his meadow reaches down to the river and the trees where, war or no war, a few pretty sheep crop and feed it.

No one walks across the grass. Only a few doves seem to have followed us. I would tell Thankful there is a rabbit feeding under the great oak tree, but he is far away in a world of his own wandering and has not spoke for so long.

I can smell the river and see it glide under the trees. There only last night I watered Nell and soaked her sore hock in the stream. I had no time to tell the smithy of her sore hock. Pray God he sees it. In the river the lazy fish flick and the water weeds tremble. Oh, Jesus, I pray thee, let me near the water once more. Thy visions of the night are as nothing to the power of the morning. I seem unable to miss any flick or hint of what's alive. I am hollow within and light as a reed from lack of sleep, and my fear grabs at my belly, insistent to be remembered. When will they come for us, when in God's name? The window ajar, the silence, the fine gentlemen's prison, the waiting, the hunger—all are policy to break us. I am near broke by it.

Thankful has that divining sense to comfort with some word.

"I have been such places in the night I have not thought of ever."

"Aie, and I too," I tell.

The door flings open, and I can see a fragment of

the great hall beyond. "No speaking there," the guard yells.

"On whose authority?" I hear Thompson's furious voice, ever demanding the right. Is he then pardoned and free? I can trust nothing, not even the consistency of a stupid man like Thompson.

One other speaks softly, and the door is left ajar. Someone listens. How is it one knows when there is an eavesdropper? What of grand importance to the state would they have us say?

I must bring Thankful to me. It is too lonesome here.

"Have I told thee of Nellie and of my son?"

"Aie, in the night you told me, how he has not your name, but name of Lacy, and how that pains you."

I have no memory of it, how much was aloud in that loft, how much a world within me. Did I tell him how there is gathered in me Charity and Lazarus and the bird woman, aie, and for that moment of his royal courage, the king, but that was all of God and smelled of blood, and none saw me seeing them in turn? Did I tell him I loved him along with Nellie and Peregrine and my son? Did I say how all this carried me to the noise and drums of armies marching, and the clank of tackle, and dust in my mouth? I wonder at the difference, for these four are chosen, but the others met me head on, intruded on my life, and mingled with me when I would have been repulsed to touch them with my hands. Both are love, the chosen and the intruders. One goads me; one guides me. I'll be blotted out not knowing what the difference between them is.

"I think for the most there is no contact but only the self reflected in another eye." That is not what I meant to say at all.

From without, the soldier grumbles, "I have orders to keep them from speaking lest they connive. . . ."

Thompson's voice orders, "Let them be."

"You must not die so, my dear, lest you die needlessly," whispers Thankful. If he were a lass or a political man, I would suspect him of seeking out that patch of sun that forms a halo, but being Thankful, he would scorn courtship had he scorn in him. He only seeks the warmth and does not know he shines, or care. "Look with charity even though they smite thee."

He makes me laugh, sitting so straight in Speaker Lenthall's carved chair and spouting Bible words as easy as he breathes and saying nothing. I must touch him nearer the quick for answer.

"Must I look so after my heart is empty?"

"Aie, even so."

"Why, that's hypocrisy."

"No," he says sadly, and falls to watching the sun crawl on the floor, "only a whistling to keep the others' spirits up," and winces and holds his bandaged arm.

"Does't hurt?"

"Aie, throbs so."

We fall awaiting again as still as stones in the river bottom.

The waiting flows through the door, and in the great hall outside they wait. The clock in the tower above us strikes eleven. It is the clock that measured our long night in the distant dark. Now, overhead, it chimes through the house more gently, with a prettier sound than I would have thought. The day yawns toward noon. What do they wait for?

What would I do if I could wander to the window, and push it open, and walk out upon the soft grass, not to run away, only to wander for a little? Every muscle longs for that, only for one more hour when this was not all happening to me. Thankful, look not into my mind now, for there are luxuries there you wot not, nor any here. My longings are unfaithful to love or cause or any.

Sometimes I weary of these solemn men whose only metaphor is God. Before I go hence, I would spend one more morning hour mooning along the river in the water meadow, scribbling of pretty lines to lovers too elegant to know and too far away to notice me and so disturb my sorrow. I would dream of their safe, soft shadows. I would do that once more. Mooning's the greatest luxury, and few do know it. There is an aristocracy of the eye, of innocence and words, all before conscience, no democracy can touch. Aie, to twiddle and twirl strong lines and fine phrases, sentiments and thoughts of God made of intelligence and secret wit! I would make glittering metaphors to clothe this raw time and wear them like a silken mask lined with fine leather. Aie, there's one, caught like a trout, no, smile's more like. I would put Priapus on Speaker Lenthall's Presbyterian grass and muse on death that's naught to do with this sick weight in me. I would make all comforting fantastics and conceits and even tell myself I wrestled with the line to catch all truth with such sugar and spice. My God, I am hungry.

To sit here listening to the doves still and the hunger rumbles of mine and Thankful's bellies, that's all too daily a morning to have so bitter an end to it as I know will be.

There's noon so slowly striking, twelve hours since we were broken.

The clock wakes the whole house out of sleep. There's the stamp of boots in some room beyond the chimney. I cannot remember what it looks like there, for we were dragged through it and flung into this room so early that we seem to live here now. There's call of orders, tumble of doors, fast walking, the crash of a pikestaff upon the stone floor. That will mean the officers have come, and we still know nothing, nothing of what has happened and who are dead.

"I am afeard," Thankful whispers.

"Aie, and I too."

Then he says, "I wish something," and I think of my dream of mooning and phrases, and he says, "I wish that I had cared a little the less. Sure there is a balance."

Cornet Thompson and Cornet Denne bring the sound of heels into our quiet room, quiet now no more. Men pour around, above us. Cornet Thompson's hands are bound behind his back. A soldier releases them and does not look at him. Every muscle of his face is clean with honest anger. Cornet Denne has been aweeping, and his face is swollen with prayer and tears. It would be grand if some had not dried as snot just beneath his nose and made him look like a boy caught in some innocent prank and afeard of whipping. They do not see us here. Thompson's at the window, all still fury, and Denne's amewling in a leathern chair. Pikemen of the Lord General's Regiment of Foot crowd out again. 'Tis Francis' regiment. They leave the door ajar, one so careful that I know it to be policy.

Thankful goes on as if the room's silence had not been plundered.

"We do not find things out, Johnny, and they do not change. We only recognize them. This is the way they have been all the time," he says, watching the meadow flattened by the noon sun. "We die of our own beliefs and of not listening to the darkness of our own whisperings."

We must face all of the terrors all of the time. How do I know that? I heard it once or dreamed it.

Thompson laughs that short fox bark of laughter and comes to us.

"Aie, lad, still in that tree house of thy pretty thoughts. Come down, 'tis all too late, damn me, damned to all."

" 'Aie, they that take the sword shall perish with the sword,' " Denne mutters.

"Oh, shut thee up, thy puling kitchen slut." When Thompson uses "thee" so, it slashes across Denne's mouth.

"I forgive thee thy angry words," Denne tells him.

"Thee thou me not," says Thompson, and forgets him. I think, from his eyes, it is to keep from falling on him and strangling him with his hands.

"We know naught of what has happened. What kind of pickle are we in here?" I must ask and know.

He catches a shiver in my voice I did not know, he always catches such, but this time he is unlikely kind. "Listen, both lads of you. You may say brother to all and keep your hats upon your heads, but even then does the heart quake before the mighty men and the men of war. 'Tis your training, like setting dogs to a whistle. Now look you, 'tis that heartquake they will play on to lessen you. . . ."

"The great gifts to God are a broken and contrite heart," Denne groans from his corner.

Thompson goes and stands over him. "Before God, Harry, if you quote and snivel at us one more time, I will beat you shitless and go to my Christ in better frame of mind." He comes back to us again.

"Please, how many were taken?" I must know.

"Of a thousand men, less than four hundred."

"All who slept in the woods escaped. They caught those who slept in houses. I feared as much. Are they dead?"

"Nay, 'tis not politic to kill them all. Only one dead, and Eyre under civil arrest. He exchanged much fire with them from an inn. My brother has escaped, so all's not lost. There are many wounded, shot as they ran out, for sport."

"Where have they took them? Are they here?"

"No." This makes Thompson bark that laugh again. "They've made the church a prison. There's fine justice in poetry, eh? The spire we rode toward. . . ."

Some voice within the great hall, risen above the rumble of the others, stops him. We hear the thump of a fist upon a table that makes the plates upon it ring. They must have eat there. Christ, I am hungry.

"I tell you, sir, you have no other way to deal with these men than to break them in pieces."

One voice, milder, answers, but we cannot hear.

Loud, and thumping on the table; then Cromwell, it is Cromwell's voice, again. "Let me tell you that which is true. If you do not break them, they will break you."

One, a fat voice, answers, "You make too great a thing of it. We can hang twenty before they hang one."

Cromwell's voice rises to preacher pitch. "Aie, break

you, and bring all the guilt of blood and treasure shed and spent in this kingdom upon your heads. . . ."

One speaks again so softly we cannot hear.

" 'Tis the Lord General Fairfax," whispers Thompson, and falls to trying to hear as we all do who can die of that argument within the great hall.

"Why do they wait so long?" I whisper to him.

"They rid forty miles yesterday and had not slept all night. Oliver said they should withdraw and pray this morning. He lisps not a syllable without fasting and praying. But truly, I think it was to wait upon a letter, yet another letter. Oh, he'll kill us with legality."

All night that dangerous sincerity of his let him not sleep. I know this.

Cromwell's voice commands us to silence. "Do you want to make void all that work, the toil and pains you have done, and so render yourselves the most contemptiblest"—and here he thumps the table again—"generation of silly, low-spirited men to be broken and routed by such a despicable, contemptible generation as these democratical, atheistic, anarchical dogs?"

"I am bound in my conscience to speak a word." 'Tis Francis now, at last, that clear, almost piercing voice when he is angry enough. "You have broke covenant with me and with these men. All the time you did assure us that you would treat with them and sent us after them to compromise and promise meeting, you did drive hard upon their heels. You have not made good your engagements with them. . . ."

"I"—'tis "we" no longer, Captain General Cromwell, not that fiction, your "I" has took over—"I have no engagements with rebellious soldiers but to break them, I tell you, Francis."

They speak as friends who quarrel there, familiar.

"They are citizen soldiers and not at war. No war's declared, no choice has been made by the citizens. They spake from duly elected Agitators as we did at Putney and Newmarket."

"Damn, sink, and blast Putney and Newmarket. I will die of them!"

"Would that it were so," Thompson whispers.

Francis' voice is near to crying and loud the way I have not ever heard him. "You have not kept covenant with us."

'Tis too late, sweet Francis. We have no room for thee in our graves.

There is the silence again, and no one enters it. Thompson is twitching, twitching of his hands, and Thankful watches calmly as his tears fall on his clouted shoes.

Francis himself must break it. "You gulled them and drove after them. You treated as an enemy free men who have set you where you are."

"I think that you should remember, Francis, this is your superior officer." Would that be Fairfax who speaks? I have not seen Black Tom before except afar, where generals are and decisions are made, within doors I have guarded. He sounds exhausted and apart. Is that the way they sound, the lords of the earth? I heard one other once, Lord Cockburn, a cousin to the Lacys, and he was fat and all damn me and sink me and all fellows now and slubbered up with Sir Valentine before ten of the morning.

"Let him speak. I stand upon the bottom of my innocence in this." Cromwell's voice is quiet but still rings in the great hall. "They have brake the army ordinance, and this is mutiny, and I have the prerogative patent to use whatever means I can to put it down."

"These are free Englishmen, duly elected, and no man has patent cver them as citizens. They have the right to speak as they please in this."

Why do they argue on, free election, prerogative patent, and on and on and Thankful's tears still fall upon his shoes? I want to shout, "Leave off your justice. You only seek the words to unlock our killing," but how I know this I know not. There is a certain sun in May that makes the looking up among the trees as looking through water.

That word "please" has stripped Cromwell to his

own truth. "I do what's for their good, not what pleases them. Cease all this. I have work to do. Without authority otherwise than themselves, these men are nothing, clouted shoes and leathern aprons with the breeding of pigs. Be wary how you let forth your foolish words, Francis, or before God, you will join them."

"I would with all my heart I had joined them, knowing what I do."

"You can be shot for that under the rules of war," says the one who before would hang twenty.

"War be damned. There is no war. . . ."

Francis, oh, hark him, Francis! Cromwell puts on a father's voice more dangerous than his anger; listen how gently he reasons. "I would ask no unlawful engagements against duty, and I would not stand against their liberty of speech and their conscience, but conscience does belong to God, not politics."

What of the doors kicked in, my general, what of the men routed from their beds and cast into the Tower for what they speak?

"I shall say as Christ said, 'Render therefore unto Caesar the things which are Caesar's; and unto God the things that are God's.' "

Thompson's hands clench now, and I am embarrassed to look at Denne, for his face is all purged and love-soft with conversion.

"Would you use such arguments to let twelve hundred dangerous men abroad who believe in no authority beyond their free elections?" Cromwell speaks the words with a contempt I did not know he had of us. "I tell you Francis, seriously, as before God, without authority from above and otherwise than yourselves, you sink. . . ."

"A hundred thousand men, aie, and women too, in London. . . ."

Cromwell laughs as one who has sought and not found, as one broken to disappointment, a whore's laugh. It rises and carries him over what abysses I know not, nor have ever seen, as if it had waited to intrude upon him and strip him and toss him there, a wave of it. Christ, spare me hearing of it. It is obscene. "And I will show you a million who do not know or care what you are talking about, you silken little fool. Do I not know of what you speak and how it can be bent and forged and used as weapon? Do you not know that I know you are the true aristocracy and would speak in the name of those who fear and despise you and so seek and need authority that if it were as weak as a hare swimming across the Thames, they would have hold of it and not let it go?"

'Tis that he speaks that empties my soul at last. Ah, Francis, Francis, why I did speak philosophies with you two years ago and let you plant this seed that can be watered by those terrible words I know not? Your fatal way of seeing all sides and all the failure of strength and all the strength of failure too that sends all abyssward with that laugh.

"They will conform to authority"—Cromwell's voice is easy now—"and they will not jump out of all engagements; it is too great a jump for this kingdom to bear. . . ."

"Conformity," says Francis, and his voice is thin and civilized again and intimate among the others, "the great Diana of the Presbyterians."

One laughs and says, "Francis, your wit is of the devil."

Why has he changed his voice now when he did defend us before, as if his energy had failed before the very conformity he mocks?

"Seriously, as before God," I hear Cromwell say, now reverent, "let us be more united in our doing," and he groans. "I tell you, Francis, I agree with your words, but when I come to act, in the presence of God, I must needs speak my heart and do my duty, and I have prayed"—his voice begins to lilt, in groans of spirit—"that God would take from me the governing of this mighty kingdom as too great a burden to bear" —and he grows angry again, that petulance that seems to lurk always behind his words—"and I have not time to treat with rebellious boys. I will break them here, now, in Burford, and have done with their blasphemies and their free speeches and their elections and all their contemptible carnal reasonings. . . ." Contempt comes too easy to this man.

Thompson walks across the floor and slams the oaken door.

"Open that door," we hear Cromwell bawl, faint through it, and when 'tis open, we know he speaks to us. "Their indulgence will never be heard of in this kingdom again. Why, there is a fault deserving death in them who are least guilty there. They must be broken. I, too, love freedom, but they go too far in it."

Thankful wipes his sleeve across his eyes and nose.

What is it we carry in us, we three, for Denne's a melted man, that makes the power of all those mighty ones set onto us to kill us?

"This I will do before my God. What else can I do?" Cromwell ends with that question. The trees turn their leaves slowly to a new breeze from up the Windrush, and there is nothing in me now but this moment so sweet so suddenly, so free 'tis like only the weight of singing. That is the question that Creon asked her, the girl with the dirt clutched in her fist; her uncle asked Antigone that final question, and she had no answer for him, for his words took place somewhere else, stars away from her, and so she turned her wrist and turns it still. Francis, you gave me greater gift than you knew with the myths you told me. She did not need to wait so politic as you think. The time came and met her. That's all that stands against their power to damn and diminish us, the turning of a wrist. The trees are turning around; I hear Thankful, far away, calling, "Put your head down between your knees, Johnny."

WHAT was it made me faint like a girl? The trees watch down on me. I lie in grass beside the river, another small prayer answered. Soldiers look down on me as neutral as the trees. It is too late to be ashamed. In the seconds before they move I must feel green all through me, the lovely wet of water on my face. Thank Christ, they have flung me on the bank, and my hand trails in sweet water and brings it to my spirit. To lie loved by grass and wind and flowing water, oh, I would have treasured all the moments of it 'til I died of treasure, ravished by the plains God gave us to be upon had I but known.

"He's come to his senses," says one in the west country tongue.

"Aie, he's come to himself again," another says, watching my eyes.

I sit up in the grass and feel so foolish.

" 'Tis one of them atheists," says one solemnly, as if they had landed a strange fish on the bank.

Across the meadow runs the boy of the dawn, his pot bouncing, and something under his arm that runs with grease down his breeks. He squats down on the grass beside me.

"I waited 'til she cooked it," he says, somewhat proud, and uncovers the goose from her tablecloth. We all sit upon the grass and tear the goose apart and eat it, then throw the bones into the Windrush and watch them float downstream.

"I would take some to my friend. He has not ate neither," I ask them.

The boy gives me a goose wing, brown and crackling, and thrusts into the carcass and pulls out the liver and apple and raisins the old woman has stuffed it with. He makes a little pile of it upon a leaf.

"I would have not caught you was I not ordered so," he tells, shy now, as if it had been only a morning's ugly task to halter and drive a fellow creature. "When did you engage with the army?"

"In forty-five." I have to think. It is so long.

"Was't at Naseby?"

"Aie."

Another interrupts. "Scrope's regiment was never at Naseby."

My heart surges as if trying to call me a liar mattered even now. "Many of us come into the regiment after our old colonel did stop our preaching and did also try to rescue the king."

"Have on. Have on." The soldier laughs because he got his rise of me.

"To kill a king!" the boy speaks, wondering.

"He's man like any another," the first says, arguing, forgetting to twit me.

"I was pressed out of a tavern a year since." The boy forgets the king in his own troubles. " 'Twas the first time I had been in such a place."

"Aie, I was pressed too," says the one who would twit me.

"And I, too," tells a third, who has a London tongue.

I know again what I knew before, that we who came toward this with such zeal are the leaven, not the bread, the voice nor yet the muscle of the leg.

"Come!" one soldier who has not spoke grabs me by the shoulder, and I wince and feel faint again.

"I broke it," I apologize, "afalling from my horse when I swerved to avoid a baby who ran into the road." Why am I braggart over this? Why do I want of a sudden for them to know I did it to avoid a baby in the road?

We march across the meadow now toward the house,

and through the window of the great hall I can see them, Cromwell and my Lord Fairfax and divers others, seated on one side of the refectory table with the fireplace beyond where the carved and painted arms of Speaker Lenthall shine so new. Thompson stands before them, as if in midstride, and I can see his face moving, and once he throws back his head. Only one at table seems to be answering, and that is Cromwell. Lord Fairfax has a face that never asked a question. It is a great room of leather and wood and linen beyond the window like a painting. They, caught there with so little movement, look not real enough to decide the ending of our futures while I march past in the tall grass and steal looks like a caught truant schoolboy.

'Tis the pressed boy who dragged him along the road who comes within and gives the leaf to Thankful.

Thankful smiles and holds it and touches it with his other hand, but he does not look up at the soldier. Something has happened, I know. His face is strange and wondering, as one in a trance. Once again they withdraw and leave us with one guard upon the door. Denne has fallen into some kind of sleep in the corner. My senses grow and grow this day. I can smell his tears. Thankful holds the leaf so long I have to take it from him.

"You do not eat." Now I know why he listens so. We can still hear the voices through the door.

"I hope we know God better." Cromwell finishes some argument, some old, old argument he has been at so long.

"They are all using God," says Thankful sadly, looking at the goose liver. "I am so filled with Christ now that strong meat would make me vomit."

"We have not withdrawn ourselves from our obedience and killed the king to yield ourselves slaves and vassals to the tyranny of our fellows." Thompson speaks as he did, thundering in the field at Salisbury to the regiment, the same words. Must they always use the same words as if saying them enough would etch them

in the air? "I am a free man of England and therefore
not to be used so." He speaks the words now of Lilburne. Has he none of his own for defending of his
very life?

"How long has he been in there?" I whisper.

"You are an officer of this army, and you are guilty
of unlawful engagement against duty." Cromwell's
voice is stronger.

"Above half an hour," Thankful says. "Oh, Johnny,
I will never be twenty. They're going to take us out
and kill us." The tears stand in his eyes. Oh, Thankful, disgrace yourself not with tears, not before these
men who will use them.

"You have plundered us, pillaged us, and violently
used us to break our necks before we should speak our
minds. You have given your mercenary and pressed
troops the flower of the army to plunder as free prize.
You have brought men who would fight for the devil
if he gave them a groat more and did feather them
with plunder to dash and break to pieces our spirits
who would not undertake the Irish service."

"Speak not so loudly. It is late, and I am weary to
the teeth," says the fat voice.

"Let him speak," says Cromwell, "he is free to speak
his mind."

Oh, Christ, he is so subtle in his heavy way, to give
a man freedom to say what he likes with only hostile
ears and hardened hearts to witness.

"You sent Francis here to gull us with cunning and
lead us to this trap."

"Not so either! You know me, Will, I would never
do aught," Francis seems to force himself to speak.
He sounds broken and mild. Why, Francis, compromise has failed you, and you have no future more than
me. You have turned aside at pitch point and must
spend your life harking back to here, apologizing for
our deaths. I wonder how you will spend the gaps of
time. I know you love women. Perhaps turn lecher,
Francis, plow your God-given life under into women,
all fallow fields, as impotent as a man who plans his

passions for seducing as a battle and discharges them only into woman in a pathetic field of pillows because he dared not act, to make or to destroy. Francis, did I not tell you not an hour since, or a day, I forget now which, that there is a place where my bird woman screams and my Lazarus lies you wot not of?

How easily the tears come to my eyes and dim the afternoon. Let me not be like Denne there, counting of his tears as if he were a miser and they coins of the realm. Of this realm they may be. These men fast and pray and weep as easily as they parcel out the land of England.

Thompson's voice rings out, desperate now. " 'Tis you are guilty. You have tried to get the disaffected and dangerous men, the men who think, who put you where you are before time had changed you and tempered you with power, away beyond the seas. You use our loyalty and Christian zeal to fan us to Ireland to plow that soil with Presbyters to fight and murder a people who have done us no harm. . . ."

Cromwell shouts, "By my Christ, Thompson, thy carnal reasoning. . . ."

Thompson. I had forgot for a moment who spoke there. Will we be forgotten? I mean will what we were be forgotten? I wonder if it happened or no. The taste of the goose is still in my mouth, and the water that ran through my fingers is cool in my body. Perkins' hand steals over to the leaf, and he falls maunching the goose wing. The clock strikes two. There is a pause as if the angel of death flew low over Speaker Lenthall's house.

Thompson's stride has turned into a strut. He passes by the window under guard and does not look toward us.

Two soldiers must pick Denne up from the chair. I would I were not so sickened by the sight of him. He wallows in his sorrow as a pig in a sty.

Have I slept? On such a day, have I? The shadows across the grass are longer, and the bees hum outside the window, and Thankful is far away again in his eyes, but quiet now, a quiet too deep for me to fathom. What has happened while I slept? The voices murmur on within. Weariness waits among the soldiers at the window. They wish us over so they can drink and sleep.

"What is it?" I whisper to Thankful's trance.

"Let me tell you, Johnny. That man in there. . . ."

"The captain general? Oliver?"

"Aie. Cromwell. I have been studying of him all the day. No one touches him to the quick. He remains a pace behind his voice and gesture, watchful of self and other, weighing all. The voice in his own head is his ever-present strength, as if some faith there to believe and halter to were better than a man beyond his eyes, and as real or more to him. Watch your tongue a little, for you have a pretty wit when you can speak at all, and it slips out, nay, dances summat. Thank Christ, for it has sweetened hours for me enough. He is not a man weakened by any wit, though I have heard he shows in his cups a bawdy kind of humor that some might mistake for it."

I had not thought the wit that had often shamed my tongue had been a part of this, much less of use to Thankful. I thought always he wotted not of it. How blindly we think we bring part when we bring all of ourselves. I reckon not to have bit my tongue as often as I thought.

Oliver seems to will Thankful to talk of him, creeps in, and demands the boy's understanding. "He is one who can divide, not knowing. 'Tis worse than if he knowed. He is sincere to his very bottom. His playing is sincere. He's played the captain general with Thompson, and now he is all baptism and groans of spirit and eyes cast up as if he could pluck his God off the chimney with Denne there."

"What will he be with us?" I must feed this fire of understanding to save my life.

"What he sees in us to be mirror of," Thankful says, and as calmly, "It was Denne who betrayed us, all along, not Francis. I do believe he thinks he done right," he adds, wondering at it.

I am glad Francis does not carry that at least. Thank God for it.

"When it happened I know not. Even as late as yesterday he spoke with the same zeal of spirit as always."

The soldiers are coming toward the door, and now they bring Denne in and close it after him. He stands and watches us as one who has seen the light of new baptism.

"I have a marvelous reverence and awe upon my spirit," he begins.

Thankful gets up slowly, and the food drops to the floor. He walks past that man, standing there all naked with the spirit, and falls to watching out of the window.

"Harden not thy heart against me, Thankful."

I let out laughter from the bottom of my gut at Thankful's Christian name in such a mouth. Denne begs Thankful's back, his face still stained and ugly with the drenching of his tears, and says—and there's an edge of pride in his confessing, that courtier's pride that lives on small attentions of the great—"We two have prayed together within, Oliver and I. We could not speak, he and I, for bitter weeping."

Thankful turns and looks at him long. I would he had died more innocent of the world, before this coldness I see had overcome him. But his voice still has that trace of wonder in it, that wonder he watches the world through, as through a finer eye than mine.

" 'Tis foul," he says. " 'Tis a foul thing done here, and I cannot tell what it is," and looks long at Denne. "I did love you and wonder at you, for I had not known so passionate a spirit before in zeal for Christ, nor one yet with such fine manners. You did never wipe your nose upon your sleeve but ever used your kerchief. Johnny, we must not trust such using of the kerchief."

". . . some of charity . . . you cannot know how I suffer . . ." Denne is mumbling at the floor.

"And what of that? 'Tis not to be broken and melted so, I tell you. And cease your gazing into empty space,"

Thankful raps at Denne as if he were giving an order. "God is no imp that hovers in empty space but is as one to another and lodges in the eye. Look at me." He waits until Denne obeys him. "Look to your murders, Harry, to find out who you are and what you want in this wicked world. We two here will be shot like Robbie Lokyar, not you, for you have done much duty I would not befoul myself with." He is harder than I have ever seen a man, burning cold in that strange light.

I keep slipping into something like sleep. He has stopped speaking, and there is buzzing in the room.

"Wrap yourself in player guilt," I hear Thankful say again, and had not known him so certain a man in his anger. I hear him walk across the room and feel his touch upon my head. " 'Tis useless, ain't it, my Johnny? How dost feel?"

"Nothing."

"Not me either. I would beshit me, though. I have had an evil business this last hour.

"I must needs shit." He goes and calls to the guards outside the window.

"Beshit thyself then," says one, and another laughs.

Denne calls out, all officer, "Let this man shit," and falls into that leaking of his eyes again as if there were enough tears to wash them clean.

A guard jumps to the sound of that authority as horse to spur and leads Thankful away across the grass.

One walks across the floor within the great hall. It is the only sound.

"He will not kill you." It is Denne again, standing over me, seeking a convert. "At worst you will be made to ride the wooden horse like the Agitators at Ware."

"You? Why not you?"

"I too, I meant. All he asks is that we see our error, our terrible error, that we did not submit to order." He must urge his zeal upon someone, and there is only me to assure to his own comfort. "When the ancient Jews had first prophets and then elected kings and did submit so to their chosen ways, and honor their fathers as God in their houses, to elect authority, and then. . . ."

Thank Christ he has run to a stop. I would that Thankful would come back. I am finding out a good thing, that it is possible to shut out a voice.

"Dost know," says Thankful beside me again; I would I did not lose this precious time, slipping in and out of sleep like this. "The privy here has arms to rest yourself on while you shit. Did you ever see the like?"

"Aie. In my father's house."

" 'Tis so?"

We are used now to the burring of the great clock as it prepares itself and begins to strike five. We have been now twelve hours in this prison of Delft china and pretty carvings.

"Corporal Thankful Perkins," one calls some way beyond the door. A guard, a musketeer, takes his arm as he tries to stand and falters. Thankful shakes the arm away, and the soldier follows him, a great lumbering man, but leaves the door ajar as delicately as woman's hand with care to obey orders. I wonder what the general will see to act toward in Thankful's face. What prayer can I have for him in there? Nothing. Nothing. I am too fatigued. I cannot think clear.

Someone says there, "Read this letter if you can read. If not, 'twill be read to you," one who sounds petty with five o'clock weariness.

"I can read." I can only barely hear Thankful's voice.

"This boy is not sixteen. What can he know?" another says, annoyed.

"I am nineteen." Thankful's light, small voice again.

One scrapes back a chair and stumps to the window. I can hear it creak open. Cromwell's voice grumbles, "We want air in here."

And another, the weary one: "Do you own this letter or no?"

"Aie. My hand is to it."

One laughs. "He has not wit enough to compose such a letter."

"God did choose the foolish things of this world to confound the mighty," I hear Thankful almost whisper and must see, see where they are and where he stands. The soldier at the window drowses, and Denne has fell to studying the floor boards. The door is not ajar enough. I can only see the man at the window. Once he puts his hand to his forehead as someone sick of an old fatigue would do. I see now the reflection of Cromwell's face, disinterested in the boy behind him. Does he not know that Thankful Perkins threatens him more than all the rest of us?

"Some I did not write," says Thankful patiently. "Give me leave . . . oh, then I must speak from memory. There where we harped upon our pay arrears. That was well known enough," and I can see him again in that room at Salisbury, marching in and out of candlelight, and hear the sharp bark of Thompson's laugh as they argue. Is it now or then? They fuse, I fight sleep and soft voices, ever saying—the passionate voice of Henry, who we loved then. . . .

"We did stoop to our fellow creatures to court them to our side with pay and reward when there is that in them to answer that we do not trust enough to call to. Policy kills, not honest dealing. . . ." No, that's never Henry Denne.

One mutters in the room beyond, "I cannot follow such rantings."

"I mean," says Thankful, "I did not treat with my brother as a man, but one to be cozened and persuaded with reward."

Cromwell speaks to his own image in the glass. "Enough of this. ' Tis late. Why did you send this letter to Bristol to be printed? Who are the printers? Damn me, they spring up like mushrooms."

They could not beard us with the letter we sent to Bristol, unless he there who argued and prayed with us did tell them we had wrote it, for it was not signed. Didst take our prayers and laughter to Cromwell's ear as well, brother Harry? I cannot fathom how a mind could dissemble so; it is another world to me, another language spoken with our words. He still cries there in the corner who has so wounded himself, and I can bear less the sin and smell of that wound than the foul sweet smell of human flesh forgotten in the sun. Were I true Christian, I would comfort this man, but I cannot, as I could not go near to the girl stampeded by the horses. I cannot even call him enemy, this blind, encumbered, neutral man who did not see us as he passed over us to save his life. There are many things I wish I did not know.

"Pardon me, brother." Thankful is answering Cromwell. " 'Tis a subversion of my liberty to question me on interrogatives and seek advantage from my mouth"
—and he raises his voice—"to make me betray my brothers."

"Can one in conscience go thus against authority?" Does Cromwell ask this of Thankful or of his own image? I cannot tell. It is Thankful, for he has drawn him from his fatigue and from the window.

"Pardon, brother." When Thankful calls him that, it makes Cromwell touch his face again in his habit of stroking his cheek. Now he stamps out of my sight, and I hear his chair drawn back. "You are not capable to judge my conscience," Thankful tells him, "only my acts, and then not in time of peace, for I am a free commoner of England. . . ."

"Boy, prate not such abuses to me. I have heard them all and from many mouths, and I say as I have said before. Where will it stop, this democratical notion? If all have rights who have no property and interest but the interest in breathing, you will bring anarchy. . . ." He stops, in midsentence, as if he were ashamed of being drawn into argument by a boy.

The weary voice interrupts now and seems to be seeking some legality to rid himself of Thankful, for he says, "It is reported that you have oft urged this equality of voice . . . whatever that may be."

"Oh, have off . . ." the fat voice mutters.

" 'Tis for the record," the weary one explains.

"Universal manhood suffrage, we do call it so. I would be grateful if you would write it so in the record," Thankful says. How can he sound so mild?

"Let them to disobedience and ambitions beyond the station God has pleased to call them. . . ." He has netted the weary one into argument.

"I did but try to give courage to my brother younger than I in learning."

"Learning," that fat one who I can never see grumbles. "He's what? Apprentice tailor, and has no more breeding than a pig, damn me by Christ's bowels."

Somehow Thankful has caught a flicker of interest from Cromwell. "Now you tell me," he says, quieter than the others, "where but division and division will such policies as yours lead us?"

"I had thought you to be concerned with this, brother." Thankful is as interested as if they spoke together across a tavern table. "How can we know that until we but try it?"

"Insolent," one mutters.

"Nay, brother," Thankful tells him, "but honest and plain dealing."

"Have you no fear in you?" Cromwell asks him.

"Oh, I did, last night, but 'twas burned out by sorrow at the world. Now you, being you, can but kill us or lose authority, your blood and bones, and I know that, so 'tis too late for fear, oh, now some shaking and freezing and running of my bowels, but that's the body in revolt, not true fear, think you?"

"I think that without authority and true obedience under God. . . ."

"Pardon me, brother, my voice of God speaks freer than yours."

"Aie, inner voice. How do you know it is but carnal reasoning?" Father voice? Minister? I cannot tell.

"Mine speaks true, that all who live have a voice in how they are governed."

The chair flings back and falls. Cromwell is at the window again.

"How do you know this?" The fat voice is amused. Thankful answers, "That I die for it." I can barely hear him now.

"Enough of this. He has condemned himself out of his own mouth." That is the weary one, and Cromwell is still intent upon the lawn where the shadows stretch all across it.

"Give me leave to ask . . ." Thankful begins again.

"Enough."

"Let him speak on. All speak free here." Cromwell has said this so often he hardly knows he says it.

"Are you so afeard of our hopes and our spirits that you must needs set men spying and listening and condemning on hearsay for conscience and private speech who lisp a syllable against you? Dost know you cannot legislate the secrecy of the heart?" Cromwell does not seem to hear Thankful, he is so still there.

"Take him out," one new voice says, preoccupied with a shuffling of papers.

They march him toward me, but he does not look at me, only at Denne as the door is slammed behind him. He stands over the huddled, broken man, and there is such a rage in him that if Denne were dying, he would not stint one word.

"Canst answer that? Canst answer? What God in you set you to watch and whisper all our thoughts and hopes to such men? It was the Bristol letter they read to me. You have done evil to me, Harry, for I go to God now with the sin upon me that I would kill you now if I could."

"I would you did so," Denne whispers.

"Add not the luxury of guilt to the life you stole from us. Johnny"—he sees me now and comes to me— "look not so surprised as if you knew not such things."

"No, 'twas not that. You cannot try him so. He is not there as we knew him. You try one we knew." I take his arm. "How was it there? I heard most but could not see."

"I was tried by a thrumming of papers and fingers. We are of no import to those grandees within, being only common soldiers and lacking wit. They did not believe that I could read. Now that hurt my feeling. I am so tired." He slumps in a chair and closes his eyes and falls into the slow breathing of sleep even as I watch.

Denne has so diminished he would seem to sleep too. The light of sundown is such perfect light for the time of this fine and graceful room. It brings a yellow glow upon the boards and the paneling and makes the plate shine soft. I sit upon fine leather, an old man with my legs stretched out and all done in my life, no running now, no dodging, but only the luxury of being alive by minutes in the evening to stretch and yawn. Why now is it my turn? Oh, Christ, how could I drowse and dream so? There is so much that I would say. I look at Thankful sleeping, his ordeal over for the time, and would to God I could speak out as he did, but I know I cannot. God give me easier speech for just that little while, I pray thee. Writing is more natural a thing to me than speech with strangers. What will Cromwell be to me? If I am in luck, he will be as lofty as he was with Thankful, that way will be less lies and more efficient killing, and not the humiliation and wounding of seeming interest in my life. I who am so brave a wit among my friends cannot be silent now.

J OHNNY, watch your tongue, and let them not offend your spirit." Thankful has waked and takes my hand. He has heard and seen before me the soldier standing in the door. The silence within the great hall is shattered with a loud voice: "Call Corporal Jonathan Church."

I can stand who has no weight, and I can breathe and am empty within at the end of this long journey to this room where I left Charity sniveling on the floor while my father prayed the morning prayer.

It is a long, slow way across the smooth-trod stone. The carved scutcheons watch from the rafters. A fire is lit now in the chimney, and a whole log burns there and casts its light across the floor. It is hard to see here. I hear someone shuffle papers like rats' scuttling. They sit in twilight, this council of old men. It smells of them. They are stretched, some slouched, some soldierly; one picks his nose and stares beyond me, a fat man, very near to sleep. The long refectory table is so black with age, so big it must have been built within this room when the monks were here. I watch hands, papers, all now sketched by firelight. The point of a pikestaff shines. The room is haunted by old, dried roses, as the rooms at Henlow. These men whisper and murmur among themselves. No one looks at me. Where is Francis? How long must I stand here? Francis, I need you. This is too final a whipping to be administered to a boy. Help me, all who have ever stood in such presences without buckling of your knees. I am where we dream of on bad nights. How mundane it is.

"Read the letter where I pointed out." One breaks the muttering among them with a command. It is Cromwell, but I dare not look at him. How great a protection from them is the stand to attention of a soldier.

"Are you listening? Answer me," the same man orders.

"Sir."

"Well, harken then."

"Here? They take up David's complaint?" He stops to check again with Cromwell and begins to read. His voice is all legality and slurring, not my passion and precision at Salisbury when I spoke these words so slow and weighed all and Thankful writ it down. I

wish they would let me read it. I have not seen my
words printed before. "It is not an open enemy that
enslaves the people, not damme Cavaliers, nor rigid,
envious, and surly Presbyters"—that is good; I like the
sound of it even in that dead voice—"but religious and
godly friends that have prayed, declared, and fought
together for freedom with them, that with their swords
have cut in sunder the chains of other tyrants."

"Get on. Get on," one says from the end of the
table.

"All the form of government"—the cold voice slurs
on across our words in some hurry now—"being corrupted and abused, the law and administration being
perverted, and the people's liberties betrayed. It was
promised that a new foundation. . . ."

"Come. Skip that," Cromwell says. His voice is mild.
He reaches for the paper and points a line. "Here.
That it should be. . . ."

"That it should be impossible for any tyrants in this
or future generations to introduce bondage among the
people."

"Enough. That is the particular I sought. Johnny
Church, look at me," and I must now look upon that
kindly, ugly, pocked face, the eyes easier with tears
than any man's in England, the mouth that fights between sternness and grief. "We have fought one with
another since Naseby." How can he know this? "I have
stayed in your father's house not three months gone."
Did you see her? Did you hear the patter of my son's
feet when you sat at food and wine? "You know me,
and you know I speak from a free heart. If there is
such iniquity as this you write of among us, help us to
find it out that we may remove such sad rebukes as
you have placed upon us."

"Sir, for the record he must own the Bristol letter,"
one interrupts.

Annoyance passes over this man's good face. "Yes.
Yes. Well, do you own the letter?"

"Yes, sir."

"Speak up. Why are you afeard here? I do not oppose you."

"Yes, sir."

"Much I believe, too, that every man might not only hold, but preach and do, in matters of religion what he must from God's voice within him. This I have fought for."

Something . . . he blots from my mind any belief that he has not acted from the bottom of his innocence. This room is so safe. All my spirit is at home in this color and twilight. I am melting, slipping into love with him who bids me so well. Where is Francis? I have been deceived and know not which deceives me. This rough soldier speaks so soft to the child within me.

"I have not slept this night for thinking of thee."

There is Francis. He will not look at me. He is angry with me because I suffer. He wants to be quit of me. I must alone, and look at this man who is fathering me.

Yes, I know you did not sleep the night and knew then that it was your candle that cast so pale a light across the dark gulf of the priory meadow, so that I, the only other one awake in Burford, was so near to you I could have spoken.

He makes me listen. "I thought of how I have sweet duties to perform that relieve me from the burden of this mighty kingdom. I have been at the arranging of a marriage for my son, and I thought of your father who cannot claim his right to see you on with life as he would have you, taking of your rightful place in the country, he who bragged so to me of your learning."

He bragged of me? Speak not. I must be wary. Why, I can feel my own heart heavy that he bragged of me and so long with my soul to turn again for blessing, to placate this man and all fathers, to be remembered by him as he sits by the fire at evening with his bandy leg upon a stool, and watch him smile a blessing at the thought of me. All I need to do is turn again and doff my hat, and this man waits so patiently for me to turn. I know it. I am naked and defenseless before him.

What was it Thompson warned? 'Tis my heartquake he plays on.

God, thou gavest me anger to do the work set out for me. Take not away that certain anger and replace it with a mealymouthed fatigue that makes the face smooth and slack to court blessing.

"This is a boy of learning?" one says at the back to Francis.

"Aie. Of learning and good parts and good family in Northamptonshire." I hear Francis speak low, sliding into the excuses for me of lands and right learning and scutcheons and connections that is an identity as deep as his blood. He does not know it has naught to do with me, stripped, standing here.

"He has only fallen among dangerous and seditious companions in the army," Cromwell explains to them. They try me together now as if I were not here. They all sound so weary of it all. I know of nothing that will satisfy these men but either my turning or my blood upon their hands. Only the general knows how he speaks and plays on one already within me to whom I am trained as dog to bend the knee, recant, and ask for the peace of forgiveness and defeat.

Will no one break this silence?

"You have much influence among these plain misguided men. You can stop a slaughter of them." Cromwell speaks as if we are alone. I am cold. Put not this burden on me, oh, Christ, put not this burden on me. "They have put their trust in you." We could be by a safe hearth with wine between us.

"I want no more than unity in this army and peace and safety. After that we can treat." Aie, as you promised before to treat? "Canst lead them back who have had a hand in their wayward guidance. . . . Show your contrition. . . ."

He has picked up a brass seal in his hand and turns it slowly, waiting for me to do what would ease this weight of expectation bred in me that fights with lonely conscience. He watches. He makes me feel foolish, such a little thing to do; my thoughts feel foolish. I have

been a man and dashed all before me and spoke out
and breathed deep; now I am a frail craft to stand in
the power of this man's certainty.

One who is less trained in patience breaks in: "We
want your words, boy, not your blood!"

Cromwell throws down the seal and leaves it tumbling across the table.

"By Christ's blood," he calls, furious, "can you not
wait? The boy's too dumb to speak quickly." The seal
thuds on the stone floor.

My mind is sweet and clear now with the tumbling
of the seal and the dropping of sweetness for that annoyance that rules those close to him. He has made
a mistake with me. He read youth and need of father
and played on that, but what he read not was my shame
at that need.

We weigh each other, he and I, and both are annoyed
by the watching of the others. He reads my inability to
turn. I cannot. Does he not know I cannot? I see in
him a longing to be forgiven that cannot be comforted
by all the power he takes upon himself to cover it.

"I would give you freedom," he says now. "I am not
so wedded and glued to forms that I cannot overlook
your transgressions."

He thinks he offers blessings when he offers bribes.
Does he no longer know the difference?

There are no more words, only the turning of the
wrist, the dropping of the dirt on the dead, obscene
face; I did not know before how inevitable the choice,
how perpetual is the taking place of the thing, the ever
asking of the question, the ever turning answer. How
frail a wrist is. There's the clock again.

"This boy is dumb with insolence," one calls. If only
he could smell this fear that nearly sinks me to my
knees. It is not insolence. It was over for me in the
night, this tired argument, and I am but a guest here.
You judge so sleepily, you Saints with the authority
that you say comes from God. Well, I never had a
choice but to join with the stumbling, slow growth of
lesser men than you, and blinder.

He knows he has lost and has no more need of me, who cannot use me. The kindness that made me tremble has gone from his face, wiped clean, and I see his fingers drum upon the table now, as when will it be over and this boy gone from me who did my best by him, and I can get on with the matters of greater import?

He thrusts back his chair and leaves the room without another glance at me. He does not do it in anger. I do not do what he says, and he can forget me for the time. One at the end of the table stretches, the council over and the shadows long. It is my Lord Fairfax, who has not suffered himself to be part of this. There is a smell of cooking, deep in the house.

Scrope, my commander, sits beside him. He finally speaks, in such calm fury. "He has condemned himself already when he owned the scandalous and seditious letter. We need no more of him." Thankful and I and all have ruined this man's career as a soldier. I had not thought of that before.

"He said not much," old Legality speaks, dissatisfied.

"He is too dumb. Have over for love of God. 'Tis late. We have been too long at this mean business." It is the fat voice. I cannot turn my head to look at him. We have indeed been at this business too long. Is the world a mad place that what these heavy old men say, will say, destroys my life? I have seen judges sit so. That one still picks and fondles at his nose. It is not our deaths, but the order and legality that are desired here that we may be blotted out from conscience, and these old men weed the young ever out of the garden they would make of England.

One clears his throat.

"A last question, I pray you, for the record." That same old Legality has stayed so upon the point all through this. "Are you an elected Agitator of this regiment?"

I cannot speak, only nod.

"Do you admit that you knew that to act so was against the law and punishable by death?"

A law we had no part in making . . . there is so much to say. I nod again. Why, these men have sat so rumbling and mumbling upon a king's death, wrestling with a convenient legality there too in some other great dark room. What have Thankful Perkins and Johnny Church in common with a king that they should fear us so and hunt us as foxes and run us to earth in Burford? No matter what old words they pile upon this fire, we are such pebbles and so soon forgotten that no horse would notice much less stumble on us. As king and Robbie and bird woman's blood mingles in me, will Thankful and I meet in some other vein?

"You must speak," he says, and I look up at him. Why, he is an old gaunt man and has his death upon him as I do.

"Yes," I say, and "Yes," I say again.

He nods, satisfied at last, and I am marched away. Behind me chairs scrape back.

Thankful catches me at the door and holds me.

"I did not doff my hat," I tell him, nearly falling.

Denne is gone. There are eight musketeers now, for we two dangerous men. They must make show of capture. They tie our hands behind us. We must march in twos, by file; a drummer leads us through the darkening garden. The muffled drum tolls out our footsteps. The evening lies softly on the town. We stop in the lane beyond the priory for a drover to drive his cattle back slowly through the village green. I am filled with the gentle peace of their lowing and the hollow pure sound of their bells.

The spire ahead of us gathers to itself the last faint light of the sun. Its stones shine pink. It was so long ago, the promise of its safety, and yet it is so calm, rising there into the sky pointing up to God. I stumble on the cobbles of the dark narrow street toward it. There are boys gathered to watch us pass. A stone hits my arm, and another my back. One hits Thankful's ear and makes him crouch for a second and straighten again. The boys rain stones now on us, easy targets, strangers and prisoners of the soldiers. The drum is

beating on ahead, ignoring our faltering. Behind the
children their parents maunch and stare. Why do these
stones hurt more than any other, who have just lost my
life that they may never kneel again?

"Aie, 'tis a long way to paradise," says Thankful,
dodging among the stones.

We are through the lich-gate and past the fine tombs
of the rich wool merchants. Over the door an idolatrous
Mary stands, her head lopped off by soldiers. We are
flung through the church door and lie there hog-tied on
the stone floor and hear the lock groan in the door
behind us. It is too dark to see. I hear one above me
call out, "Stand off there. Make room."

IREMEMBER that someone did take my
arm and haul me up and lead me through the darkness
and the sound of bodies and a seeming corridor of men
who called out, "Johnny," and, "Johnny, what's to
happen?" as if I were still leader and one to ask, and
there was a dry whispering, a warning of something not
yet words, and only one spoke loud, " 'Tis they that
cozened us," and then an old man's voice, "I know he."
The one who held my arm muttered, "Shut your mouth
and scratch your pox," and the words turned to the
sound of scratching that stayed in my ears.

Then I was lying down and could feel nothing because whatever the ordeal was, it was over, and I had
won in my eyes and not lost that in me, that core. I
could feel nothing but the core still there, untouched,
unmelted, as real as my heart or all those parts of me
I have always took for granted. It is that they will have
to shoot out of me.

I am getting used to the dim light that filters from
the windows, so high that some early light shadows the
vaulted concave of the nave. All along the walls the
stone tombs stand. Carved figures kneel in prayer in
their ruffs and pantaloons of other times. One, a woman,
lies asleep upon stone, faint light upon the brackish
blue of her old painted dress.

Outside somewhere one chops wood; the distant dull
thud of the mindless ax tolls at my nerves and draws
me into naked wakefulness.

It is growing lighter. All this night I must have slept
like one dead. Someone has spread straw for me on
this table tomb I lie on and made my bed. Such thought
of one unknown tears at me. I am too weak to bear
the kindness. 'Tis lighter. They are going to take me
out and kill me. My heart beats and my breath flows.
Oh, Christ. Let me be comforted just this little while.
Let someone touch me.

Faint, faint, the sounds of men awake and trying to
be quiet so as not to wake the others, and now the
darkness of the floor begins to pale, a floor of tomb-
size stones. All across it, flung down in sleep, leaning
against the arches, huddled among the tombs, there are
still stone lumps of men, far from one another. One
man lifts his head and seems to study the carvings of
faces at the roof beams, a laughing imp, a griffin, the
sad face of a woman, the corroded heads of lepers.
He scans them, sightless, and retreats again. His head
sinks into his own chest.

There must be three hundred men at least here, isolated among the tombs, as far as I can see along the
aisles, the nave, the side chapels, these lumps of men
waiting, penitent, alone.

The first light colors them. As those in prison,
quieter than the free, they seem to make the stone
floor begin to move, slow as old men, who were so
young yesterday or day before and wore passion on
their shoulders. Dawn shapes them among the richer
stones where the faces of bland men belie with art the
things rotting below these floors. How, now that I see

it as a prison, could men have thought to call on sweet God in this charnel house? These monuments among these hungry silent men; why, the bones below them have murmured and muttered in this place, reading Jesus into their desires, as the bumbling of the doves when I used to be in the loft then, bumbling to wit Jesus meant this, and to woo he meant no such thing, depending on who hungers and who owns the food, cross twisting prayers, dippling runs of words as the doves moan, but the eyes are the same and the beaks take in, take in, take in, and by God's grace give me a finer tomb than other to hide my death.

One moans. He lies below me, propped against my bed, and I see another, and another leaning there. I do not know this man, but I see something I know there in his eyes. He is what name? Will. Little Will we used to call him, for he is fifteen and has not yet his full growth. It was his golden curls we teased him for; he was so full of pride for them. He used to push his pot back when he thought none watched, so the girls could see his hair when we rode through the towns and he psalm singing loud and knowing the girls were watching his hair. The obedient Saints have cropped him for sport, as they do who are only the law removed from castrating after their wild rage after Naseby when some were hung for what they did there to tear away from the ungodly all trace of sex and carnal desire.

Will watches me, and I think he has for some while, waiting for me to wake. He is all naked and abashed, shrunk, his pate raw and obscene.

"Will?" I whisper.

"Aie, 'tis me." His chin bobbles that I must ask, but he does not let himself cry.

"They took naught that will not grow back."

"Not this time." He touches his ears and begins to smile, and then he stops and, prim as a girl, says, " 'Tis to punish me for vanity and carnal desire."

"No, Will. 'Twas in evil sport."

Why, his embarrassment is like a wound and calls for staunching. "Will, I am ashamed of you. God gave

you anger. Put it not away because of some mealymouthed fatigue that some would tell you is Christian
penitence."

My eyes cannot take in the wreck that has foundered
here. There is a smell of rags and blood I know for
wounds that fester. Too much fear and time have made
me silly. It is hard to pick out men I know at first, they
are so changed. I begin to see now what I knew would
be. There are many townsmen here, for the country
and woodfolk among us only sleep in peace near the
smell of forests, the scent that tells them they are free
men who know how to run where a horse cannot follow.

What rags they have made from their shirttails are
all they have to make their bandages. The light reaches
to the corners and finds men out who have crawled
there and flung themselves down apart. Men who can
are getting up. One starts to move, looks around, and
sinks down upon the straw litter that makes the church
a stabling for men as beasts, rises again, looks to satisfy himself that no one sees him, and then, his face
down, ashamed, hidden by his hair, he goes behind
the font, and I can hear his piss hit the stone wall. He
comes back again, past me, seeing nothing, and leans
down and mutters to one who leans against my tomb
who has been wounded in his shoulder.

"I'll help thee up, Praise God," he whispers, so as
not to wake the others who lie near.

We are too gentle with each other.

"Nay, I cannot," the one, Praise God, whispers back.

I cannot bear this tenderness, too near to tears.
They are being broken around me by the waiting, the
neglect, as carefully as a colt is broken to harness.

"What's this?" My voice is harsh. I make it so.
The Lord preserveth the simple.

I lean down beside this wounded man, whose eyes,
in animal surprise, look up at me, wondering.

"I have trouble," he whispers, and with his good
hand holds his stomach.

"Art wounded there as well?"

"Nay," the other tells me, above his head. " 'Tis that he cannot piss or shit within the church."

" 'Tis not right." Something of a twinge in his shoulder makes his face twinge. " 'Tis the house of God."

"I think a place is called what it is used for," I say to help him. "All fine tombs and gaudy glass make not a church here but a prison."

"Aie, I told him that. Come, try again, Praise God."

"Have you still the bullet in your shoulder?"

"Aie." He tries to save his own hurt as we help him up and let him lean on us. We move along a narrow path of stone, over the flung arms of sleeping men, and watched by some whose eyes only follow us as we pass, but do not see us. How wise Cromwell was in the evil he thinks of as his necessity to put these simple men within a church and use the awe they're bred to to melt them.

In the chapel where a lady and her husband lie under a fine canopy, on a carved bed, their hands met on their stomachers, their fingers pointed in perpetual prayer, they have put buckets, and the stench befouls the air to sickness.

Praise God squats obediently on a stinking bucket. "Look there." He points beneath the stone bed and tries to rise from the bucket. " 'Tis a skeleton of a man."

" 'Tis nothing. A conceit. 'Tis only carven there of stone."

"Didst ever see the like?" Praise God squats again and begins to strain.

Over his head I must ask the other, "How long have you been here?"

"Since Monday night or first dawn Tuesday morning. I was cudgeled out and all pillaged from me."

" 'Tis Wednesday. I marked the wall," another says. "Have et?"

"Nay." The man laughs. "That was a mighty trick upon us. They brought straw and water and buckets for to shit, and then did stand, one cornet I never saw before, and offer them that was penitent money to buy food. Some took it, but 'twas all a cruelty upon us. What food is left in Burford is hidden for higher price than we could pay. The soldiers have picked other clean."

"I cannot do it," moans Praise God.

"Come then." He plays the impatient mother. "They would have thee so. Dost give in so easy?"

All around us men sit upon the buckets, shrunk from each other, as if such withdrawing within their own skin could give them privacy. More wounded wait their turn, brought in by their fellows. I am fine tuned this gray cold time of morning, tuned to their playing on me. No one speaks to me who would two days gone have jostled at me and called my name out loud and played the fool with me. When I step out of the chapel, there is a little eddy away from me.

I say to one before he can turn and pretend not to hear me, "Where is Perkins?"

Too eager and ashamed of himself, he points across into the shadows of the far aisle.

Beside him, a man waiting to shit grins and says, "No popish incense and fine candle wax smell now."

The hollow morning is within my hollows.

They have avoided the place that was the high altar with their sleeping. There is a wide swath neglected around it, and beyond it, Thankful is propped against a tomb, staring at the east window, all scarlet, blue, and yellow of old saints and apostles whose glass feet are frozen on the glass green. Christ holds a lamb, and it stares down at Thankful.

"I know it to be idolatory, but it is fine to catch the light," he says, seeing me.

"No one speaks to me."

"No. Nor me either."

I can see all, as when in battle or hunting, all hungry and bright, but I can put no words. The blue is bluer, red redder, the yellow pierces me. I am hungry. Why, those old pains, those old wounds of the night are luxury to this bright hunger honing us for policy.

TIME is space now. I stare at the sun from the east window, traveling along the south wall all day long, until it filters in the window to the west, and I know the spire rides the sun over us, its shadow timing our spacious day. We forget each other and are forgot here. Talk tries to rise sometimes and sinks again. One or another moans in pain or heavy sleep, and no one moves to him. We are being carved as the tombs by waiting. No one comes to empty the buckets, and they overflow into the chapel floor, and the stench crawls toward us. All day no one has come near Thankful and me. Come, Johnny, my dear, did you not ask for the spire to cover you and give you rest? The inevitable granting of prayer is a fearsome thing. My soul cries out a fine whimper only. I wonder if these stones hear the rats scutter over them or my thin soul's wailing? Hell is made by men, carved slowly on one another.

My soul cries out a fine scree, this need not be. We use the tools of belief or cruelty or blindness or sport or old anger or quest for power, and all this need not be. There's a boy who has crawled into a corner and sleeps as if to sleep it all away until some trapdoor opens for him and he is free. Freedom's no fine thing; it is as simple as the opening of a door, or a ceasing of persuasions upon you, or a blessing. The east window is dull with evening. To bless and grant freedom are the same. We are in prisons of other men's beliefs. God made us; we make beliefs. What was it I was thinking just then? Aie, of the boy asleep. I would not now desire to put so much as the weight of my breath upon

him or diminish a hair of his head, my heart there
snoring, whose face I cannot see. If he is let out of
here, and it is night, and he is by some fire in a room
he knows he can leave, then much that is of Christ will
be there in him, unnamed, naked, and sweet. Perhaps
he will laugh of a sudden, and one ask why, and he
will say, "I know not." I could only have opened the
door for him, and not even that now, for freedom's no
thing of air and argument, but 'tis as simple as the
opening of a door; no fine thing, but as rare as the
pearl of Jesus.

How many days here? My mind is dim. Some, I
think, have spoken with us, but I cannot recall them.
What was unthinkable? Something that was unthinkable we did and now is thinkable and can never bury
itself and be forgot again. We walked forth in green
fields for a while without the blessing of our fathers.
Let me be. Leave off shaking of my arm. By the darkness it is some nightfall, somewhere. . . .

"Johnny, Johnny! God damn me, what easing off is
this?" One shakes my arm again. Why am I here,
crouched below the font? When did Thankful and I
move here, to these heavy shadows?

"Aie, where's my young statesman, you sniveling
boy?" The words flow strong, like wind into my
bowels. 'Tis Gideon MacKarkle, thank Christ, come
to chide me, and I thought him dead. Why do I thank
God for his capture? Here he is as naked and scarecrow
as when I first saw him. "I thought you dead," I
whisper.

"I fell in an orchard and played dead until 'twas
quiet, but they cotched me at the river anyhow."

"What day is it?"

"Still Wednesday. You asked me that before."

"No one's come?"

"I heard nothing from without but the dogs bark.
We're left to cool our heels. None has yet died." He
answers a question I have not asked. "And thee?"

I had persuasions in me once; but they are gone, and

I am clean of them, weightless, empty of all. Surprised, I tell him, "I dreamed something."

He settles down to hear the story, as he has always done. I cannot persuade this gnarled tree that one can go to Oxford for anything beside learning astrology and the reading of dreams.

"I dreamed that all that sets men apart from the beasts is the act without hope of reward."

"Oh, that." He looks away, disappointed. "Then there's little man and much beast in us. I like not the temper of the men. Who would have thought that old Ironsides would be quick enough to use hunger to ruin us?"

"God told him to," says Thankful, who has not spoken for so long I had forgot him. He laughs in a way I have not heard him do before.

"I have never heard you cynical." I pull at his doublet to make him look at me, and when he does, it is with the same surprised smile as ever.

"It is no cynicism to see what is true," he tells me.

"Aie, he hath a convenient God in his ear." Mac-Karkle understands as I do not.

Silence interrupts and covers us again. A few pitch-pine torches have been lit by the men and cast a cold light along the aisles, not the warm yellow glow of beeswax cast from the altar here once onto worshiping faces and softening them, but intruding on us, seeking us out, making the arches jut out in the dark like bones.

"Hast heard news?" Perkins asks MacKarkle.

"Naught. We are in Coventry."

This waiting is knife-sharp and edged to screaming.

"THIS IS NONE OTHER THAN THE HAND OF GOD THAT YOU ARE BROUGHT SO LOW!" one, far away in the nave, screams out, flushes up, panicked; his shadow grows to the roof beams beyond the harsh light.

"I expected this," MacKarkle says.

One calls, "Shut that man up. He is sent to delude us."

Already the spirit moves one and then another. They are rising up from the floor.

A man calls, "Repent ye, for the day of the Lord is at hand!"

Someone calls out, "Another sent to cozen us."

But men are beginning to roll upon the floor, the spirit upon them, and moan and move, waking to some thing so new and terrible that I would I had died before I saw it begin. Their bodies flicker, dancing on the stones. One sobs; another swears. Thankful shouts, "Quit! Ye play into his hands!" He runs among them, grabbing at their shirts. One scratches his face, screaming no words.

I would rather have died than see how we are maneuvered into this distrust of one another. I must run forward and pick the man off Thankful and lead him back to us by the font. He says nothing.

Is this the way we are defeated, without a blow from them, to be torn from one another and left all alone in fear of one another's whispers, our words used as weapons of mistrust, our sorrows held in, as Thankful does now, so that others might not have to pay for them? So we have come to be afraid to speak to one another but wait for doors to open and die of waiting. The dead will seem to win if they make us dream only of past or future, as men in prison mark the days upon a wall. This crying out below reason offends me; this penitence, this jump to the lash within, this fear, stink in my nostrils.

Someone flings the church door wide, and the tongue of last evening light shows men fallen to their knees and sobbing against the arches. Christ crucified! No one looked at us when we were still brave. This they have waited for.

SHADOWS whip high up the walls of the temple. One shadow soldier lifts a scourge and brings it down on another. How brotherly are shadows. They are clearing the aisle, sweeping it with whips. There is only the flogging and moan and scurry of men as they try to get out of their way.

Musketeers file in and stand guard while the solemn officers flow through their ranks, lit by tapers carried before and behind. Such ceremony is false pitched to my hunger.

"I thought it," MacKarkle whispers. "Earlier they sent in townsmen to clean the shit and burn pine."

I have been too deep in this dark waiting and had not seen it. The air is indeed new and scented with pine. Somewhere high in the spire, they have climbed up from the outside and opened windows.

"What is it of churches that makes men move so slow?" says Thankful, not to me, but to MacKarkle. "It looks so foolish."

"There is Henry Denne with them."

"Art surprised?" Thankful could be teasing with me.

"I wonder when we first knew of him?" I have forgot this.

"Some. . . . I cannot think. . . . His movements were writ too black . . . somewhat not his own. Hast noticed how Henry's penitence takes him ever upward?"

There is an unhallowed thing in this church, lit as an armed camp. The wind-tossed pitch-pine torches make our eyes blink against the thrusts of light. One is ensconced below the pulpit. It exposes the soldier's face who climbs there, and his helmet tosses huge against the wall behind. All the rest is plunged into darkness, and the men loom out of it, white-faced, caught in white light.

Why is there a rolling of drums and the officers standing so before the altar? They make a stage, and Harry is before them, his hands chained, suffering too much in too much light.

Pray, God, let him not speak.

The drums stop, and the silence that had retreated to the walls covers us again. Fear is a hollow thing. MacKarkle puts his hand upon my shoulder.

"That whereas the Lord General Fairfax hath appointed officers to his command to sit upon a council of war for the trying of various and sundry soldiers of Scrope's and Ireton's regiments on charges of mutiny and the spreading of disaffection and dangerous sedition among the army in time of war. . . ."

"There is no war!" one calls, and I hear the running of feet, a blow, silence.

Little Will has edged closer to us. Ahead of us there is a wall of soldiers, packed close, mild in the light of the pulpit.

"And whereas when apprehended by their lawful officers they did raise up arms against them. . . ."

"Aie, a fine fight in our shirttails," mutters Mac-Karkle.

"And for other crimes and misdemeanors against the Commonwealth of England, the findings of this court are as follows: that for the crimes of sedition, mutiny, and high treason, Cornet Thompson and Cornet Denne are condemned to be taken from this prison and to die before a firing squad by shooting."

Harry sways and would fall but that an officer steps forth and grabs his arm. I cannot see Thompson or Francis. Would you not watch this, Francis? Is the shutting of your eyes your absolution?

"That for sedition and the dangerous spreading of disaffection by the writing of false letters and the putting them among the soldiers and for leading them so in the way of mutiny and disobedience, the two elected Agitators, elected against the law and discipline of the army, Corporal Thankful Perkins and Corporal Jonathan Church will be taken from thence and put to death before a firing squad of their fellow soldiers."

I thought to have known this before, but now I hear it, 'tis a wall of stone. MacKarkle's hand is light upon my shoulder. The flares spread and swim before my eyes. Let no water fall from my eyes, lest the soldiers think I betray them by penitence. It is only that I am twenty years old.

"That there be a fault deserving of death in them that are least guilty among the mutinous troops, all these men captured here are condemned to death by shooting before a firing squad."

What will they do with us? Why, we will make a charnel pile that reaches to heaven. The light touches the stone merchants praying. The lady in the painted blue dress lies with her fingers pointed so delicately to God. What a pretty thing. Will no one speak?

"Mark Hurst, death."

"Matthew Brown, death."

They have made a form of this to suit the prison. All stand still as for a muster roll, read by that one who flickers there. The names are tolled out in the dark spaces.

"John Roper, death."

"Simeon Roper, death."

Brother's name falls on a wild sobbing.

"Anthony Sedley, death."

"Gideon MacKarkle, death."

"I thought to die in battle, not like this, just stood up there and shot," he says, and I do not think he knows he spoke.

"William Dogood, death." Now they will cut all of you down, not just your pretty hair.

"Praise God Thomas, death."

"William Pinck, death."

" 'Tis Panck," says a mild voice behind me. He is forever correcting of his name.

"John Cantloe, death."

How long has this been going on, this tolling of the names? A hundred now? Two hundred? The lights grow brighter and the shadows black. Every man's face is like no other in this world was. The east window is a black mouth. The light fingers the bottom and brightens the green glass field, the lamb of glass. To be prepared so bravely for to die and to know the when and where of it are a different thing.

"Thomas Atkins, death." That man's hope must have grown, thinking himself forgot. He is the last. The torch burns low. The pulpit is empty.

Now another is helped into the pulpit. Hark him stagger and fall against the wood. A new torch is lit and flows up over the livid face of Henry Denne. He raises his head and eyes to pick God from the rafters and bring Him down among us, and he groans a great groan. How familiar the voice is. How many times he's played on us.

"Brothers, I stand before you as one condemned to death, and I have so much remorse of conscience for being the occasion to lead others in this way of mutiny and disobedience that I know I am not worthy of mercy. I am more ashamed to live than afeared to die." His voice hits hard against the stone. "Oh, God forgive me." He is reveling in this, rolling in guilt and revelation. He sings, "Thou hast spared me by thy terrible sword of justice from the sin of plunging this land into more misery and ruin. Look down upon they children. Melt their hearts and cleanse them who are condemned here to death with me for their transgressions."

He is using their sorrow and trying his words in their ears. I could kill him now, and God forgive me for it. He will change these hungry men and mold them to shame. Will no one stop him, no one cry him nay?

"Good God, what a damned lick ass is here!" Mac-Karkle speaks loud enough to turn the soldiers toward him, but they are stopped by the loud clanking of Harry's chains on the pulpit.

"Out of jealousy and repinings at the felicity of our betters we have condemned the generation of the just, and out of the unthankfulness of our hearts we have acted on flying reports. My deep crime, oh, by God's body that died for us, I do abhor it. We have helped to mislead the well affected of this nation. . . ."

Thankful leans forward slowly, and the vomit pours from his mouth. I hold his body and feel it heave under my hands.

"When's he et?" MacKarkle holds the other side of his body. "I fear the dry heaves."

Somewhere Harry keeps on yelling; it is not enough that he befouls us, but he must do it long and loud.

"We would have made a breach in this victorious army by forcing one in fury to destroy the other to bring down upon us a more desperate condition than before and to hamstring the sinews of this mighty land."

"Them be not even his own pocky words," I hear a man say behind me. "Hamstring the sinews. The general speaks that way."

Another answers him. " 'Tis all well with him, that ranting and raving. No officers are shot. They are always pardoned before and the soldiers shot." Thank God he has not played on them.

One of the musketeers moves forward now, close to us to hear us.

"But we have been led out of this desperate and dangerous enterprise by God's hand."

"What of your brothers, Harry, what of all men in the kingdom of their building?"

I must have whispered, for Thankful answers me. He is sweating and paper white. "Now, Johnny, quit that. He does nothing we knew not in our hearts he would do if needs must." He seems relieved. He has vomited out Denne.

MacKarkle takes a piece of jerk from his shirt. "Here, I did save it. Chew it slow, get not shot apuking. It has no dignity."

I never knew I had been caught in this crying around

us until Thankful wipes my face with the palm of his
hand.

"Johnny, nobody asked for our lives. We offered
them. Aie, and our love too for that matter. Nobody
asked." He who I would comfort comforts me.

Denne is saying something to make these men melt
and sway.

"You would go back to your farms and your wives
and children and the place in life God has seen fit
to bless you withal, see spring, plant crops, and fish
the seas of God's bounty. . . ."

One sobs, another moans and moans, will nothing
stop this man's obscenity who stands there and breaks
them of their sweet new pride?

"But at least ye need not go to your Saviour without
the penitence that cleanses you as I am cleansed before
you." He waits and knows he has succeeded. Before
God, that man is sincere in the evil he does and even
joins them howling and weeping so that he does lead
them in song. Suddenly his voice rises clear over the
shadows.

"We have therefore cause to say blessed be the Lord
who gave us up into the hands of Oliver who has followed us here like the one who sought out the lost
sheep, and blessed be His Excellency of the Lord who
has been so happy an instrument to withhold our
hands from the blood and ruin of our nation."

Now those who have crowded near him wail and
sway as they are wont to have done always when he
spoke to them, but some are moving back so close to
us that I am trapped by them, by our sweat and stench
of animal fear that no courage of spirit can take from
our bodies.

"We are going to die," Harry cries in a loud voice,
and then, nearly whispering, "Justly does the Lord dis-
own us to teach all men that he is a God of law and
order and just authority and not of confusion."

Now at last, he stops, and someone cries "Amen,"
and another is sobbing for his mother. One near us, a

quiet man, is swearing as deep as prayer, "A foul pox on that traitorous canting son of a mangy bitch."

Harry throws up his manacled hands as one blind and is led down from the pulpit, suppliant to the air. Why have I fallen into calling him Harry? I do not know this man.

The very floor and air are crawling. Out of sight behind the men close-packed around us, some have fallen in prayer, for I hear snatches of it in the dark and the lilt of some taken by the spirit. Oh, my sweet Lord, hold me up, I pray thee, for this is a contagion; it fair pulls me down. Thankful and MacKarkle and I hold hard to each other to keep from falling among them. It is not what he has said, those false and studied words, but the calling out of my brave friends so mild and beaten. I cannot look at them, but only at my old boots. Thankful's vomit has splashed on them. No matter. I'll find more. Now that is strange, never to need boots more, or simple things.

Denne has been led down among the men. Some of them fawn on him, push at each other to get nearer.

Over me, MacKarkle and Thankful comment with the cool irony of angels. I am bogged down, foundered here between them. Their whisperings are my shore in this foul sea of sorrow.

"That man knows well what ears to place his guilt in. Look at Oliver," MacKarkle whispers. The general sits in the bishop's chair, with his head down and cupped in his hand. "And them there. Some dogs love men the more by how much they beat them."

"They are only weak and scared and hungry," Thankful answers.

So I too must watch. Did I say in the night that I must face all of the terrors all of the time? Beyond this there may be light, if I'll not fail now. Come, Johnny, leave off the gazing at your own boots and watch him there, blessing his flock with manacled hands. Oh, 'tis a noble and martyred gesture, that. It will not be women as with Francis that Denne waits out his life with. It will be prayer and a parish like to this one, and he will cringe before some man like my father, who will sit stern in the front pew and weigh his puny living by what he speaks.

But he will always see us.

I must have spoke aloud again, for Thankful answers, "Nay, you make him see with your own eyes. It is a sweet fault with you, Johnny. I think he will be somewhat content and have a luxury of life and guilt more airy and less named." His voice is gentle, as always, but his hands tremble as one with drink. He can hardly get the jerk to his mouth.

"Some here have prepared a letter," a new voice calls from the pulpit. They are taking turns at playing on these backs.

"I'd admire to know when," MacKarkle is muttering. "I would have thought that breaking covenant with us was enough."

"Hell's fire, 'tis only their turn today. 'Twill be ours tomorrow," I hear, and one beyond the voice says, "Amen, brother," and can laugh, but they speak their bravery low so the soldiers with the knouts will not hear.

"I will go to Virginia, God damn it," says the one pressed against the font.

"You will go nowhere," MacKarkle answers him, and they laugh between them.

There is much scrambling and shuffling at the pulpit, a rumble of talk, and finally the stage is ready again. It is one of their horse preachers Cromwell likes so well, and he holds the paper up of this paper war that is waged to our deaths.

"Out of the deep penitence and sorrow and that they may go to God with clean hands of repentance, that they may be washed in the Lamb's most precious blood. . . ."

"Get on," an officer whispers behind him, but we can hear.

"To His Excellency Thomas Lord Fairfax Lord General of all the Parliament's Forces."

"Damn, sink fuck, and bugger his excellency." The

man against the font speaks a quiet litany while the preacher pauses for effect.

Something hurries his voice for once in his life, to slide upon the words he reads, "The humble petition of the sad and heavyhearted prisoners remaining in the church of Burford. In all humbleness showeth, that your petitioners are very sensible of the odious wickedness of their fact, how liable it renders them to the wrath and displeasure of God, how destructive the same might have been to the being of this nation, and therefore cannot but acknowledge the sentence of death passed upon them by your excellency and the Council of War, very just and equal. . . ."

"Why, they prepared the letter before the sentence was read," MacKarkle must speak what we all know.

"Your petitioners nevertheless do most earnestly and heartily beg and implore your mercy toward them, by omitting the severity and strictness of their just deserved sentence. . . ."

The men are listening as carefully as if they had indeed wrote the letter, pondered on it and argued as we did at Salisbury.

Now he goes so fast that I cannot follow and, as the end of the letter comes near, reads slower and with the same unction he would use for the word of God of a Sunday.

". . . and extend the bowels of your compassion toward them by omitting the execution of your just sentence and inflicting such other punishment upon them as they are able to bear, which will very much magnify your excellency's Christian temper, in receiving such detestable offenders to mercy. So it will ever engage and endear us to your excellencies and the Commonwealth's service. And your poor heavyhearted petitioners, as in duty bound, shall daily pray for your excellency."

"Them's Denne's words. 'Tis a right ugly thing," Thankful whispers to me.

"Aie, I know them to be, but they do not. I fear they may think we writ it as the other."

Oh, my sweet and broken lads, do not crowd so to sign that thing and go to death ashamed of yourselves. Some hold their hands up into the light. I cannot see them for the thick darkness, only their white hands.

The preacher is speaking down into their hands, low, I cannot hear him. I would I had not seen this. I fear me I will learn more of life in these hours before my death than in all the twenty foggy years before. What weighs is not evil, we knew and fought that, but the bowing of our friends before it. Resist not evil? Aie, but do not rename it for the convenience of your souls and bow and scrape and call it Christian living.

The shadow of his hand moves down the wall as he passes the paper below him. The swaying shadow men that climb and bend along the arches and flow across the faces of the stone lepers and ladies seem to watch down on us, then dance and twist, and pause again as the soldiers come among the men with their torches, hauling them to their feet where some still kneel in prayer to sign their names or make their marks.

I can only see by the turning of their heads as they lean into the light that it moves slowly, signed and signed again. But I lose heart, my ever-grievous fault. MacKarkle does not move, nor Little Will, nor that man at the font base, nor that one leaning against a praying stone landlord. As many are falling back toward us, as if we were the center that they choose. What a final choice is this for them. One even looks over his shoulder and winks and bites his thumb.

I would see better. What is happening? The soldier with the paper comes toward us through the clutch of men. Musketeers beat his way. He thrusts now the paper toward Little Will.

"I will not sign that. I never writ no such thing." His voice is clear and carrying.

A musketeer has took his arm and pulls at it.

"Nay," Little Will calls out, "I will not sign. You are going to kill me anyhow."

The musketeer does force him to the floor, and he

with the paper, I do not know him, he is not of us, stands over him.

"Nay, I will not," we hear from the floor.

The gun barrel rises, shadowed mast high along the wall, and it seems to move down slowly and churn up to the eaves and down again, thumping and thumping against a body. I can hear it on his flesh. Musketeers have forced their way through the crowd and hold us all away. There is only the drumming on the flesh of his body and silence all around.

They leave him there, still on the floor, and when they have marched away, one leans down and lifts him up. His face is bloody, and his eyes are glazed over. We bring him to the font, where there is water.

"I did not sign, did I?" he mumbles through his swollen lips.

"Nay, didst not," Thankful speaks softly.

But he has already forgot. "Tell me I did not sign," he begs and clutches at Thankful's jerkin and smears his blood on him.

It has all changed behind us. This beating has hardened them somewhat, and they turn away when the letter is brought near. Little Will has freed us for this moment. We had lodged on fear and now float up from it. The men watch, unmoved now, as the soldiers pass. One runs to them and whispers, and they move back along a file of men toward the pulpit. The men watch as calmly as if they watched players at a fair. I cannot see over them until one, no, the same preacher climbs up to the pulpit stairs into the light, fumbling with his red cap. He holds the letter up.

Cromwell is in a fury. I can tell. He would want all to sign, all of them to make a legality for him. He does not look at us as the preacher starts to speak again.

"Your sad and heavyhearted plea does not remain unanswered." Someone laughs, and the soldiers move in toward the laughter.

"Your penitence has so moved the heart of our General Cromwell that he has prayed of His Excellency Lord Fairfax. . . ."

"Damn and sink that cipher. He would have us believe that a man rides under orders of his horse," MacKarkle grumbles.

The preacher knows well how to pause, indeed.

"And . . . by God's grace . . . I am so touched I cannot speak. . . . He has pardoned thee."

Something pent within this church goes out, a great sigh, and one says, "Thanks be to God," and another, "Amen." In their relief they do not hear the gun butt on the body of the man who laughed too loudly.

"But for those who have been your ringleaders, Cornets Thompson and Denne and Corporals Perkins and Church, they will be taken thence and put to death by shooting, God be praised, as a warning to all high and peremptory rebellious men who would lead the simple men of this Commonwealth into mutiny, anarchy, and rebellion."

"While God has such men on earth to preach his word, we need no hell," MacKarkle says.

Thankful is as serious with his answer as if he had not been twice condemned. "I believe not in hell. We make it so. Aie, and heaven too. 'Tis only politics that sets it so all safely before and after," and falls again to listening to the preacher so that I wonder if he has heard the sentence. He only puts his hand up to his eyes, and bows his head, then drops his hand and straightens again, and I know he has heard.

It was only a glimpse of the doors opening with us. I am so far from you who will live longer. Some emptiness has opened between us too great to cross. I want to apologize, I know not what for.

T HE spirit of the Lord has called upon Oliver.

My bowels are water. What prayers I have now! Oh, God, let me not befoul myself before the others.

The man stands, waiting up there above us, as one stopped in midstride, who yearns to be let alone, but will attend to us for a pause between some private matters, though it pain him. It is pain he shows, as if he could only bear it in silence, lest interruption break the bloody thread of it. When he turns his head slowly sideways, as one who listens, and his eyes roll upward out of the light that the torches toss across his face, it makes him look as one already dead.

"By God's wounds," he calls at last, a harsh call, angered with righteousness, "I will not have the stealing of your hearts and the splitting of this great army I have made into peremptorous and hotheaded factions." His voice is risen as if it would break like a boy's, and he must needs control it and speak more simply. "By the hard labor of my soul before my God I have come to what I must say to you. In these latter days. . . ." He speaks alone with air as one now who prays aloud, and his face speaks beyond his words, a man tormented, as if he cried out instead, let me do that for them they do not fathom and let them not weary me so while I am about it. For a pause he seems to forget we are before him in the flesh, but only a preoccupation for his singular and wandering spirit.

"Oh, Oliver"—MacKarkle speaks low and in a new

sorrow to him—"how we have fed and watered thee and let thee grow to this!"

Then, with a hard mastery of himself, visible in his muscles, he remembers we are before him, and he must be something to us, something . . . and seems to shake his head to clear it.

"I am but a poor farmer like you, a father like some, a son as all are whose mother is even at this moment in her last hour. But you will henceforth go out in peace into the bowels of England and live your lives without so mighty a burden as I carry on me. For it will be I who am driven by God to care for you, dearest hearts who have been led astray and who have fretted against the will of God. I am not ashamed to kneel before you here. God must first be sought for his guidance by you who have been given new life."

And all, some shirttailed, even the musketeers and pikemen, are falling to their knees. I hear their armor clank as they arrange themselves, kneeling in their apology to this wounded man. This bending of the knee is a mighty current that tries to pull me down among them, for there is that in me, too, who is only at home when I am filled with prayer's spacious lodging. But I must not fall; I must not. I must make my prayer straight and keep my wits high and be a man to those who kneel there, not child bending so, for it trains the knee to evil things. Oh, Jesus, my body does long to cringe, to cry, to fall. But then I will not, no, God's grace keep me from it. Thankful beside me does not kneel, for the first time since I have known him when prayer was called.

What shame of soul is in this bending of the knee. I think the conscience that can be played on lodges there, for it obliterates all in its zeal to obey. They can kneel before one who with a scratch of goose quill took all their lives and with another scratch has granted it again. I cannot, though one within me is betraying me by crying to go home in old clothes of beliefs that no longer fit me. Then I would be unworthy in my eyes, but not in him who would defeat me, for such a shame of soul is food to his vision of himself up there. He would give me, too late, full favor, love, the fatted calf at the wrong time and for the wrong reasons, my cowardice mistook as Christian courage.

And still they pray. One hauls his weight from one ham to the other, and still they wait for him to say that their prayer is over. They will go back to poverty, stripped of all, who see their liberty now as fields and fathers, and lilac and laburnum and the love of a woman. He calls them dearest hearts and is grief-stricken that they have fretted against the will of his God. Fret! So small a word for so much blood. How nimble he is by nature; why, his soldier-father awkwardness is nimble. I, who would not harm so much as a hair of their heads kneeling there, must watch while they diminish themselves, plunder and strip their own souls on this stone floor, leak out their man's pride, break their own spirits under those clouded eyes, and give up their credulous innocency as a gift to him who would cleanse them as rust from his private kingdom.

Thankful has turned and took me in his arms.

I thought that with the work we have done that never again would the son kneel in his father's presence, but treat with him as a man, and father no longer have power to withhold blessing from his growth, for to bless and grant freedom are the same. Not the gun butt or the cudgel conquers them, but the infinite sadness of the turned head and the closed door, the mind's curse unspoken, the power of the sigh.

And still they pray on, and still Thankful holds my head against his shoulder, and still there is the movement of their bodies, and once a sneeze. They do not break, they melt, for freedom's a costly thing and rare, and they grow tired. Why do they let themselves be brutalized by those who do not see them separately in the street, but a mass to conjure with; why teach a doctrine in Christ's name that murders many a poor heart that is bashful and simple and cannot speak for itself?

No one needs to seek the sheep that is lost, for it

wanders back from its own break for freedom, from being too long its own father.

They are all rising with Oliver, who stands now and calls in some ecstacy, "Blessed are the pure in heart was what I heard from my Lord!" His weariness is gone. He has been fed there, on his knees, by the silence of his demanding and the breaking of their spirits. Why, he looks rested. We few who did not kneel have been culled from his mind, already, not dead, but forgotten.

Will is with us still and has not knelt, and those others who came toward us at the signing of the letter have stayed close, though they did kneel.

"The pure in heart who have been so misled from the place God has seen fit to put them and led into envy and malice. How my heart went out to you when I was told how you did refuse money for food in such contrition and Christian humility, saying 'twas more meet to prepare for heaven than the things of earth."

He believes this, and now I see that they believe it, too. Yet there is no reaching out between him and them. He speaks from behind a wall of terrible certainty.

"Why, Thankful, yonder man is crazy in his health," I whisper.

"I do believe it; then the more dangerous."

"You innocent and penitent . . ." he calls over their heads.

"At least, thank Christ I ain't innocent and I ain't penitent," MacKarkle says aloud, but he looks around without knowing to see if he has been heard by other ears. Is this what you have done, turned even Mac-Karkle's blood to buttermilk to make him glance over his shoulder so? Damn you. That clears the last compassion for your sickness from me, and I am freed of pity. I send you anger to your face, and I need no more of Thankful's shoulder to lean on.

"They have conspired to mislead you and influence you to your public destruction and ruin. What they told you was liberty of conscience was but carnal reasoning writ large. . . ."

Someone behind us yells out, "It's your turn today, but 'twill be our turn tomorrow. . . ."

The musketeers move forward from the walls. Cromwell does not flinch at the sound of the gun butts. "I would that all men should seek God in the way that God calls them. You know me for a Seeker as one of you, but I will say, as Christ said of such matters. My kingdom is not of this world."

"The devil it is not, damn you," MacKarkle mumbles and picks his nose.

"They cozen you who say other and let envyings and strife place greater burdens on those whom God has called to rule over you in peace, even so your fathers, your magistrates, your appointed officers. If all men have a voice in their own ruling and think and worship as they please, even Jesuits and atheists and libertines and other disordered men, and men without any interest but their own opinions, who have naught to lose in the things of this world, where will it end but in anarchy when there is no bound or limit set? Give me leave to tell it you again. We must set aside these misguided notions and carry on our business, which is God's business of subduing Ireland."

MacKarkle throws his snot toward the pulpit. "Unless we fetch all our water from his well. . . ."

It is too hard to listen or think. I know he is still there, but I cannot keep track of his raving. No matter, for it is old words, and he is already an old man, usurping in our hearts our father's place. I need you not, Oliver, as metaphor for my father, but there's your danger, for father's a fathom's deeper need than lover, and the war with you is ever-lasting, for it is against the slavery within and the easy fall of the knees. Some see themselves grown great in you and clothe themselves in Cromwell. As for the others, why, you have not touched them but only took their horses so they will have to limp away, that is all.

"We will cleanse this land of confusions!" Now, by

his yelling like a fishwife Ranter, he intrudes again on me. "I have a warrant from God to do my duty to make this land of England a place fit for the Saints. I promise you, I promise you"—he is tired and has lost the thread again—"I promise you as our God has promised me"—he pauses and his voice speaks poetry —" 'Thou shalt no more be termed Forsaken; neither shall thy land any more be termed Desolate: but thou shalt be called Hephzibah, and thy land Beulah: for the Lord delighteth in thee, and thy land shall be married!' "

"Thou pocky whore's son." MacKarkle comforts himself.

Thankful must giggle and turn it to a cough because it is Scripture and a sin to laugh.

Finally he is finished with us and sits again, his head in his hand, back to whatever preoccupation he was called out from to speak to us.

IT is dark, thank God, and they are gone at last. What's waked me? There is only left from their presence here a faint scent of pine in the blackness. I sense a sad, exhausted peace here in dark, as men after lust.

When will they kill us? In the morning, with the cows driven past, will they blot me out, or afternoon, keeping the children from play to watch so that they will be scarred in their minds with what happens to rebellious children? Will some bird woman be there, blaming me for her sorrow as that one did blame the king?

"Who is awake?" I whisper. "Thankful, are you awake?"

"Aie."

"What doing?"

" 'Comfort ye, comfort ye my people.' " It was that whisper woke me. "I have got to there. It is so beautiful a thing, Isaiah, that I thought to say it all to myself and savor it once again."

In and out of sleep I try to drive off now and cannot. I drift through the night hours and Thankful's murmuring.

" 'Hast thou not known?' " I hear him once. " 'Hast thou not heard, that the everlasting God, the Lord, the Creator of the ends of the earth, fainteth not, neither is weary?' " His words flow, there is the sound of scratching and too much black space. " 'There is no searching of his understanding. He giveth power to the faint; and to them that have no might he increaseth strength. Even the youths shall faint and be weary, and the young men shall utterly fall.' " It is the scratching of Thankful's nails on the stone. He is searching for my hand, and now he clasps it. Thank my God for that warmth more than words of men and promises.

" 'But they that wait upon the Lord shall renew their strength; they shall mount up with wings as eagles; they shall run, and not be weary; and they shall walk, and not faint. Keep silence. . . .' "

Must drift . . . must not waste these hours. I would hold them with his voice. There is a faint lifting of the darkness, the vague line of a tomb there. His hand lies against mine, as if it were asleep and not he. His voice flows on: . . . " 'to open the blind eyes, and bring out the prisoners from the prison, and them that sit in the darkness out of the prison house.' " That has driven him to tears. Why, that's a child crying there.

I can see the wall now, and the sleeping men, and the upthrust of those perpetual stone hands. I know one of my father, foul and old, who is fed gold powder to keep alive and so turns privilege and acres into life.

Thankful has gone beyond Isaiah and sobbed himself to sleep, his arm flung out, his body open and tender, as sleep brings trust back to his limbs.

I must not sleep, must see, be at the edge of my life for the time left. Something is urgent. I know not what its name is. Oh, I am quiet this side of a great howl my body pulls me to, its sperm and blood and humors, me here, my flow of me. Oh, how graceful a man is, and never one like the other. What silent songs his life sings.

In the first dawn I see the space around us. We smell of death to them. In the night the others, not knowing what they do, have crawled away from us as animals ring around the dying and make a fairy circle. It is too fearsome for them to come closer, for they see us no longer as leaders or bearers of tidings, but crying, clinging, fearsome, honest souls. MacKarkle has not left us, nor Little Will either. His bare pate is cradled on MacKarkle's leg, the blood dried on his face.

I did dream it or did hear sometime in the darkest night that they plan to go to the colonies, to Virginia. They were bolstering one another up with tales of fine acres just for the taking and the girdling of some trees.

"Not so either," one beyond them said. "The land is took up by the grandees there as here. Ye go all that way and still ye pay to some landlord somewhere." I think of my father and his investments in the New World to bolster his illusions in the Old.

"Why, ye can go into the Indian lands." I heard another voice.

"Aie, and lose your hair," another added, and began to sing softly:

Give ear unto a maid,
That lately was betrayed
And sent into Virginia, O,
In brief I shall declare
What I have suffered there
When I was weary, weary, weary, weary, O. . . .

And weary, weary lulled us all asleep again.

I dreamed there was a great deep sea and beyond it all Virginia, where the savages were red and ten feet tall and dressed all in ostrich plumes. After all the terrors of abandoning to the sea, the other shore was just as this one is, and I thought, I can dream only what I already know, even though I have come here. One served me comfit upon a china tray as gentry does and curtsied, with great ribbons in her hair. It was Thankful's pretty little Ranter slut. All was the same as before when the sea went back from them after the heartbreak of the crossing over.

But I heard another voice say, and it was not a dream, "I am freeborn and bow to no man nowhere."

MacKarkle answered him, whispering, "Nay, you take yourself. I cannot uproot my whole family again. They already boo-hoo for the Highlands. Walk to Bristol, lad, you must needs walk there to sign on for a ship. . . ."

Dreaming, I flowed in the sea again, and on the horizon were the ships, slowly moving, courageous, and blind in the water that receives our tears and does not concern itself with the source of its rolling strength.

There now are the cries of the birds of every morning. Morning breaks and brings color through the stained glass windows. Thankful is waked by them and turns and opens his eyes and stares at me as if I were a stranger.

"Where are we?"

"In the church still."

He puts his arm behind his head. "You know, I had all those persuasions in me, but they are gone, and I am cleared of the weight of them. I feel much joy in me."

Away in the distance the clock over the priory strikes. No time. No matter now. Was all this done in vain, all this blood and wounds and fear? I know not. It is too late to play at such questions.

Thankful touches me. "Break not thy pretty spirit, Johnny. Send on defiance."

Aie, I will that, for I have learned defiance of a king's gesture and a bird woman. I pray they will murder a free heart.

We are watched to see how men look who die this way, not plunging toward it in a chosen fight or fading into it from old age, but stopped dead in their tracks.

T HE soldiers are flinging back the doors. The morning hits us, and we, all huddled there, look shipwrecked and abandoned in the raw light. Will it be more speaking or dying now? I think dying, for all is exposed, empty, and personless. I should be praying as Thankful does there, but I am too adrift and cannot. I should bring Nellie close to me. In plays they do that, take a last embrace. How far from this dread blank of spirit is that. How will they tell my father? Why, one will call on him all sadness and formality at Henlow and break the news in a low voice that befits the place and time, and she will overhear and be alone as I am and speak nothing. He will make mourning for a son, she for a lover. Who will for me here, now, in Burford churchyard? I would admire for someone to set a stone in the grass there to mark where we were put. Surely they will do that, not just plow us under. It would be so lonely to lie forever among strangers in a market town, unmarked.

Through the west door near us there is the smell of new morning. What noise the soldiers make. The churchyard wall is there across the wet grass. The stones that mark the graves have sunk awry in it, grow down into the ground with age and neglect. I am so far from the smell of green and dew and early sun.

In the corner of the chapel the soldiers are forcing open a little long-unused door. MacKarkle wanders over near them to see what they are doing.

He comes back and hunkers down beside us. " 'Tis foul. They are going to whip us onto the roof of the church and make us watch thee."

"What time is it?" Thankful asks. I say I know not.

As if it were important, he studies the sun without and says, "I think near nine."

The men are being fed into the little door. No one needs whipping. They shuffle along as stunned and docile as men in sleep. Some, as they pass, steal glances at us and then look quickly down and away. I must walk well for them so as not to scar them with more fear. My body looks to them so quiet, but I am racing at full speed, without past, without what I hoped to yearn for, not Nellie, not my son, I cannot find them to shore me up with their warmth. Was it so long ago in my life that I wandered into that loft where my soul met all? I cannot bring it back. My mind twitters. I would dwell on all the luxuries of God and love but must needs be excused for the present and put all life into my knees that they will not betray me. If my fellows here forget my words, and God knows they will do that, there are so many words, at least they can remember that my legs did not buckle, and I did not befoul the way we came together by weeping and howling and begging God's forgiveness for using the heart he gave me and my sight to see.

The men move so slowly through the little door to climb the stairs into the church leads. They are being funneled out toward heaven. I can see the day, and the scent of it is in me now. All we need is someone who will say no to all this. 'Tis a simple thing.

One, I do not know him, a weedy, ragged man, spry in his leaping beyond the soldiers, falls ashaking of my hand, and nodding, and saying, "Yes, yes, oh, indeed, yes," until they cudgel him into the ranks again, and then he turns and winks his prayer for me and his yes.

Gideon, leave go of me and Thankful. Why, he holds us in his heavy arms, near squeezing the life from us, and Little Will is grabbing and plucking at us until they both are hauled away and thrust through the little door.

Now there are only the guards and the silent, empty church. They have laden us with irons. Thankful and I can only clasp our fingers together by standing nearly back to back. Outside we hear the orders barked and the drums that make my heart tumble down in me. They march and halt before the door, soldiers like any other, in rank and file. Those who are left to guard us do not speak; they do obey orders with their eyes locked forward. I did that once and understand.

Someone is being brought in at the north door, for I hear a growl of men from the roof as he passes. It is Thompson. His chains clank on the stone floor. How could I have been close to him or anyone? Is this your punishment, Cromwell, that you force me to be as alone as you?

Thankful, why laughter that moves a soldier toward you? He has seen first what drags and clanks along behind Thompson. Here comes Denne. He has put himself already in his shroud, as one dead; even in this he must make too wide a bow.

"For shame of yourself, Harry!" Thankful calls and makes the stone echo. "Why do you mock us so?"

He stands in the midst of the empty hollow nave, shrouded, silly.

"It is a conceit," I say.

"Well, what is that then?"

"A serious thing turned joke perhaps"—I look carefully for how to say it—"a gesture that means more than it seems"——and I would cling to the word even now—"a metaphor."

"Oh, I know. A lie."

"A kind of lie."

"Pray with me in my last hour." Denne stumbles on his long skirt as he tries to kneel.

"Scratch not thy back on me, Harry," Thankful calls to him, so far away. He is not even cruel. "Get from my mind. I have this thing to do and no time for thee."

"Why, Thankful," I tell him, "you would have turned man of wit had they but let you live." I am still thinking of the metaphor, the lie.

"No, not. I think the stink of death's done this. Had I lived, I would have been encumbered with Harry's trappings."

"Will you not pray with me then?" Why, the man is begging.

"All you want of me is some forgiveness. Oh, well." Slowly, for the chains are heavy, Thankful drags himself across the floor. He leans forward and kisses Denne's cheek. "You will . . . no matter now."

"Why, I am to die with thee." He looks up, still begging to be believed.

"No, Harry. You will play the martyr and be pardoned. You take no part in us for all your winding sheet." He comes back to me, dragging the irons across the stone as one crippled and old.

Thompson, at least, has the grace not to come near or speak to us, so that I know that he, too, has been broken to asking pardon.

The drums roll across the air, so loud that as they unlock his chains we can hardly hear them fall. He is taken out. They roll and roll. How can I tremble so and stand so still?

We cannot see. The firing squad is ranked before the door. The drum roll will not stop. I see beyond the soldiers only a fragment of his back as he is led up to the wall. He stumbles once.

The drums stop. His weak voice trembles. "It is just what does befall me here," and pauses as one who has learned words and forgot them for a moment. "God has not owned the ways I went. I beg the general's pardon for offending him. I desire"—he fumbles again at the words; the sky is so big he sounds small under it—"your prayers who are appointed to shoot me and so do your duty."

No one speaks. No orders. We wait his pardon.

I see their backs change as they raise their muskets and hear the order, "Fire." Silence closes over the shots. Smoke and the smell of sulphur drift in on us.

The facts of life beyond himself have finally touched poor Denne. He falls, and as they lift him up again, I see he has befouled his winding sheet.

The ranks part, and the soldiers carry in Thompson's body that was so stupid and brave a man. He is shot clean, not bloody. His eyes stare up. The private part of him that plowed so arrogantly into women has shot his last lust into his breeks. He leaks sperm and blood as she, the raggle-taggle bird woman, did once.

Denne is sobbing as they unlock him and take him out between the parted ranks into the sun. I see him before they close, half fall, half kneel against the wall. His eyes beg heaven, beg all. His voice is almost a scream. Denne, show us not such shame who must go after you. There is a way of gracefulness.

He is dribbling his words, and we cannot make them out, but when he stops I hear the voice of the general. "God hath pardoned thy transgressions, Henry Denne, henceforth serve him."

He is brought in again, past Thompson, who was too dangerous to live on, even though at the last they brought him down so low in his recanting.

"God has forgiven me." He tries to touch Thankful but the soldiers have already taken Thankful's arms and are unlocking his chains, and there's no room for Denne. They fall around him, and he stands free. Thankful, will no one say no? Will it not stop here?

"The general forgave you, Harry, and will kill me. I think you set your God too high in the state." He shakes away the soldier's hands, and we hold each other. "Thank thee for thy love, Johnny. I will see thee in paradise."

I must drink deep of this last man, his small, thin

hands made for such neat ways, his sun-catching hair
that makes wings down his cheeks, heavy young hair,
his almost frail strong face, his eyes. I am taller than
him by a head. I forgot I was tall and must look down
to him. Search his eyes. A smile is left, I think, in
them. A soldier drags at him. His eyes go blank with
fear, then clear again, fighting to see me, and as he
makes himself see again, his gentleness comes forth,
and they are full of joy. I could touch the light that
seems to come from him. His back is straight. He goes
out between the soldiers like that and pauses for a
stop in the doorway, black against the sun. A soldier
pushes him as if he faltered, but I know he only pauses
to look. We have been so long locked here he wants a
single breath of freedom and morning air.

God, thank thee that thou hast clothed my Thankful
in such armor of joy that I saw. The drums stop. I had
not heard them.

This wait is acres long. His voice now is strong. "I
see you are drawn out to murder me. God forgive you,
for I do freely. But I wonder that you are so unwise."

The shots blast air; the birds escape and cry. I hear
the men who watch groan once. Smoke drifts in the
doorway. There is a taste of salt in my mouth. Through
it a new sound strips me. Thankful is screaming.

They are bringing him in, or something that once
held his spirit. They have shot off his mouth, and he is
not yet quite dead, but the bloody hole that was his
face howls. The blood from him is pumping out onto
the floor. Denne, praying, does not look.

"Shoot him for love of God," I am screaming; help
me not to join your screaming, Thankful, and so dis-
honor you. They did not shoot true. Some, too late,
have shriven themselves by shooting over his head.
There were not enough true bullets to kill him. A
fountain of blood bursts from the howl and drowns it.
Thankful is dead, spent there and thrown aside. I pray
you, someone close his eyes.

They have took my arms. The drum roll has begun
again. I feel the chains fall from me. I must fight

against the bending of my knees. I should be praying. Blood of the bird woman, blood of the king, blood of one I killed, blood of Robbie, blood from Thankful's mouth, I am making a track of it across the floor. Oh, Christ, I pray thee control my body so I can walk out of that door as Thankful did. It is too late for other prayer.

The sun is blinding for a minute. Let me see. My God, someone speak a word. Hast forgot how to say no? Will no one cry cease? Will no one look at me? There they are, ranged along the church leads above me as far as eye can see, and over them the spire is riding the air, as it will do when I am gone from here and promise peace to other men. I hear a man clear his throat. I did not hear the drums stop. Someone is sobbing. Most of them have clasped their hands and pray me to the heaven I leave behind me. Will no one look at me so I am not alone?

I must walk carefully across the grass for it is slippery with blood and dew. I turn. I face the spire now. Why is that cow lowing? It is too early to milk. She must be in calf. This doublet is too heavy for the shot. I must take it off and spread my arms so that the shot will find true. Those who are ranked there before me look through and past me.

Are my eyes a tawny color or brown? I think an autumn color, as my hair. I can feel the wind under my shirt and the muscles of my chest. I think they wait for me to speak. Are there expectations, even in this?

This is so good an earth. I am touched of the sun and warmed. The grass is wet against my legs.

What can I say who have said so much? Shoot true, and God forgive us for what we do to one another? Thankful has said it all. You are unwise.

There are no words. I am empty.

I stretch wide my arms.

I step forward.

ABOUT MARY LEE SETTLE

Mary Lee Settle is one of this country's finest contemporary writers. She was born in Charleston, West Virginia, in 1918—a region that in many ways remains the central base for much of her fiction. Ms. Settle spent two years at Sweet Briar College in Virginia before moving to New York in pursuit of an acting and modeling career. In 1942 she went to England and joined the Women's Auxiliary of the RAF, an experience she recounts in ALL THE BRAVE PROMISES. After the war ended, she returned to the States, working as a journalist for various publications and writing novels and plays in the interim. In addition to the four completed books of the Beulah Quintet (PRISONS, O BEULAH LAND, KNOW NOTHING, and THE SCAPEGOAT), she is also the author of THE LOVE EATERS, THE KISS OF KIN, THE CLAM SHELL, and BLOOD TIE—winner of the 1978 National Book Award for fiction. Ms. Settle has taught creative writing at Bard College and is currently at the University of Virginia, while living in the Tidewater city of Norfolk, Virginia.

ABOUT ROGER SHATTUCK

Roger Shattuck is the co-winner of the National Book Award in 1975 for MARCEL PROUST. He is the author of THE BANQUET YEARS: THE ORIGINS OF THE AVANT GARDE IN FRANCE, 1885– World War I, and THE FORBIDDEN EXPERIMENT: The Story of the Wild Boy of Averyron. At present, Roger Shattuck is Commonwealth Professor of French at the University of Virginia.

PAUL THEROUX

"...will successively startle you...shock you ...impress you ... but never, never bore you!"*

The best
in modern fiction from
BALLANTINE

20   G-3